WHAT ANSWER?

CLASSICS IN BLACK STUDIES

WHAT ANSWER?

Anna E. Dickinson

WITH AN INTRODUCTION BY

J. Matthew Gallman

Humanity Books

an imprint of Prometheus Books
59 John Glenn Drive, Amherst, New York 14228-2197

Cover image: Courtesy of J. Matthew Gallman

Published by Humanity Books, an imprint of Prometheus Books

Inquiries should be addressed to
Humanity Books
59 John Glenn Drive
Amherst, New York 14228–2197
VOICE: 716–691–0133, ext. 207
FAX: 716–564–2711
WWW.PROMETHEUSBOOKS.COM

07 06 05 04 03   5 4 3 2 1

What Answer? originally published: Boston : Fields, Osgood, & Co., 1869.

Library of Congress Cataloging-in-Publication Data

Dickinson, Anna E. (Anna Elizabeth), 1842–1932.
    What answer? / Anna E. Dickinson ; with an introduction by J.
Matthew Gallman.
        p. cm. — (Classics in Black studies)
    ISBN 1–59102–050–6 (paper : alk. paper)
    1. United States—History—Civil War, 1861–1865—African
Americans—Fiction. 2. United States—History—Civil War, 1861–1865—
Fiction. 3. Draft Riot, New York, N.Y., 1863—Fiction. 4. Racially mixed
people—Fiction. 5. Interracial marriage—Fiction. 6. Philadelphia (Pa.)—
Fiction. 7. Passing (Identity)—Fiction. 8. African Americans—Fiction.
9. New York (N.Y.)—Fiction. 10. Racism—Fiction. I. Title. II. Series.

PS1538 .W48 2002
813'.3—dc21   2002032910

Printed in the United States of America on acid-free paper

ANNA ELIZABETH DICKINSON was born on October 28, 1842, in Philadelphia. She was the youngest of five children of Quakers John Dickinson, a dry-goods merchant, and Mary Edmondson Dickinson. Her father died when she was two years old. She received her early education from her mother and had five years of formal education, mainly at Friends' Select School of Philadelphia. Raised in modest circumstances, at age fifteen Dickinson went to work as a copyist and later as a schoolteacher.

The Dickinson home was reportedly a station on the Underground Railroad. At age thirteen Dickinson had an antislavery article published in William Lloyd Garrison's paper, the *Liberator*. In 1860 she gave her first public speech, addressing the Pennsylvania Anti-Slavery Society. In 1861 she gave her first paid lecture on "The Rights and Wrongs of Women," arguing for women's suffrage and their entrance into the professions.

In 1861 Dickinson lost the job she then held at the U.S. Mint in Philadelphia, for accusing General George B. McClellan of treason in the loss of the Battle of Ball's Bluff. She again turned to the lecture circuit, where the press hailed her as the "juvenile Joan of Arc." In 1863 Radical Republican leaders in New Hampshire and Connecticut hired her as a campaign speaker. In January 1864 she addressed a gathering, including President and Mrs. Lincoln, in the hall of the House of Representatives, calling for Lincoln's reelection.

After the Civil War Dickinson was an important

speaker on the lyceum circuit, lecturing on racial prejudice, big business, the double standard of sexual behavior, and the liberation of women from the financial and legal control of fathers and husbands. She published *What Answer?* (1868), a novel about interracial marriage; *A Paying Investment* (1876), on various social reforms; and a memoir, *A Ragged Register: Of People, Places, and Opinions* (1879).

By 1873 Dickinson's popularity as a lecturer declined, and she turned to writing and acting for the theater. In 1876 she appeared in her own play, *A Crown of Thorns*, but critics ridiculed her work. While most of her other plays remained unproduced, *An American Girl* was a success for actress Fanny Davenport in 1880. After she was ridiculed for her portrayal of Hamlet, Dickinson retired from public view.

In 1888 Dickinson again appeared as a platform speaker for the Republican National Committee, but it is alleged that her language was so caustic she was an embarrassment and was let go. In 1891 she was involuntarily confined for a short stay in the State Hospital for the Insane in Danville, Pennsylvania. Upon her release she sued those responsible for committing her and was awarded nominal damages.

After 1891 Dickinson lived in several places in New York and Pennsylvania, and finally settled at Goshen, New York, where she died on October 22, 1932.

INTRODUCTION

"It is one of those books which belong to the class of *deeds* not *words*," declared Harriet Beecher Stowe. "If anybody can read that book unmoved, we have only pity for him." With these words, the celebrated author of *Uncle Tom's Cabin* announced her official approval of Anna Elizabeth Dickinson's new novel, *What Answer?*[1] Privately, Mrs. Stowe wrote the twenty-six-year-old Dickinson a short note:

> I lay on my sofa all alone on Saturday night & read your book all through & when I got through I rose up mentally . . . & said Well done good & faithful Anna—daughter of my soul—I thank you for this. Your poor old grandma in the work rejoices to find it in your brave young hands. . . . Don't mind what any body says about it as a work of art. Work of art be hanged!—You had a braver thought than that.[2]

Anna Dickinson's *What Answer?*—assisted by Stowe's widely circulated review—attracted tremendous interest when it first appeared in the fall of 1868. Set in the midst of the Civil War, the controversial novel traced the tragic history of an interracial marriage doomed to disaster within a northern society that refused to accept racial equality. The topic was certainly timely, as postwar Americans struggled with the political and cultural implications of emancipation. Reformers like Stowe praised the book's courageous stance, while other reviewers recoiled in disgust at the relationship at the book's core, or belittled the young author for her naïve beliefs and sometimes unwieldy plot and prose. Whatever its strengths and defects, *What Answer?*—like its author—was not destined to produce moderate responses.

Although *What Answer?* was her first book, Anna Dickinson was a very familiar name to northern readers in 1868. During the Civil War, Dickinson had emerged as one of the nation's most celebrated orators, captivating audiences across the Northeast with calls for emancipation, racial justice, and women's rights. She rose to fame as the darling of the abolitionists—counting William Lloyd Garrison, Wendell Phillips, Lucretia Mott, and Susan B. Anthony among her early mentors and supporters—but Dickinson quickly bridged the gap between radical reform and partisan politics. During the crucial elections of 1863 and 1864, Dickinson became a favorite Republican speaker, traveling across Pennsylvania, Connecticut, New York, and much of New England supporting Republican candidates and warning of the dangers of Copperheadism.[3]

Anna Dickinson was by all accounts a captivating speaker. Her supporters celebrated Dickinson's charisma and oratorical gifts, while her detractors insisted that she was no more than an attractive young mouthpiece for tired radical rhetoric. Certainly part of her fame accompanied the fact that she was a woman trespassing into a political world that was ordinarily reserved for men, and she did so at a remarkably young age. In fact, Dickinson first entered the public arena at age thirteen when she published an essay on abolitionism in Garrison's abolitionist newspaper, the *Liberator*. Five years later, on the eve of the Civil War, Dickinson attended a forum on women's rights in Philadelphia and found herself delivering an impassioned speech from the floor. Before long she was entertaining invitations to speak on women's rights and abolitionism around Philadelphia, and then later in Boston. By 1862, before her twentieth birthday, Dickinson was earning occasional fees for her oratory. And by the time she became a Republican stump speaker, Dickinson was a national celebrity, demanding substantial fees for her labors. In January 1864 Dickinson accepted an invitation signed by over a hundred Republican congressmen and senators to speak before them in the hall of the House of Representatives. Although the radical Dickinson was an outspoken critic of Abraham Lincoln and his moderate administration, the president and first lady joined the packed crowd in time to hear the fiery young speaker somewhat grudgingly endorse his renomination in the upcoming election.

By the close of the Civil War Anna Dickinson was, at age twenty-two, among the nation's most famous women. Several photographers, including Mathew Brady, had taken her portrait and small *cartes de visite* of her image circulated widely among her friends and admirers. Complete strangers wrote to Dickinson seeking advice, offering praise, or simply asking for an autograph. After Appomattox, Dickinson remained in the public eye, traveling across the nation delivering public lectures to packed houses. In an age when Americans attended lectures for entertainment as well as edification, Dickinson became one of the nation's most active and best-paid public speakers. Dickinson concentrated on reform themes, generally speaking on the condition of women, the status of African Americans, and the state of postwar Reconstruction. During each off season she toiled away on research and writing in preparation for the next year's tour. In this fashion, Dickinson supported herself and her family while also maintaining her voice in public affairs and her position as a national celebrity.

When Anna Dickinson wrote *What Answer?* the nation was deeply divided about the future of race relations in both the Reconstruction South and across the North. Although new amendments to the Constitution had abolished slavery and extended the rights of citizenship to African Americans, and the Reconstruction Acts of 1867 had mandated Black suffrage in the conquered southern states, northern states continued to resist manhood suffrage in their own backyards. In Dickinson's native Philadelphia, and across the North, African Americans endured a postwar world of continuing social and legal segregation, despite the fact that African American soldiers had helped preserve the Union.

The ironies and the challenges of race in postwar America were not lost on the young orator. The child of abolitionist Quakers, Dickinson and her family counted some of the Philadelphia area's most prominent African Americans—including the Purvises and the Fortens—among their friends and acquaintances. During and after the war, Frederick Douglass, the great orator and Black leader, was a regular houseguest at the Dickinsons' Locust Street home. Only days after the battle of Gettysburg, Dickinson shared a platform with Douglass at a Philadelphia mass meeting to promote enlistment into the United States Colored Troops. One of her close friends and correspondents, James C. Beecher, served as a White officer with the USCT, and Robert Purvis's son, Charles, fought as a volunteer in the United States Colored Troops. When Dickinson chose to write her first novel about race relations in the postwar North, she selected themes that she cared about deeply and knew perhaps as well as any White woman of her day was likely to know them.

✳   ✳   ✳   ✳   ✳   ✳

At its core, *What Answer?* is a rather familiar tale of for-
bidden love. The hero is Willie Surrey, the charming,
handsome heir to a New York foundry fortune. In the
novel's first pages Willie spots the lovely Francesca Ercildoune walking down Broadway, and immediately vows
that he will someday know the enchanting young woman.
Before long Willie encounters Francesca at a school con-
cert, where he is thoroughly smitten with her powerful
reading of an antislavery poem. Willie—like the reader—
does not realize that Francesca is of mixed racial parentage
and only able to move freely within White society because
few New Yorkers know her true racial identity. Although
she is so light-skinned that she can easily "pass" as White,
Francesca seethes at the prejudice around her and becomes
mistakenly convinced that her new suitor is cut from the
same racist cloth and that thus they could never be
together.

   When news of the firing on Fort Sumter rocks the
nation, Willie enlists in the Union army without having an
opportunity to speak with Francesca, who has fled to
Philadelphia in dismay over their last conversation. He
spends the next two years in the army, convinced that
Francesca has spurned his affections. Finally, Willie returns
home having lost an arm to the cause and seeks out his lost
love. Francesca first sends him away, but soon Willie discovers her secret and manages to convince Francesca—and

her father and brother—that his love knows no racial barriers. The two marry, over the objections of the Surrey family and the disapproval of most of Willie's friends. Now a committed activist, Willie sets out to raise a brigade of Black freedmen to fight for the cause of Union and Emancipation. But before he can begin recruiting, Willie finds himself in the midst of the terrible New York City draft riots of July 1863. The mob lynches Abram Franklin, a sickly African American friend from Willie's youth, and then accosts Willie as he is trying to get Abram's mother to safety. Willie, the one-armed war hero, dies at the hands of the mob only moments before Francesca arrives on the scene. Then, in a moment that perhaps Dickinson hoped would call to mind Shakespearean tragedy, Francesca is hit by a stray bullet and dies alongside her husband. And if that irony were not enough, the reader learns that the two fell only feet from the Surreys' front door.

[margin note: seems to have same defeated end as the death of Mr. Mrs. Garie.]

This central love story caught the attention of Dickinson's supporters and critics alike. To portray such a relationship only three years after the Civil War was to many an act of remarkable audacity. Dickinson's friends praised the power of her tale and the poignancy of the lovers' demise. Some critics voiced disgust at the very notion of miscegenation, and more cynical readers argued that Dickinson had really danced around the critical issues by portraying Francesca as nearly White in her physical appearance. After all, they noted, Willie Surrey fell in love with a highly educated, well-bred woman whom he thought

[margin note: so different levels of allowance for skin color → "passing" deemed not as bad as dark skin?]

was White and whose true identity he did not even know for half the novel. What does such a story really have to do with racial equality or even tolerance?

Perhaps it is true that Dickinson opted to mute the power of the story by painting Francesca as a woman of almost White features. On the other hand, that choice also allowed her to critique, and even mock, contemporary notions of racial identity. At a crucial moment in the novel, Willie's Aunt Augusta travels to Philadelphia to deliver a letter from Willie to Francesca. She knows Francesca as a highly "respectable" young woman of great "gifts and graces" (p. 171)* and she is happy to assist the young lovers. That is, she is happy to encourage the relationship until she meets Mr. Ercildoune, Francesca's dark-skinned father. Immediately Francesca changes in Aunt Augusta's eyes into an unworthy creature who must be kept from her nephew. In this fashion, Dickinson eloquently illustrates the fundamental arbitrariness of racial definitions and divisions. What is one to make of a society that embraces a young woman for her personal character and bearing, only to reject her when it discovers the true nature of the blood running through her veins?

Readers who concentrated too hard on the story of Willie and Francesca were liable to miss Dickinson's much broader indictment of racial injustice. If Francesca Ercildoune symbolized the fundamental incoherence of a social structure built upon racial hierarchy, numerous other char-

---

*Pagination in this edition.

acters and events in *What Answer?* forced the reader to confront the vast range of racism's evils. Consider Dickinson's depiction of Abram Franklin, the African American man who was grotesquely lynched by the draft rioters. We learn in the novel's early chapters that Abe and Willie were childhood friends, and that Willie had arranged for Abe to get a job in his father's factory. When Mr. Surrey discovered that Abe had been secretly assisting the factory's incompetent bookkeeper, he took the unusual step of firing his White worker and replacing him with the talented young Black man. But this recognition of merit over race backfires on poor Abe when the factory's 272 White workers vote unanimously to strike if he remains on the job. Faced with this seemingly impossible dilemma, Mr. Surrey caves in to his workers and fires Abe. A distraught Willie finds Abe a new position, but broods over his inability to change the larger society. Two years later, Willie is visiting his old friend at his sickbed when the rioters break into the Franklins' home and drag Abe into the streets to his death. Willie is powerless to aid the Black man, and in fact loses his life moving Mrs. Franklin to safety. What is the reader to make of these events, which move parallel to the relationship between Francesca and Willie? Dickinson is clearly illustrating the evils of racism within northern society, but she also appears to be questioning the power of a single good-hearted individual to change such a society.

In other episodes, Dickinson illustrates the pernicious

evils of northern segregation. Although Abe Franklin is lame, he has to limp back and forth to work because he is not allowed to ride the city's streetcars. Later in the novel, Dickinson sets an entire chapter on a crowded Philadelphia streetcar in 1863. Among the car's passengers are Francesca, several well-dressed men and women, and a filthy, drunken coal-heaver. As the chapter opens, two passengers are discussing the sad irony that the coal-heaver is allowed to ride the cars whereas "a nice, respectable colored person can't" so long as the private streetcar companies refuse to serve African Americans. Just then the conductor, ignoring the company's rules, stops to pick up a uniformed Black soldier with one missing leg. Not only do the passengers accept this new rider, but a Quaker man actually gives up his seat to the wounded soldier and they engage in lively conversation as social equals. But the spell is broken when the coal-heaver (almost certainly intended to be an Irish immigrant) awakens and demands that the Black man be removed. One "gentleman" on the cars joins in this demand, and the conductor is forced to acquiesce and stops to eject the soldier. Once again, the tide on the car starts to turn as several passengers raise their voices in objection, led by none other than Francesca Ercildoune. The irate gentleman turns his wrath on Francesca and is apparently just about to reveal her true racial identity when Willie Surrey—who has just boarded the car—steps forward and knocks him down, much to the satisfaction of most of the riders. After the gentleman flees the scene, the rest of the passengers band together and demand that the drunkard be removed from the cars for disturbing the peace.[4]

With this small morality play Dickinson is doing much more than providing a context for Willie and Francesca to be reunited after two years. She is also reiterating the fundamental inconsistencies in a society that rejects the respectable Black man while embracing the drunken White man. And of course the point is dramatized when the Black man at the center of the turmoil is a wounded veteran. Moreover, the chapter suggests the power of popular outrage, and specifically the power of a few voices raised in protest, in overturning racial segregation. But even here Dickinson seems to be acknowledging the limits of this solution. After all, both the Black soldier and the coal-heaver are ejected from the streetcar in fullfillment of rules and laws, and not merely because of the collective demands of the passengers.

The Black soldier on the Philadelphia streetcar draws a link between the home-front narrative set in New York and Philadelphia, and the parallel narrative involving events at the seat of war. In addition to Willie himself, several other central characters join the army, including Willie's friend Tom Russell, his father's old foreman Jim Given, and Francesca's brother Robert Ercildoune. In a series of intertwined subplots and isolated episodes, Dickinson portrays a range of Black characters demonstrating great heroism and character, consistently shaping their own lives rather than being mere pawns in a power struggle between Southern and Northern Whites. While stationed on Morris Island, Jim Given encounters two escaped slaves who prove instrumental in rescuing Tom Russell and several other escaped prisoners of war. At the chapter's conclusion, one of the newly free Black men—also named Jim—sacrifices his life to save a boatload of Union soldiers stranded on a sandbar. The following chapter features a powerful description of the storming of Fort Wagner by Black troops of the famed Fifty-fourth Massachusetts regiment. Among the heroes of the assault is Robert Ercildoune, who risks his life and is badly wounded saving the regiment's colors.

With such episodes Dickinson celebrates not only the bravery of African Americans, but their direct agency in emancipating themselves and in defeating the Confederacy. These episodes, in turn, prompt Dickinson's White characters to rethink their racial assumptions. Although Willie was deeply troubled by the condition of Blacks before the war began, Tom Russell and James Given represent more mainstream White opinions about racial difference. After Jim—the escaped slave—sacrifices his life on the sandbar, James Given declares that he would fight any soldier who doubted that the Black man was the equal to the White man. On the hospital ship heading home, Jim Given discovers that Robert Ercildoune is on board and leads his comrades in three cheers for the hero of Fort Wagner. By the close of the novel, Tom Russell and Robert Ercildoune have become fast friends, brought together by a common military experience and a shared grief over the deaths of Francesca and Willie, but the two men truly bonded because they were both "of the gentle blood, [with] tastes and instincts in common" (pp. 308–309). Through the experiences of Jim and Tom, Dickinson is suggesting another answer to the book's central quandry. The solution to the nation's race problem, she seems to suggest, must begin with individual evolution from racist hostility or ignorance to the embracing of commonalities through experience.

Events set in the wartime South also suggest that Dickinson recognized the potential role of law and government in recasting race relations. Early in the war, before the Emancipation Proclamation turned the conflict into a war for liberation, we meet an enslaved man named Sam who had discovered a dead Union soldier, buried his body, and hidden the soldier's money and papers until he could hand them over to Federal troops. The Union soldier who told Surrey this story came away so impressed with Sam that he had embraced abolitionism, and openly decried the government policy that was still in effect forbidding slaves from finding freedom behind Union lines. Later, Sam and his elderly Virginian owner approach the Union troops with a pass through the Union lines on their way to Fairfax. The Virginian orders his slave to hand the pass to the soldiers, and Willie and Jim cleverly interpret that paper—which reads "pass the bearer"—as pertaining only to the man who personally handed it over. Therefore, they let

Sam pass through the lines but refuse to allow his master to follow.

The two episodes involving Sam are really quite minor, and certainly one of Dickinson's goals is to lampoon the pompous Virginia gentleman who is tricked by the Union soldiers. But the story also suggests another path to racial justice. The pass that the Virginia gentleman carried functioned as a legal document, with the Union soldiers serving in a judicial capacity. Willie and Jim were able to thoroughly befuddle the elderly Rebel simply by treating Sam and his supposed owner as equals, and thus equally eligible to be the "bearer" in the printed pass. In effect, the episode was anticipating life in the South under Reconstruction, when freedmen would enjoy the same citizenship rights as Whites, but only when protected at the point of a Union bayonet.

Critics of *What Answer?* questioned Dickinson's decision to continue the novel for three chapters after the climactic scene of the New York City draft riots. After all, they asked, why continue a story after the hero and heroine have died tragically? Rather than dismissing this as the foolish decision of an inexperienced author, we should consider what happens in the three final chapters following the deaths of Francesca and Willie. With the main characters gone, Dickinson shifts her attention to the romance between Sallie and Jim, two working-class New Yorkers who had been dating since before Fort Sumter. Jim had been wounded in the war and returned home with a newfound respect for African

Americans. In the meantime, Francesca had taken Sallie in and given her work doing sewing for the Ercildoune family. In the book's final chapter, the reunited lovers marry, with Sallie wearing a dress and jewels given to her by Robert Ercildoune. And after the wedding the two newlyweds move into a small house given to them by Mr. Ercildoune, in memory of his fallen daughter.

Here we have a strange inversion of the familiar social order. Rather than imagining a world in which good-hearted White northerners reach out their arms, and their pocketbooks, to needy African Americans, Dickinson has challenged her readers with a much more radical vision where the people of color are politically disenfranchised but materially privileged and offering their friendship and aid to working-class Whites. But such a vision was on the one hand too extreme, and on the other hand too limited, to provide the template for racial justice. In the novel's final scene Tom Russell insists that Robert Ercildoune join him at the polls. Although the wounded Black war hero walks with a cane and has one empty sleeve pinned to his shoulder, Robert is blocked from voting. "1860 or 1865?—is the war ended?" Robert asks (p. 311). The answer is clear to Tom, and to the reader. The war would not be over until *all* the men who had sacrificed their lives, and their bodies, to the Union could participate in the nation's future. By ending the novel at this point, Dickinson made it clear that the answer to the book's title lay—first and foremost—at the voting booth.

* * * * * *

Many of Dickinson's friends joined Harriet Beecher
Stowe in celebrating *What Answer?* as a great political statement, although not necessarily an entirely successful work
of art. The novel was, to Oliver Johnson, a "powerful blow
against the Satanic spirit of caste."[5] Theodore Tilton—
another of Dickinson's old abolitionist allies—agreed that
she had "rendered a noble service to [her] day and gener-
ation."[6] Author Charles Dudley Warner, one of Dickinson's closest friends and mentors, declared that any
reader would be "profoundly moved" by *What Answer?* and
radical Republican Senator Charles Sumner revealed to a
friend that the novel "did make my eyes overflow."[7] Perhaps the most blunt critique from Dickinson's own inner
circle came from the *New York Tribune*'s Whitelaw Reid, a
close confidant and political sparring partner from early in
the war. The caustic Reid acknowledged that it was a
"powerful" book, but doubted if its political aims were
"worthy of the prominence" Dickinson gave them. Moreover, the editor found that although there were "passages
. . . of wonderfully vivid force," there were also "frequent
phrases that offend a critical taste."[8] Many of the published
responses to the novel shared Reid's double-edged
response. "Take away the moral inspiration of the book,"
commented one reviewer, "and it would be little more
than an enthusiastic love story, eloquently written, but rad-
ically commonplace and imitative."[9] The Democratic *New*

York World, long a critic of Dickinson's public appearances, belittled the author's political idealism and dismissed the book as only "called a novel by the cunning of good-natured publishers" who shared her agendas.[10]

There is no question that if *What Answer?* deserved a place on the same shelf as *Uncle Tom's Cabin,* it was because of the novel's political passion rather than its technical sophistication. The plot is quite ambitious for such an inexperienced author, including various subplots and shifts in time and place. That complexity enables Dickinson to pack a wide range of characters and situations into her novel, but along the way she periodically resorts to awkward plot devices. Entire chapters are built around long letters filling in missing information, or extended anecdotes told in the voice of minor characters. The result is what the *New York Herald Tribune* termed a series of "impassioned sketches" rather than a single, coherent plot.[11]

Contemporary readers were most impressed with Dickinson's writing when she described actual events, and for today's reader *What Answer?* becomes a valuable—if impressionistic—historical source. Like Stowe's portrayal of *Uncle Tom's Cabin,* Dickinson insisted that "almost every scene in this book is copied from life" (p. 313). The two most celebrated scenes were the storming of Fort Wagner and the New York City draft riots. Free of the limitations of her sometimes unwieldy dialogue, and writing in a style reminiscent of her popular oratory, Dickinson's prose was at its best when she inserted her fictional characters into these dramatic historic events. The heroic color-sergeant who fell on the parapet at Fort Wagner was quite real, as was his comrade—recast as Robert Ercildoune—who picked up the fallen colors and pressed on. Willie Surrey's death during the draft riots was based on the celebrated demise of Colonel O'Brien, and Dickinson modeled the terrible murder of Abram Franklin on a reported episode. Dickinson also found inspiration for the character of Francesca Ercildoune, and her noble father and heroic brother, in the lives of her friend Harriet Purvis and her family.[12]

It should come as no surprise that Anna Dickinson's fiction was most powerful when she wrote closest to the facts. Although a work of fiction, *What Answer?* was distinctly a political statement, addressing the concerns of postwar America and more specifically the immediate political landscape in 1868. Thus, when Dickinson recounted the events surrounding the 1863 draft riots she devoted several pages to attacking the behavior of New York's wartime governor, Horatio Seymour, who was the Democratic candidate for president in the approaching 1868 election. Moreover, only six months after the novel's publication Congress would pass the Fifteenth Amendment, expanding the right to vote to African American men, while disappointing advocates of woman suffrage. By writing and speaking in support of Black suffrage, Dickinson broke ranks with many of her former allies in the women's movement who had urged that the vote be extended to all men and women. For several years Dickinson's close friend Susan B. Anthony had been urging the young orator to speak out more emphatically for woman suffrage, but although Dickinson certainly supported woman suffrage she ended up casting her lot with those reformers who declared that it was "the Black man's hour." In this context, it is particularly noteworthy that *What Answer?* is so exclusively focused on Black issues with no passing nod to woman suffrage. That omission was not lost on the leaders of the women's movement. In reviewing *What Answer?* for the *Revolution*, Elizabeth Cady Stanton tweaked Dickinson for failing to further the cause of women's rights in her first novel, a critique which prompted a published defense from Theodore Tilton.[13] Privately, Susan B. Anthony told Dickinson that she thought that the book "was a terrific experiment" but in the same letter she asked, "What answer—. . . when will you speak for the women[?]"[14]

Anna Dickinson remained in the public eye for two more decades, but she never attempted another novel. Dickinson did publish one short book on public policy, and a travel narrative based on her letters home from the road, but she generally maintained that she preferred the platform to the pen.[15] When opportunities for lecturing diminished, Dickinson turned to the stage as both an actress and playwright. But although she remained a celebrated public figure—even campaigning for Horace Greeley in the presidential election of 1872—Dickinson never quite matched her earlier fame.

Dickinson's public career took an unhappy turn in 1891 when her sister arranged for her to be committed to an insane asylum. After securing her release, Dickinson devoted much of her energies over the next decades to suing those responsible for her incarceration and to restoring her damaged public reputation. In a sad ironic twist, Dickinson's friendship with Robert Purvis and his family dissolved when she discovered that during her time in the asylum he had lent his name to a fund-raising letter describing her supposed mental illness.[16]

For today's reader, *What Answer?* provides an excellent portrait of race relations during the Civil War era, as well as a fascinating window into Dickinson's radical critique of that world. Dickinson's novel also invites broader reflection about the nature of racial identity formation, the power of racial stereotyping, and the various strategies for pursuing racial justice. Although set quite firmly in a particular time and place, readers of *What Answer?* may discover that Dickinson's central insights and critiques remain quite relevant to contemporary discourse.

J. Matthew Gallman
Henry R. Luce Professor of the Civil War Era
Gettysburg College

NOTES

1. *Hartford Courant*, n.d., clipping in scrapbook, 1863–1876, Anna E. Dickinson Papers, Library of Congress, Washington, D.C., microfilm. Hereafter AED Papers. At least one reprint of this review also appears in the scrapbook, and several reviews and letters refer to the Stowe article.

2. Harriet Beecher Stowe to AED, n.d., AED Papers.

3. "Copperheads" was the term used to describe antiwar Democrats.

4. Chapter X. In her "Note" to the novel, Dickinson says that she personally witnessed the episode described in this chapter. For the battle to desegregate the Philadelphia streetcars see Philip S. Foner, "The Battle to End Discrimination Against Negroes on Philadelphia Streetcars," two parts, *Pennsylvania History* (1973): 261–90, 355–79.

5. Oliver Johnson to AED, 30 September 1858, AED Papers.

6. Theodore Tilton to AED, 9 October 1868, AED Papers.

7. Charles Dudley Warner to AED, 12 September 1870; Susan Dickinson to AED, 16 March 1873, AED Papers.

8. Whitelaw Reid to AED, 12 October 1868, AED Papers.

9. The *Morning Post*, 21 September 1868, Dickinson scrapbook. (Publication location unknown.)

10. *New York World*, 30 September 1868, Dickinson scrapbook.

11. *New York Herald Tribune*, 29 September 1868, Dickinson scrapbook.

12. On Robert Purvis, Harriet's father, see Roger Lane, *Roots of Violence in Black Philadelphia, 1860–1900* (Cambridge, Mass.: Harvard University Press, 1986), p. 47 and *passim*. On the African American elite in antebellum Philadelphia, including the Purvises, see Julie Winch, *Philadelphia's Black Elite: Activism, Accommodation, and the Struggle for Autonomy, 1787–1848* (Philadelphia: Temple University Press, 1988).

13. *The Revolution*, 5 November 1868, Dickinson scrapbook.

14. Susan B. Anthony to AED, 15 October 1868, AED Papers.

15. *A Paying Investment* (Boston: J. R. Osgood and Company, 1876); *A Ragged Register* (New York: Harper and Bros., 1879).

16. The author is engaged in writing a biography of Anna Dickinson. For a short biographical essay focusing on the Civil War years see J. Matthew Gallman, "Anna Dickinson: Abolitionist Orator," in Steven E. Woodworth, ed., *The Human Tradition in the Civil War and Reconstruction* (Wilmington, Del.: SR Books, 2000), pp. 93–110.

WHAT ANSWER?

CHAPTER I

"In flower of youth and beauty's pride."
DRYDEN

ACROWDED New York street,—Fifth Avenue at the height of the afternoon; a gallant and brilliant throng. Looking over the glittering array, the purple and fine linen, the sweeping robes, the exquisite equipages, the stately houses; the faces, delicate and refined, proud, self-satisfied, that gazed out from their windows on the street, or that glanced from the street to the windows, or at one another,—looking over all this, being a part of it, one might well say, "This is existence, and beside it there is none other. Let us dress, dine, and be merry! Life is good, and love is sweet, and both shall endure! Let us forget that hunger and sin, sorrow and self-sacrifice, want, struggle, and pain, have place in the world." Yet, even with the words, "poverty, frost-nipped in a summer suit," here and there hurried by; and once and again through the restless tide the sorrowful procession of the tomb made way.

More than one eye was lifted, and many a pleasant greeting passed between these selected few who filled the street and a young man who lounged by one of the overlooking windows; and many a comment was uttered upon him when the greeting was made:—

"A most eligible *parti!*"

"Handsome as a god!"

"O, immensely rich, I assure you!"

"*Isn't* he a beauty!"

"Pity he wasn't born poor!"

"Why?"

"O, because they say he carried off all the honors at college and law-school, and is altogether overstocked with brains for a man who has no need to use them."

"Will he practise?"

"Doubtful. Why should he?"

"Ambition, power,—gratify one, gain the other."

"Nonsense! He'll probably go abroad and travel for a while, come back, marry, and enjoy life."

"He does that now, I fancy."

"Looks so."

And indeed he did. There was not only vigor and manly beauty, splendid in its present, but the "possibility of more to be in the full process of his ripening days,"—a form alert and elegant, which had not yet all of a man's muscle and strength; a face delicate, yet strong,—refined,

yet full of latent power; a mass of rippling hair like bur-
nished gold, flung back on the one side, sweeping low
across brow and cheek on the other; eyes

> "Of a deep, soft, lucent hue,—
> Eyes too expressive to be blue,
> Too lovely to be gray."

People involuntarily thought of the pink and flower of
chivalry as they looked at him, or imagined, in some indis-
tinct fashion, that they heard the old songs of Percy and
Douglas, or the later lays of the cavaliers, as they heard his
voice,—a voice that was just now humming one of these
same lays:—

> "Then mounte! then mounte, brave gallants, all,
>   And don your helmes amaine;
> Death's couriers, Fame and Honor, call
>   Us to the field againe."

"Stuff!" he cried impatiently, looking wistfully at the
men's faces going by,—"stuff! *We* look like gallants to ride
a tilt at the world, and die for Honor and Fame,—we!"

"I thank God, Willie, you are not called upon for any
such sacrifice."

"Ah, little mother, well you may!" he answered,
smiling, and taking her hand,—"well you may, for I am
afraid I should fall dreadfully short when the time came;
and then how ashamed you'd be of your big boy, who

took his ease at home, with the great drums beating and the trumpets blowing outside. And yet—I should like to be tried!"

"See, mother!" he broke out again,—"see what a life it is, getting and spending, living handsomely and doing the proper thing towards society, and all that,—rubbing through the world in the old hereditary way; though I needn't growl at it, for I enjoy it enough, and find it a pleasant enough way, Heaven knows. Lazy idler! enjoying the sunshine with the rest. Heigh-ho!"

"You have your profession, Willie. There's work there, and opportunity sufficient to help others and do for yourself."

"Ay, and I'll *do* it! But there is so much that is poor and mean, and base and tricky, in it all,—so much to disgust and tire one,—all the time, day after day, for years. Now if it were only a huge giant that stands in your way, you could out rapier and have at him at once, and there an end,—laid out or triumphant. That's worth while!"

"O youth, eager and beautiful," thought the mother who listened, "that in this phase is so alike the world over,—so impatient to do, so ready to brave encounters, so willing to dare and die! May the doing be faithful, and the encounters be patiently as well as bravely fought, and the fancy of heroic death be a reality of noble and earnest life. God grant it! Amen."

"Meanwhile," said the gay voice,—"meanwhile it's a pleasant world; let us enjoy it! and as to do this is within the compass of a man's wit, therefore will I attempt the doing."

While he was talking he had once more come to the window, and, looking out, fastened his eyes unconsciously but intently upon the face of a young girl who was slowly passing by,—unconsciously, yet so intently that, as if suddenly magnetized, a flicker of feeling went over it; the mouth, set with a steady sweetness, quivered a little; the eyes—dark, beautiful eyes—were lifted to his an instant, that was all. The mother beside him did not see; but she heard a long breath, almost a sigh, break from him as he started, then flashed out of the room, snatching his hat in the hall, and so on to the street, and away.

Away after her, through block after block, across the crowded avenue to Broadway. "Who is she? where did she come from? *I* never saw her before. I wonder if Mrs. Russell knows her, or Clara, or anybody! I will know where she lives, or where she is going at least,—that will be some clew! There! she is stopping that stage. I'll help her in! no, I won't,—she will think I am chasing her. Nonsense! do you suppose she saw you at the window? Of course! No, she didn't; don't be a fool! There! I'll get into the next stage. Now I'll keep watch of that, and she'll not know. So—all right! Go ahead, driver." And happy with some new happiness, eager, bright, the handsome young fellow sat watching that other stage, and the stylish little lace bonnet that was all he could see of his magnet, through the interminable journey down Broadway.

How clear the air seemed! and the sun, how splendidly it shone! and what a glad look was upon all the people's faces! He felt like breaking out into gay little snatches of song, and moved his foot to the waltz measure that beat time in his brain till the irate old gentleman opposite, whom nature had made of a sour complexion and art assisted to corns, broke out with an angry exclamation. That drew his attention for a moment. A slackening of speed, a halt, and the stage was wedged in one of the inextricable "jams" on Broadway. Vain the search for *her* stage then; looking over the backs of the poor, tired horses, or from the sidewalk,—here, there, at this one and that one,—all for naught! Stage and passenger, eyes, little lace bonnet, and all, had vanished away, as William Surrey confessed, and confessed with reluctance and discontent.

"No matter!" he said presently,—"no matter! I shall see her again. I know it! I feel it! It is written in the book of the Fates! So now I shall content me with something"— that looks like her he did not say definitely, but felt it none the less, as, going over to the flower-basket near by, he picked out a little nosegay of mignonette and geranium, with a tea-rosebud in its centre, and pinned it at his button-hole. "Delicate and fine!" he thought,—"delicate and fine!" and with the repetition he looked from it down the long street after the interminable line of stages; and somehow the faint, sweet perfume, and the fair flower, and the dainty lace bonnet, were mingled in wild and charming confusion in his brain, till he shook himself, and laughed at himself, and quoted Shakespeare to excuse himself,—"A mad world, my masters!"—seeing this poor old earth of ours, as people always do, through their own eyes.

"God bless ye! and long life to yer honor! and may the blessed Virgin give ye the desire of yer heart!" called the Irishwoman after him, as he put back the change in her hand and went gayly up the street. "Sure, he's somebody's darlint, the beauty! the saints preserve him!" she said, as she looked from the gold piece in her palm to the fair, sunny head, watching it till it was lost in the crowd from her grateful eyes.

Evidently this young man was a favorite, for, as he passed along, many a face, worn by business and care, brightened as he smiled and spoke; many a countenance stamped with the trade-mark, preoccupied and hard, relaxed in a kindly recognition as he bowed and went by; and more than one found time, even in that busy whirl, to glance for a moment after him, or to remember him with a pleasant feeling, at least till the pavement had been crossed on which they met,—a long space at that hour of the day, and with so much more important matters—Bull and Bear, rise and fall, stock and account—claiming their attention.

Evidently a favorite, for, turning off into one of the side streets, coming into his father's huge foundry, faces heated and dusty, tired, stained, and smoke-begrimed, glanced up from their work, from forge and fire and engine, with an expression that invited a look or word,— and look and word were both ready.

"The boss is out, sir," said one of the foremen, "and if you please, and have got the time to spare, I'd like to have a word with you before he comes in."

"All right, Jim! say your say."

"Well, sir, you'll likely think I'm sticking my nose into what doesn't concern me. 'Tain't a very nice thing I've got to say, but if I don't say it I don't know who in thunder will; and, as it's my private opinion that somebody ought to, I'll just pitch in."

"Very good; pitch in."

"Very good it is then. Only it ain't. Very bad, more like. It's a nasty mess, and no mistake! and there's the cause of it!" pointing his brawny hand towards the door, upon which was marked, "Office. Private," and sniffing as though he smelt something bad in the air.

"You don't mean my father!" flame shooting from the clear eyes.

"Be damned if I do. Beg pardon. Of course I don't. I mean the fellow as is perched up on a high stool in that there office, this very minute, poking into his books."

"Franklin?"

"You've hit it. Franklin,—Abe Franklin,—that's the ticket."

"What's the matter with him? what has he done?"

"Done? nothing! not as I know of, anyway, except what's right and proper. 'Tain't what he's done or's like to do. It's what he is."

"And what may that be?"

"Well, he's a nigger! there's the long and short of it. Nobody here'd object to his working in this place, providing he was a runner, or an errand-boy, or anything that it's right and proper for a nigger to be; but to have him sitting in that office, writing letters for the boss, and going over the books, and superintending the accounts of the fellows, so that he knows just what they get on Saturday nights, and being as fine as a fiddle, is what the boys won't stand; and they swear they'll leave, every man of 'em, unless he has his walking papers,—double-quick too."

"Very well; let them. There are other workmen, good as they, in this city of New York."

"Hold on, sir! let me say my say first. There are seven hundred men working in this place: the most of 'em have worked here a long while. Good work, good pay. There ain't a man of 'em but likes Mr. Surrey, and would be sorry to lose the place; so, if they won't bear it, there ain't any that will. Wait a bit! I ain't through yet."

"Go on,"—quietly enough spoken, but the mouth shook under its silky fringe, and a fiery spot burned on either cheek.

"All right. Well, sir, I know all about Franklin. He's a bright one, smart enough to stock a lot of us with brains and have some to spare; he don't interfere with us, and does his work well, too, I reckon,—though that's neither here nor there, nor none of our business if the boss is satisfied; and he looks like a gentleman, and acts like one, there's no denying that! and as for his skin,—well!" a smile breaking over his good-looking face, "his skin's quite as white as mine now, anyway," smearing his red-flannel arm over his grimy phiz; "but then, sir, it won't rub off. He's a nigger, and there's no getting round it.

"All right, sir! give you your chance directly. Don't speak yet,—ain't through, if *you* please. Well, sir, it's agen nature,—you may talk agen it, and work agen it, and fight agen it till all's blue, and what good'll it do? You can't get an Irishman, and, what's more, a free-born American citizen, to put himself on a level with a nigger,—not by no manner of means. No, sir; you can turn out the whole lot, and get another after it, and another after that, and so on to the end of the chapter, and you can't find men among 'em all that'll stay and have him strutting through 'em, up to his stool and his books, grand as a peacock."

"Would they work *with* him?"

"At the same engines, and the like, do you mean?"

"Yes."

"Nary time, so 'tain't likely they'll work under him. Now, sir, you see I know what I'm saying, and I'm saying it to *you*, Mr. Surrey, and not to your father, because he won't take a word from me nor nobody else,—and here's just the case. Now I ain't bullying, you understand, and I say it because somebody else'd say it, if I didn't, uglier and rougher. Abe Franklin'll have to go out of this shop in precious short order, or every man here'll bolt next Saturday night. There! now I've done, sir, and you can fire away."

But as he showed no signs of "firing away," and stood still, pondering, Jim broke out again:—

"Beg pardon, sir. If I've said anything you don't like, sorry for it. It's because Mr. Surrey is so good an employer, and, if you'll let me say so, because I like you so well," glancing over him admiringly,—"for, you see, a good engineer takes to a clean-built machine wherever he sees it,—it's just because of this I thought it was better to tell you, and get you to tell the boss, and to save any row; for I'd hate mortally to have it in this shop where I've worked, man and boy, so many years. Will you please to speak to him, sir? and I hope you understand."

"Thank you, Jim. Yes, I understand; and I'll speak to him."

Was it that the sun was going down, or that some clouds were in the sky, or had the air of the shop oppressed him? Whatever it was, as he came out he walked with a slower step from which some of the spring had gone, and the people's faces looked not so happy; and, glancing down at his rosebud, he saw that its fair petals had been soiled by the smoke and grime in which he had been standing; and, while he looked a dead march came solemnly sounding up the street, and a soldier's funeral went by,—rare enough, in that autumn of 1860, to draw a curious crowd on either side; rare enough to make him pause and survey it; and as the line turned into another street, and the music came softened to his ear, he once more hummed the words of the song which had been haunting him all the day:—

"Then mounte! then mounte, brave gallants, all,
      And don your helmes amaine;
Death's couriers, Fame and Honor, call
      Us to the field againe,"—

sang them to himself, but not with the gay, bright spirit of
the morning. Then he seemed to see the cavaliers, brilliant
and brave, riding out to the encounter. Now, in the same
dim and fanciful way, he beheld them stretched, still and
dead, upon the plain.

CHAPTER II

"Thou—drugging pain by patience."
ARNOLD

"LACES cleaned, and fluting and ruffling done here,"—that was what the little sign swinging outside the little green door said. And, coming under it into the cosey little rooms, you felt this was just the place in which to leave things soiled and torn, and come back to find them, by some mysterious process, immaculate and whole.

Two rooms, with folding-doors between, in which through the day stood a counter, cut up on the one side into divers pigeon-holes filled with small boxes and bundles, carefully pinned and labelled,—owner's name, time left, time to be called for, money due; neat and nice as a new pin, as every one said who had any dealings there.

The counter was pushed back now, as always after

seven o'clock, for the people who came in the evening were few; and then, when that was out of the way, it seemed more home-like and less shoppy, as Mrs. Franklin said every night, as she straightened things out, and peered through the window or looked from the front door, and wondered if "Abram weren't later than usual," though she knew right well he was punctual as clock-work,—good clock-work too,—when he was going to his toil or hurrying back to his home.

Pleasant little rooms, with the cleanest and brightest of rag carpets on the floor; a paper on the walls, cheap enough, but gay with scarlet rosebuds and green leaves, rivalled by the vines and berries on the pretty chintz curtains; chairs of a dozen ages and patterns, but all of them with open, inviting countenances and a hospitable air; a wood fire that *looked* like a wood fire crackling and sparkling on the hearth, shining and dancing over the ceiling and the floor and the walls, cutting queer capers with the big rocking-chair,—which turned into a giant with long arms,—and with the little figures on the mantel-shelf, and the books in their cases, softening and glorifying the two grand faces hanging in their frames opposite, and giving just light enough below them to let you read "John Brown" and "Phillips," if you had any occasion to read, and did not know those whom the world knows; and first and last, and through all, as if it loved her, and was loath to part with her for a moment, whether she poked the flame, or straightened a chair, or went out towards the little kitchen to lift a lid and smell a most savory stew, or came back to the supper-table to arrange and rearrange what was already faultless in its cleanliness and simplicity, wherever she went and whatever she did, this firelight fell warm about a woman, large and comfortable and handsome, with a motherly look to her person, and an expression that was all kindness in her comely face and dark, soft eyes,—eyes and face and form, though, that might as well have had "Pariah" written all over them, and "leper" stamped on their front, for any good, or beauty, or grace, that people could find in them; for the comely face was a dark face, and the voice, singing an old Methodist hymn, was no Anglo-Saxon treble, but an Anglo-African voice, rich and mellow, with the touch of pathos or sorrow always heard in these tones.

"There!" she said, "there he is!" as a step, hasty yet halting, was heard on the pavement; and, turning up the light, she ran quickly to open the door, which, to be sure, was unfastened, and to give the greeting to her "boy," which, through many a year, had never been omitted.

Her boy,—you would have known that as soon as you saw him,—the same eyes, same face, the same kindly look; but the face was thinner and finer, and the brow was a student's brow, full of thought and speculation; and, looking from her hearty, vigorous form, you saw that his was slight to attenuation.

"Sit down, sonny, sit down and rest. There! how tired you look!" bustling round him, smoothing his thin face and rough hair. "Now don't do that! let your old mother do it!" It pleased her to call herself old, though she was but just in her prime. "You've done enough for one day, I'm sure, waiting on other people, and walking with your poor lame foot till you're all but beat out. You be quiet now, and let somebody else wait on you." And, going down on her knees, she took up the lame foot, and began to unlace the cork-soled, high-cut shoe, and, drawing it out, you saw that it was shrunken and small, and that the leg was shorter than its fellow.

"Poor little foot!" rubbing it tenderly, smoothing the stocking over it, and chafing it to bring warmth and life to its surface. Her "baby," she called it, for it was no bigger than when he was a little fellow. "Poor, tired foot! ain't it a dreadful long walk, sonny?"

"Pretty long, mother; but I'd take twice that to do such work at the end."

"Yes, indeed, it's good work, and Mr. Surrey's a good man, and a kind one, that's sure! I only wish some others had a little of his spirit. Such a shame to have you dragging all the way up here, when any dirty fellow that wants to can ride. I don't mind for myself so much, for I can walk about spry enough yet, and don't thank them for their old omnibuses nor cars; but it's too bad for you, so it is,—too bad!"

"Never mind, mother! keep a brave heart. 'There's a good time coming soon, a good time coming!' as I heard Mr. Hutchinson sing the other night,—and it's true as gospel."

"Maybe it is, sonny!" dubiously, "but I don't see it,— not a sign of it,—no indeed, not one! It gets worse and worse all the time, and it takes a deal of faith to hold on; but the good Lord knows best, and it'll be right after a while, anyhow! And now *that's* straight!" pulling a soft slipper on the lame foot, and putting its mate by his side; then going off to pour out the tea, and dish up the stew, and add a touch or two to the appetizing supper-table.

"It's as good as a feast,"—taking a bite out of her nice home-made bread,—"better'n a feast, to think of you in that place; and I can't scarcely realize it yet. It seems too fine to be true."

"That's the way I've felt all the month, mother! It has been just like a dream to me, and I keep thinking surely I'm asleep and will waken to find this is just an air-castle I've been building, or 'a vision of the night,' as the good book says."

"Well, it's a blessed vision, sure enough! and I hope to the good Lord it'll last;—but you won't if you make a vision of your supper in that way. You just eat, Abram! and have done your talking till you're through, if you can't do both at once. Talking's good, but eating's better when you're hungry; and it's my opinion you ought to be hungry, if you ain't."

So the teacups were filled and emptied, and the spoons clattered, and the stew was eaten, and the baked potatoes devoured, and the bread-and-butter assaulted vigorously, and general havoc made with the good things and sub-

stantial things before and between them; and then, this
duty faithfully performed, the wreck speedily vanished
away; and cups and forks, spoons and plates, knives and
dishes, cleaned and cupboarded, Mrs. Franklin came, and,
drawing away the book over which he was poring, said,
while she smoothed face and hair once more, "Come,
Abram, what is it?"

"What's what, mother?" with a little laugh.

"Something ails you, sonny. That's plain enough. I
know when anything's gone wrong with ye, sure, and
something's gone wrong to-day."

"O mother! you worry about me too much, indeed
you do. If I'm a little tired or out of sorts,—which I
haven't any right to be, not here,—or quiet, or anything,
you think somebody's been hurting me, or abusing me, or
that everything's gone wrong with me, when I do well
enough all the time."

"Now, Abram, you can't deceive me,—not that way.
My eyes is mother's eyes, and they see plain enough, where
you're concerned, without spectacles. Who's been putting
on you to-day? Somebody. You don't carry that down
look in your face and your eyes for nothing, I found that
out long ago, and you've got it on to-night."

"O mother!"

"Don't you 'O mother' me! I ain't going to be put off
in that way, Abram, an' you needn't think it. Has Mr.
Surrey been saying anything hard to you?"

"No, indeed, mother; you needn't ask that."

"Nor none of the foremen?"

"None."

"Has Snipe been round?"

"Hasn't been near the office since Mr. Surrey dismissed him."

"Met him anywhere?"

"Nein!" laughing, "I haven't laid eyes on him." *German???*

"Well, the men have been saying or doing something then."

"N-no; why, what an inquisitor it is!"

" 'N-no.' You don't say that full and plain, Abram. Something *has* been going wrong with the men. Now what is it? Come, out with it."

"Well, mother, if you *will* know, you will, I suppose; and, as you never get tired of the story, I'll go over the whole tale.

"So long as I was Mr. Surrey's office-boy, to make his fires, and sweep and dust, and keep things in order, the men were all good enough to me after their fashion; and if some of them growled because they thought he favored me, Mr. Given, or some one said, 'O, you know his mother was a servant of Mrs. Surrey for no end of years, and of course Mr. Surrey has a kind of interest in him'; and that put everything straight again.

"Well! you know how good Mr. Willie has been to me ever since we were little boys in the same house,—he in the parlor and I in the kitchen; the books he's given me, and the chances he's made me, and the way he's put me in of learning and knowing. And he's been twice as kind to me ever since I refused that offer of his."

"Yes, I know, but tell me about it again."

"Well, Mr. Surrey sent me up to the house one day, just while Mr. Willie was at home from college, and he stopped me and <u>had a talk with me, and asked me in his pleasant way, not as if I were a 'nigger,' but just as he'd talk to one of his mates, ever so many questions about myself and my studies and my plans; and</u> I told him what I wanted,—how hard you worked, and how I hoped to fit myself to go into some little business of my own, not a barber-shop, or any such thing, but something that'd support you and keep you like a lady after while, and that would help me and my people at the same time. For, of course," I said, "every one of us that does anything more than the world expects us to do, or better, makes the world think so much the more and better of us all."

"What did he say to that?"

"I wish you'd seen him! He pushed back that beautiful hair of his, and his eyes shone, and his mouth trembled, though I could see he tried hard to hold it still, and put up his hand to cover it; and he said, in a solemn sort of way, 'Franklin, you've opened a window for me, and I sha'n't forget what I see through it to-day.' And then he offered to set me up in some business at once, and urged hard when I declined."

"Say it all over again, sonny; what was it you told him?"

"I said that would do well enough for a white man; that he could help, and the white man be helped, just as people were being and doing all the time, and no one would think a thought about it. But, sir," I said, "everybody says we can do nothing alone; that we're a poor, shiftless set; and it will be just one of the master race helping a nigger to climb and to stand where he couldn't climb or stand alone, and I'd rather fight my battle alone."

"Yes, yes! well, go on, go on. I like to hear what followed."

"Well, there was just a word or two more, and then he put out his hand and shook mine, and said good by. It was the first time I ever shook hands with a white *gentleman*. Some white hands have shaken mine, but they always made me feel that they *were* white and that mine was black, and that it was a condescension. I felt that, when they didn't mean I should. But there was nothing between us. I didn't think of his skin, and, for once in my life, I quite forgot I was black, and didn't remember it again till I got out on the street and heard a dirty little ragamuffin cry, 'Hi! hi! don't that nagur think himself foine?' I suspect, in spite of my lameness, I had been holding up my head and walking like a man."

In spite of his lameness he was holding up his head and walking like a man now; up and down and across the little room, trembling, excited, the words rushing in an eager flow from his mouth. His mother sat quietly rocking herself and knitting. She knew in this mood there was nothing to be said to him; and, indeed, what had *she* to say save that which would add fuel to the flame?

"Well!"—a long sigh,—"after that Mr. Surrey doubled my wages, and was kinder to me than ever, and watched me, as I saw, quite closely; and that was the way he found out about Mr. Snipe.

"You see Mr. Snipe had been very careless about keeping the books; would come down late in the mornings, just before Mr. Surrey came in, and go away early in the afternoons, as soon as he had left. Of course, the books got behindhand every month, and Mr. Snipe didn't want to stay and work overhours to make them up. One day he found out, by something I said, that I understood book-keeping, and tried me, and then got me to take them home at night and go over them. I didn't know then how bad he was doing, and that I had no business to shield him, and all went smooth enough till the day I was too sick to get down to the office, and two of the books were at home. Then Mr. Surrey discovered the whole thing. There was a great row, it seems; and Mr. Surrey examined the books, and found, as he was pleased to say, that I'd kept them in first-rate style; so he dismissed Mr. Snipe on the spot, with six months' pay,—for you know he never does anything by halves,—and put me in his place.

"The men don't like it, I know, and haven't liked it, but of course they can't say anything to him, and they haven't said anything to me; but I've seen all along that they looked at me with no friendly eyes, and for the last day or two I've heard a word here and there which makes me think there's trouble brewing,—bad enough, I'm afraid; maybe to the losing of my place, though Mr. Surrey has said nothing about it to me."

Just here the little green door opened, and the foreman whom we have before seen—James Given as the register had him entered, Jim Given as every one knew him— came in; no longer with grimy face and flannel sleeves, but brave in all his Sunday finery, and as handsome a b'hoy, *bowery boy* they said, at his engine-house, as any that ran with the machine; having on his arm a young lady whom he apostrophized as Sallie, as handsome and brave as he.

"Evening,"—a nod of the head accompanying. "Miss Howard's traps done?"

"I wish you wouldn't say 'traps,' Jim," corrected Sallie, *sotto voce*: "it's not proper. It's for a collar and pair of cuffs, Mrs. Franklin," she added aloud, putting down a little check.

"Not proper! goodness gracious me! there spoke Snipe! Come, Sallie, you've pranced round with that stuck-up jackanapes till you're getting spoiled entirely, so you are, and I scarcely know you. Not proper,—O my!"

"Spoiled, am I? Thank you, sir, for the compliment! And you don't know me at all,—don't you? Very well, then I'll say good night, and leave; for it wouldn't be *proper* to take a young lady you don't know to the theatre,—now, would it? Good by!"—making for the door.

"Now don't, Sallie, please."

"Don't what?"

"Don't talk that way."

"Don't yourself, more like. You're just as cross as cross can be, and disagreeable, and hateful,—all because I happen to know there's some other man in the world besides yourself, and smile at him now and then. 'Don't,' indeed!"

"Come, Sallie, you're too hard on a fellow. It's your own fault, you know well enough, if you *will* be so handsome. Now, if you were an ugly old girl, or I was certain of you, I shouldn't feel so bad, nor act so neither. But when there's a lot of hungry chaps round, all gaping to gobble you up, and even poor little Snipes trying to peck and bite at you, and you won't say 'yes' nor 'no' to me, how do you expect a man to keep cool? Can't do it, nohow, and you needn't ask it. Human nature's human nature, I suppose, and mine ain't a quiet nor a patient one, not by no manner of means. Come, Sallie, own up; you wouldn't like me so well as I hope you do if it was,—now, would you?"

Mrs. Franklin smiled, though she had heard not a word of the lovers' quarrel, as she put a pin in the back of the ruffled collar which Sallie had come to reclaim. A quarrel it had evidently been, and as evidently the lady was mollified, for she said, "Don't be absurd, Jim!" and Jim laughed and responded, "All right, Sallie, you're an angel! But come, we must hurry, or the curtain'll be up,"—and away went the dashing and handsome couple.

Abram, shutting in the shutters, and fastening the

door, sat down to a quiet evening's reading, while his
mother knitted and sewed,—an evening the likeness of a
thousand others of which they never tired; for this mother
and son, to whom fate had dealt so hard a measure, upon
whom the world had so persistently frowned, were more
to each other than most mothers and sons whose lines had
fallen in pleasanter places,—compensation, as Mr.
Emerson says, being the law of existence the world over.

CHAPTER III

"Every one has his day, from which he dates."
OLD PROVERB

"YOU see, Surrey, the school is something extra, and the performances, and it will please Clara no end; so I thought I'd run over, and inveigled you info going along for fear it should be stupid, and I would need some recreation."

"Which I am to afford?"

"Verily."

"As clown or grindstone?—to make laugh, or sharpen your wits upon?"

"Far be it from me to dictate. Whichever suits our character best. On the whole, I think the last would be the most appropriate; the first I can swear wouldn't!"

"*Pourquoi?*"   French?

"O, a woman's reason,—because!"

57

"Because why? Am I cross?"

"Not exactly."

"Rough?"

"As usual,—like a May breeze."

"Cynical?"

"As Epicurus."

"Irritable?"

"'A countenance [and manner] more in sorrow than in anger.' Something's wrong with you; who is she?"

"She!"

"Ay,—she. That was a wise Eastern king who put at the bottom of every trouble and mischief a woman."

"Fine estimate."

"Correct one. Evidently he had studied the genus thoroughly, and had a poor opinion of it."

"No wonder."

"Amazing! *you* say 'no wonder'! Astounding words! speak them again."

"No wonder,—seeing that he had a mother, and that she had such a son. He must needs have been a bad fellow or a fool to have originated so base a philosophy, and how then could he respect the source of such a stream as himself?"

"Sir Launcelot,—squire of dames!"

"Not Sir Launcelot, but squire of dames, I hope."

"There you go again! Now I shall query once more, who is she?"

"No woman."

"No?"

"No, though by your smiling you would seem to say so!"

"Nay, I believe you, and am vastly relieved in the believing. Take advice from ten years of superior age, and fifty of experience, and have naught to do with them. Dost hear?"

"I do."

"And will heed?"

"Which?—the words or the acts of my counsellor? who, of a surety, preaches wisely and does foolishly, or who does wisely and preaches foolishly; for preaching and practice do not agree."

"Nay, man, thou art unreasonable; to perform either well is beyond the capacity of most humans, and I desire not to be blessed above my betters. Then let my rash deeds and my prudent words both be teachers unto thee. But if it be true that no woman is responsible for your grave countenance this morning, then am I wasting words, and will return to our muttons. What ails you?"

"I am belligerent."

"I see,—that means quarrelsome."

"And hopeless."

"Bad,—very! belligerent and hopeless! When you go into a fight always expect to win; the thought is half the victory."

"Suppose you are an atom against the universe?"

"Don't fight, succumb. There's a proverb,—a wise

one,—Napoleon's, 'God is on the side of the strongest bat-
talions.'"

"A lie,—exploded at Waterloo. There's another proverb,
'One on the side of God is a majority.' How about that?"

"Transcendental humbug."

"A truth demonstrated at Wittenberg."

"Are you aching for the martyr's palm?"

"I am afraid not. On the whole, I think I'd rather enjoy
life than quarrel with it. But"—with a sudden blaze—"I
feel today like fighting the world."

"Hey, presto! what now, young'un?"

"I don't wonder you stare"—a little laugh. "I'm talking
like a fool, and, for aught I know, feeling like one, aching
to fight, and knowing that I might as well quarrel with the
winds, or stab that water as it flows by."

"As with what?"

"The fellow I've just been getting a good look at."

"What manner of fellow?"

"Ignorant, selfish, brutal, devilish."

"Tremendous! why don't you bind him over to keep
the peace?"

"Because he is like the judge of old time, neither fears
God nor respects his image,—when his image is carved in
ebony, and not ivory."

"What do you call this fellow?"

"Public Opinion."

"This big fellow is abusing and devouring a poor little
chap, eh? and the chap's black?"

"True."

"And sometimes the giant is a gentleman in purple and fine linen, otherwise broadcloth; and sometimes in hodden gray, otherwise homespun or slop-shop; and sometimes he cuts the poor little chap with a silver knife, which is rhetoric, and sometimes with a wooden spoon, which is raw-hide. Am I stating it all correctly?"

"All correctly."

"And you've been watching this operation when you had better have been minding your own business, and getting excited when you had better have kept cool, and now want to rush into the fight, drums beating and colors flying, to the rescue of the small one. Don't deny it,—it's all written out in your eyes."

"I sha'n't deny it, except about the business and the keeping cool. It's any gentleman's business to interfere between a bully and a weakling that he's abusing; and his blood must be water that does not boil while he 'watches the operation' as you say, and goes in."

"To get well pommelled for his pains, and do no good to any one, himself included. Let the weakling alone. A fellow that can't save himself is not worth saving. If he can't swim nor walk, let him drop under or go to the wall; that's my theory."

"Anglo-Saxon theory—and practice."

"Good theory, excellent practice,—in the main. What special phase of it has been disturbing your equanimity?"

"You know the Franklins?"

"Of course: Aunt Mina's son—what's his name?—is a sort of *protégé* of yours, I believe: what of him?"

"He is cleanly?"

"A nice question. Doubtless."

"Respectable?"

"What are you driving at?"

"Intelligent?"

"Most true."

"Ambitious?"

"Or his looks belie him."

"Faithful, trusty, active, helpful, in every way devoted to my father's service and his work."

"With Sancho, I believe it all because your worship says so."

"Well, this man has just been discharged from my father's employ because seven hundred and forty-two other men gave notice to quit if he remained."

"The reason?"

"His skin."

"The reason is not 'so deep as a well, nor so wide as a church-door, but it is enough.' Of course they wouldn't work with him, and my uncle Surrey, begging your pardon, should not have attempted anything so Quixotic."

"His skin covering so many excellent qualities, and these qualities gaining recognition,—*that* was the cause. They worked with him so long as he was a servant of servants: so soon as he demonstrated that he could strike out strongly and swim, they knocked him under; and, proving that he could walk alone, they ran hastily to shove him to the wall."

"What! quoting my own words against me?"

"Anglo-Saxon says we are the masters: we monopolize the strength and courage, the beauty, intelligence, power. These creatures,—what are they? poor, worthless, lazy, ignorant, good for nothing but to be used as machines, to obey. When lo! one of these dumb machines suddenly starts forth with a man's face; this creature no longer obeys, but evinces a right to command; and Anglo-Saxon speedily breaks him in pieces."

"Come, Willie, I hope you're not going to assert these people our equals,—that would be too much."

"They have no intelligence, Anglo-Saxon declares,— then refuses them schools, while he takes of their money to help educate his own sons. They have no ambition,— then closes upon them every door of honorable advancement, and cries through the key-hole, Serve, or starve. They cannot stand alone, they have no faculty for rising,— then, if one of them finds foothold, the ground is undermined beneath him. If a head is seen above the crowd, the ladder is jerked away, and he is trampled into the dust where he is fallen. If he stays in the position to which Anglo-Saxon assigns him, he is a *worthless* nigger; if he protests against it, he is an *insolent* nigger; if he rises above it, he is a nigger not to be tolerated at all,—to be crushed and buried speedily."

"Now, Willie, 'no more of this, an thou lovest me.' I

came not out today to listen to an abolition harangue, nor
a moral homily, but to have a good time, to be civil and
merry withal, if you will allow it. Of course you don't like
Franklin's discharge, and of course you have done something to compensate him. I know—you have found him
another place. No,—you couldn't do that?

"No, I couldn't."

"Well, you've settled him somewhere,—confess."

"He has some work for the present; some copying for
me, and translating, for this unfortunate is a scholar, you
know."

"Very good; then let it rest. Granted the poor devils
have a bad time of it, you're not bound to sacrifice yourself for them. If you go on at this pace, you'll bring up
with the long-haired, bloomer reformers, and then—God
help you. No, you needn't say another word,—I sha'n't
listen,—not one; so. Here we are! school yonder,—well
situated?"

"Capitally."

"Fine day."

"Very."

"Clara will be charmed to see you."

"You flatter me. I hope so."

"There, now you talk rationally. Don't relapse. We will
go up and hear the pretty creatures read their little pieces,
and sing their little songs, and see them take their nice
blue-ribboned diplomas, and fall in love with their dear
little faces, and flirt a bit this evening, and to-morrow I

shall take Ma'm'selle Clara home to Mamma Russell, and
you may go your ways."

"The programme is satisfactory."

"Good. Come on then."

All Commencement days, at college or young ladies'
school, if not twin brothers and sisters, are at least first
cousins, with a strong family likeness. Who that has passed
through one, or witnessed one, needs any description
thereof to furbish up its memories. This of Professor
Hale's belonged to the great tribe, and its form and features
were of the old established type. The young ladies were
charming; plenty of white gowns, plenty of flowers, plenty
of smiles, blushes, tremors, hopes, and fears; little songs,
little pieces, little addresses, to be sung, to be played, to be
read, just as Tom Russell had foreshadowed, and proving
to be—

"Just the least of a bore!" as he added after listening
awhile; "don't you think so, Surrey?"

"Hush! don't talk."

Tom stared; then followed his cousin's eye, fixed
immovably upon one little spot on the platform. "By
Jove!" he cried, "what a beauty! As Father Dryden would
say, 'this is the porcelain clay of humankind.' No wonder
you look. Who is she,—do you know?"

"No."

"No! short, clear, and decisive. Don't devour her, Will.
Remember the sermon I preached you an hour ago.
Come, look at this,"—thrusting a programme into his

face,—"and stop staring. Why, boy, she has bewitched you,—or inspired you,"—surveying him sharply.

And indeed it would seem so. Eyes, mouth, face, instinct with some subtle and thrilling emotion. As gay Tom Russell looked, he involuntarily stretched out his hand, as one would put it between another and some danger of which that other is unaware, and remembered what he had once said in talking of him,—"If Will Surrey's time does come, I hope the girl will be all right in every way, for he'll plunge headlong, and love like distraction itself,—no half-way; it will be a life-and-death affair for him." "Come, I must break in on this."

"Surrey!"

"Yes."

"There's a pretty girl."

No answer.

"There! over yonder. Third seat, second row. See her? Pretty?"

"Very pretty."

"Miss—Miss—what's her name? O, Miss Perry played that last thing very well for a school-girl, eh?"

"Very well."

"Admirable room this, for hearing; rare quality with chapels and halls; architects in planning generally tax ingenuity how to confuse sound. Now these girls don't make a great noise, yet you can distinguish every word,—can't you?"

No response.

"I say, can't you?"

"Every word."

Tom drew a long breath.

"Professor Hale's a sensible old fellow; I like the way he conducts this school." (Mem. Tom didn't know a thing about it.) "Carries it on excellently." A pause.

Silence.

"Fine-looking, too. A man's physique has a deal to do with his success in the world. If he carries a letter of recommendation in his face, people take him on trust to begin with; and if he's a big fellow, like the Professor yonder, he imposes on folks awfully; they pop down on their knees to him, and clear the track for him, as if he had a right to it all. Bless me! I never thought of that before,— it's the reason you and I have got on so swimmingly,—is it not, now? Certainly. You think so? Of course."

"Of course,"—sedately and gravely spoken.

Tom groaned, for, with a face kind and bright, he was yet no beauty; while if Surrey had one crowning gift in this day of fast youths and self-satisfied Young America, it was that of modesty with regard to himself and any gifts and graces nature had blessed him withal.

"Clara has a nice voice."

"Very nice."

"She is to sing, do you know?"

"I know."

"Do you know when?"

No reply.

"She sings the next piece. Are you ready to listen?"

"Ready."

"Good Lord!" cried Tom, in despair, "the fellow has lost his wits. He has turned parrot; he has done nothing but repeat my words for me since he sat here. He's an echo."

"Echo of nothingness?" queried the parrot, smilingly.

"Ah, you've come to yourself, have you? Capital! now stay awake. There's Clara to sing directly, and you are to cheer her, and look as if you enjoyed it, and throw her that bouquet when I tell you, and let her think it's a fine thing she has been doing; for this is a tremendous affair to her, poor child, of course."

"How bright and happy she is! You will laugh at me, Tom, and indeed I don't know what has come over me, but somehow I feel quite sad, looking at those girls, and wondering what fate and time have in store for them."

"Sunshine and bright hours."

"The day cometh, and also the night,"—broke in the clear voice that was reading a selection from the Scriptures.

Tom started, and Willie took from his button-hole just such a little nosegay as that he had bought on Broadway a fortnight before,—a geranium leaf, a bit of mignonette, and a delicate tea-rosebud, and, seeing it was drooping, laid it carefully upon the programme on his knee. "I don't want that to fade," he thought as he put it down, while he looked across the platform at the same face which he had so eagerly pursued through a labyrinth of carriages, stages, and people, and lost at last.

"There! Clara is talking to your beauty. I wonder if she is to sing, or do anything. If she does, it will be something dainty and fine, I'll wager. Helloa! there's Clara up,—now for it."

Clara's bright little voice suited her bright little face,—like her brother's, only a great deal prettier,—and the young men enjoyed both, aside from brotherly and cousinly feeling, cheered her "to the echo" as Willie said, threw their bouquets,—great, gorgeous things they had brought from the city to please her,—and wished there was more of it all when it was through.

"What next?" said Willie.

"Heaven preserve us! your favorite subject. Who would expect to tumble on such a theme here?—'Slavery; by Francesca Ercildoune.' Odd name,—and, by Jove! it's the beauty herself."

They both leaned forward eagerly as she came from her seat; slender, shapely, every fibre fine and exquisite, no coarse graining from the dainty head to the dainty foot; the face, clear olive, delicate and beautiful,—

> "The mouth with steady sweetness set,
>   And eyes conveying unaware
> The distant hint of some regret
>   That harbored there,"—

eyes deep, tender, and pathetic.

"What's this?" said Tom. "Queer. It gives me a heartache to look at her."

"A woman for whom to fight the world, or lose the world, and be compensated a million-fold if you died at her feet," thought Surrey, and said nothing.

"What a strange subject for her to select!" broke in Tom.

It was a strange one for the time and place, and she had been besought to drop it, and take another; but it should be that or nothing, she asserted,—so she was left to her own device.

Oddly treated, too. Tom thought it would be a pretty lady-like essay, and said so; then sat astounded at what he saw and heard. Her face—this schoolgirl's face—grew pallid, her eyes mournful, her voice and manner sublime, as she summoned this Monster to the bar of God's justice and the humanity of the world; as she arraigned it; as she brought witness after witness to testify against it; as she proved its horrible atrocities and monstrous barbarities; as she went on to the close, and, lifting hand and face and voice together, thrilled out, "I look backward into the dim, distant past, but it is one night of oppression and despair; I turn to the present, but I hear naught save the mother's broken-hearted shriek, the infant's wail, the groan wrung from the strong man in agony; I look forward into the future, but the night grows darker, the shadows deeper and longer, the tempest wilder, and involuntarily I cry out, 'How long, O God, how long?' "

"Heavens! what an actress she would make!" said somebody before them.

"That's genius," said somebody behind them; "but what a subject to waste it upon!"

"Very bad taste, I must say, to talk about such a thing here," said somebody beside them. "However, one can excuse a great deal to beauty like that."

Surrey sat still, and felt as though he were on fire, filled with an insane desire to seize her in one arm like a knight of old, and hew his way through these beings, and out of this place, into some solitary spot where he could seat her and kneel at her feet, and die there if she refused to take him up; filled with all the sweet, extravagant, delicious pain that thrills the heart, full of passion and purity, of a young man who begins to love the first, overwhelming, only love of a lifetime.

CHAPTER IV

" 'Tis an old tale, and often told."
SIR WALTER SCOTT

THAT evening some people who were near them were talking about it, and that made Tom ask Clara if her friend was in the habit of doing startling things.

"Should you think so to look at her now?" queried Clara, looking across the room to where Miss Ercildoune stood.

"Indeed I shouldn't," Tom replied; and indeed no one would who saw her then. "She's as sweet as a sugar-plum," he added, as he continued to look. "What does she mean by getting off such rampant discourses? She never wrote them herself,—don't tell *me*; at least somebody else put her up to it,—that strong-minded-looking teacher over yonder, for instance. *She* looks capable of anything, and something worse, in the denouncing way; poor little beauty was her cat's-paw this morning."

"O Tom, how you talk! She is nobody's cat's-paw. I can tell you she does her own thinking and acting too. If you'd just go and do something hateful, or impose on somebody,—one of the waiters, for instance,—you'd see her blaze up, fast enough."

"Ah! philanthropic?"

Clara looked puzzled. "I don't know; we have some girls here who are all the time talking about benevolence, and charity, and the like, and they have a little sewing-circle to make up things to be sold for the church mission, or something,—I don't know just what; but Francesca won't go near it."

"Democratic, then, maybe."

"No, she isn't, not a bit. She's a thorough little aristo-crat: so exclusive she has nothing to say to the most of us. I wonder she ever took me for a friend, though I do love her dearly."

Tom looked down at his bright little sister, and thought the wonder was not a very great one, but didn't say so; reserving his gallantries for somebody else's sister.

"You seem greatly taken with her, Tom."

"I own the soft impeachment."

"Well, you'll have a fair chance, for she's coming home with me. I wrote to mamma, and she says, bring her by all means,—and Mr. Ercildoune gives his consent; so it is all settled."

"Mr. Ercildoune! is there no Mrs. E.?"

"None,—her mother died long ago; and her father has not been here, so I can't tell you anything about him. There: do you see that elegant-looking lady talking with Professor Hale? that is her aunt, Mrs. Lancaster. She is English, and is here only on a visit. She wants to take Francesca home with her in the spring, but I hope she won't."

"Why, what is it to you?"

"I am afraid she will stay, and then I shall never see her any more."

"And why stay? do you fancy England so very fascinating?"

"No, it is not that; but Francesca don't like America; she's forever saying something witty and sharp about our 'democratic institutions,' as she calls them; and, if you had looked this morning, you'd have seen that she didn't sing The Star-Spangled Banner with the rest of us. Her voice is splendid, and Professor Hale wanted her to lead, as she often does, but she wouldn't sing that, she said,—no, not for anything; and though we all begged, she refused,—flat."

"Shocking! what total depravity! I wonder is she converting Surrey to her heresies."

No, she wasn't; not unless silence is more potent than words; for after they had danced together Surrey brought her to one of the great windows facing towards the sea, and, leaning over her chair, there was stillness between them as their eyes went out into the night.

A wild night! great clouds drifted across the moon, which shone out anon, with light intensified, defining the stripped trees and desolate landscape, and then the beach, and

> "Marked with spray
> The sunken reefs, and far away
> The unquiet, bright Atlantic plain,"

while through all sounded incessantly the mournful roar of buffeting wind and surging tide; and whether it was the scene, or the solemn undertone of the sea, the dance music, which a little while before had been so gay, sounded like a wail.

How could it be otherwise? Passion is akin to pain. Love never yet penetrated an intense nature and made the heart light; sentiment has its smiles, its blushes, its brightness, its words of fancy and feeling, readily and at will; but when the internal sub-soiling is broken up, the heart swells with a steady and tremendous pressure till the breast feels like bursting; the lips are dumb, or open only to speak upon indifferent themes. Flowers may be played with, but one never yet cared to toy with flame.

There are souls that are created for one another in the eternities, hearts that are predestined each to each, from the absolute necessities of their nature; and when this man and this woman come face to face, these hearts throb and are one; these souls recognize "my master!" "my mistress!"

at the first glance, without words uttered or vows pronounced.

These two young lives, so fresh, so beautiful; these beings, in many things such antipodes, so utterly dissimilar in person, so unlike, yet like; their whole acquaintance a glance on a crowded street and these few hours of meeting,—looked into one another's eyes, and felt their whole nature set each to each, as the vast tide "of the bright, rocking ocean sets to shore at the full moon."

These things are possible. Friendship is excellent, and friendship may be called love; but it is not love. It may be more enduring and placidly satisfying in the end; it may be better, and wiser, and more prudent, for acquaintance to beget esteem, and esteem regard, and regard affection, and affection an interchange of peaceful vows: the result, a well-ordered life and home. All this is admirable, no doubt; an owl is a bird when you can get no other; but the love born of a moment, yet born of eternity, which comes but once in a lifetime, and to not one in a thousand lives, unquestioning, unthinking, investigating nothing, proving nothing, sufficient unto itself,—ah, that is divine; and this divine ecstasy filled these two souls.

Unconsciously. They did not define nor comprehend. They listened to the sea where they sat, and felt tears start to their eyes, yet knew not why. They were silent, and thought they talked; or spoke, and said nothing. They danced; and as he held her hand and uttered a few words, almost whispered, the words sounded to the listening ear like a part of the music to which they kept time. They saw a multitude of people, and exchanged the compliments of the evening, yet these people made no more impression upon their thoughts than gossamer would have made upon their hands.

"Come, Francesca!" said Clara Russell, breaking in upon this, "it is not fair for you to monopolize my cousin Will, who is the handsomest man in the room; and it isn't fair for Will to keep you all to himself in this fashion. Here is Tom, ready to scratch out his eyes with vexation because you won't dance with him; and here am I, dying to waltz with somebody who knows my step,—to say nothing of innumerable young ladies and gentlemen who have been casting indignant and beseeching glances this way: so, sir, face about, march!" and away the gay girl went with her prize, leaving Francesca to the tender mercies of half a dozen young men who crowded eagerly round her, and from whom Tom carried her off with triumph and rejoicing.

The evening was over at last, and they were going away. Tom had said good night.

"You are to be in New York, at my uncle's, Clara tells me."

"It is true."

"I may see you there?"

For answer she put out her hand. He took it as he would have taken a delicate flower, laid his other hand softly, yet closely, over it, and, without any adieu spoken, went away.

"Tom always declared Willie was a little queer, and I'm sure I begin to think so," said Clara, as she kissed her friend and departed to her room.

CHAPTER V

"A breathing sigh, a sigh for answer,
A little talking of outward things."
JEAN INGELOW

Ah, the weeks that followed! People ate and drank and slept, lived and loved and hated, were born and died,—the same world that it had been a little while before, yet not the same to them,—never to seem quite the same again. A little cloud had fallen between them and it, and changed to their eyes all its proportions and hues.

They were incessantly together, riding, or driving, or walking, looking at pictures, dancing at parties, listening to opera or play.

"It seems to me Will is going it at a pretty tremendous pace somewhere," said Mr. Surrey to his wife, one morning, after this had endured for a space. "It would be well to look into it, and to know something of this girl."

"You are right," she replied. "Yet I have such absolute faith in Willie's fine taste and sense that I feel no anxiety."

"Nor I; yet I shall investigate a bit to-night at Augusta's."

"Clara tells me that when Miss Ercildoune understood it was to be a great party, she insisted on ending her visit, or, at least, staying for a while with her aunt, but they would not hear of it."

"Mrs. Lancaster goes back to England soon?"

"Very soon."

"Does any one know aught of Miss Ercildoune's family save that Mrs. Lancaster is her aunt?"

"If 'any one' means me, I understand her father to be a gentleman of elegant leisure,—his home near Philadelphia; a widower, with one other child,—a son, I believe; that his wife was English, married abroad; that Mrs. Lancaster comes here with the best of letters, and, for herself, is most evidently a lady."

"Good. Now I shall take a survey of the young lady herself."

When night came, and with it a crowd to Mrs. Russell's rooms, the opportunity offered for the survey, and it was made scrutinizingly. Surrey was an only son, a well-beloved one, and what concerned him was investigated with utmost care.

Scrutinizingly and satisfactorily. They were dancing, his sunny head bent till it almost touched the silky blackness of her hair. "Saxon and Norman," said somebody near who was watching them; "what a delicious contrast!"

"They make an exquisite picture," thought the mother, as she looked with delight and dread: delight at the beauty; dread that fills the soul of any mother when she feels that she no longer holds her boy,—that his life has another keeper,—and queries, "What of the keeper?"

"Well?" she said, looking up at her husband.

"Well," he answered, with a tone that meant, well. "She's thorough-bred. Democratic or not, I will always insist, blood tells. Look at her: no one needs to ask *who* she is. I'd take her on trust without a word."

"So, then, you are not her critic, but her admirer."

"Ah, my dear, criticism is lost in admiration, and I am glad to find it so."

"And I. Willie saw with our eyes, as a boy; it is fortunate that we can see with his eyes, as a man."

So, without any words spoken, after that night, both Mr. and Mrs. Surrey took this young girl into their hearts as they hoped soon to take her into their lives, and called her "daughter" in their thought, as a pleasant preparation for the uttered word by and by.

Thus the weeks fled. No word had passed between these two to which the world might not have listened. Whatever language their hearts and their eyes spoke had not been interpreted by their lips. He had not yet touched her hand save as it met his, gloved or formal, or as it rested on his arm; and yet, as one walking through the dusk and stillness of a summer night feels a flower or falling leaf brush his check, and starts, shivering as from the touch of a disembodied soul, so this slight outward touch thrilled his inmost being; this hand, meeting his for an instant, shook his soul.

Indefinite and undefined,—there was no thought beyond the moment; no wish to take this young girl into his arms and to call her "wife" had shaped itself in his brain. It was enough for both that they were in one another's presence, that they breathed the same air, that they could see each other as they raised their eyes, and exchange a word, a look, a smile. Whatever storm of emotion the future might hold for them was not manifest in this sunny and delightful present.

Upon one subject alone did they disagree with feeling,—in other matters their very dissimilarity proving an added charm. This was a curious question to come between lovers. All his life Surrey had been a devotee of his country and its flag. While he was a boy Kossuth had come to these shores, and he yet remembered how he had cheered himself hoarse with pride and delight, as the eloquent voice and impassioned lips of the great Magyar sounded the praise of America, as the "refuge of the oppressed and the hope of the world." He yet remembered how when the hand, every gesture of which was instinct with power, was lifted to the flag,—the flag, stainless, spotless, without blemish or flaw; the flag which was "fair as the sun, clear as the moon," and to the oppressors of the earth "terrible as an army with banners,"—he yet remembered how, as this emblem of liberty was thus apostrophized and saluted, the tears had rushed to his boyish eyes, and his voice had said, for his heart, "Thank God, I am an American!"

One day he made some such remark to her. She answered, "I, too, am an American, but I do not thank God for it."

At another time he said, as some emigrants passed them in the street, "What a sense of pride it gives one in one's country, to see her so stretch out her arms to help and embrace the outcast and suffering of the whole world!"

She smiled—bitterly, he thought; and replied, "O just and magnanimous country, to feed and clothe the stranger from without, while she outrages and destroys her children within!"

"You do not love America," he said.

"I do not love America," she responded.

"And yet it is a wonderful country."

"Ay," briefly, almost satirically, "a wonderful country, indeed!"

"Still you stay here, live here."

"Yes, it is my country. Whatever I think of it, I will not be driven away from it; it is my right to remain."

"Her right to remain?" he thought; "what does she mean by that? she speaks as though conscience were involved in the thing. No matter; let us talk of something pleasanter."

One day she gave him a clew. They were looking at

the picture of a great statesman,—a man as famous for the
grandeur of face and form as for the power and splendor
of his intellect.

"Unequalled! unapproachable!" exclaimed Surrey, at last.

"I have seen its equal," she answered, very quietly, yet
with a shiver of excitement in the tones.

"When? where? how? I will take a journey to look at
him. Who is he? where did he grow?"

For response she put her hand into the pocket of her
gown, and took out a velvet case. What could there be in
that little blue thing to cause such emotion? As Surrey saw
it in her hand, he grew hot, then cold, then fiery hot
again. In an instant by this chill, this heat, this pain, his
heart was laid bare to his own inspection. In an instant he
knew that his arms would be empty did they hold a universe in which Francesca Ercildoune had no part, and that
with her head on his heart the world might lapse from him
unheeded; and, with this knowledge, she held tenderly and
caressingly, as he saw, another man's picture in her hand.

His own so shook that he could scarcely take the case
from her, to open it; but, opened, his eyes devoured what
was under them.

A half-length,—the face and physique superb. Of what
color were the hair and eyes the neutral tints of the picture
gave no hint; the brow princely, breaking the perfect oval
of the face; eyes piercing and full; the features rounded, yet
clearly cut; the mouth with a curious combination of sadness and disdain. The face was not young, yet it was so

instinct with magnificent vitality that even the picture impressed one more powerfully than most living men, and one involuntarily exclaimed on beholding it, "This man can never grow old, and death must here forego its claim!"

Looking up from it with no admiration to express for the face, he saw Francesca's smiling on it with a sort of adoration, as she, reclaiming her property, said,—

"My father's old friends have a great deal of enjoyment, and amusement too, from his beauty. One of them was the other day telling me of the excessive admiration people had always shown, and laughingly insisted that when papa was a young man, and appeared in public, in London or Paris, it was between two police officers to keep off the admiring crowd; and," laughing a gay little laugh herself, "of course I believed him! why shouldn't I?"

He was looking at the picture again. "What an air of command he has!"

"Yes. I remember hearing that when Daniel Webster was in London, and walked unattended through the streets, the coal-heavers and workmen took off their hats and stood bareheaded till he had gone by, thinking it was royalty that passed. I think they would do the same for papa."

"If he looks like a king, I know somebody who looks like a princess," thought the happy young fellow, gazing down upon the proud, dainty figure by his side; but he smiled as he said, "What a little aristocrat you are, Miss Ercildoune! what a pity you were born a Yankee!"

"I am not a Yankee, Mr. Surrey," replied the little aristocrat, "if to be a Yankee is to be a native of America. I
was born on the sea."

"And your mother, I know, was English."

"Yes, she was English."

"Is it rude to ask if your father was the same?

"No!" she answered emphatically, "my papa is a Virginian,—a Virginia gentleman,"—the last word spoken
with an untransferable accent,—"there are few enough of
them."

"So, so!" thought Willie, "here my riddle is read.
Southern—Virginia—gentleman. No wonder she has no
love to spend on country or flag; no wonder we couldn't
agree. And yet it can't be that,—what were the first words
I ever heard from her mouth?" and, remembering that terrible denunciation of the "peculiar institution" of Virginia
and of the South, he found himself puzzled the more.

Just then there came into the picture-gallery, where
they were wasting a pleasant morning, a young man to
whom Surrey gave the slightest of recognitions,—well-
dressed, booted, and gloved, yet lacking the nameless
something which marks the gentleman. His glance, as it
rested on Surrey, held no love, and, indeed, was rather
malignant.

"That fellow," said Surrey, indicating him, "has a queer
story connected with him. He was discharged from my
father's employ to give place to a man who could do his
work better; and the strange part of it"—he watched her

with an amused smile to see what effect the announcement would have upon her Virginia ladyship—"is that number two is a black man."

A sudden heat flushed her cheeks: "Do you tell me your father made room for a black man in his employ, and at the expense of a white one?"

"It is even so."

"Is he there now?"

Surrey's beautiful Saxon face crimsoned. "No: he is not," he said reluctantly.

"Ah! did he, this black man,—did he not do his work well?"

"Admirably."

"Is it allowable, then, to ask why he was discarded?"

"It is allowable, surely. He was dismissed because the choice lay between him and seven hundred men."

"And you"—her face was very pale now, the flush all gone out of it—"you have nothing to do with your father's works, but you are his son,—did you do naught? protest, for instance?"

"I protested—and yielded. The contest would have been not merely with seven hundred men, but with every machinist in the city. Justice *versus* prejudice, and prejudice had it; as, indeed, I suppose it will for a good many generations to come: invincible it appears to be in the American mind."

"Invincible! is it so?" She paused over the words, scrutinizing him meanwhile with an unconscious intensity.

"And this black man,—what of him? He was flung out to starve and die; a proper fate, surely, for his presumption. Poor fool! how did he dare to think he could compete with his masters! You know nothing of *him*?"

Surely he must be mistaken. What could this black man, or this matter, be to her? yet as he listened her voice sounded to his ear like that of one in mortal pain. What held him silent? Why did he not tell her, why did he not in some way make her comprehend, that he, delicate exclusive, and patrician, as the people of his set thought him, had gone to this man, had lifted him from his sorrow and despondency to courage and hope once more; had found him work; would see that the place he strove to fill in the world should be filled, could any help of his secure that end. Why did the modesty which was a part of him, and the high-bred reserve which shrank from letting his own mother know of the good deeds his life wrought, hold him silent now?

In that silence something fell between them. What was it? But a moment, yet in that little space it seemed to him as though continents divided them, and seas rolled between. "Francesca!" he cried, under his breath,—he had never before called her by her Christian name,— "Francesca!" and stretched out his hand towards her, as a drowning man stretches forth his hand to life.

"This room is stifling!" she said for answer; and her voice, dulled and unnatural, seemed to his strangely confused senses as though it came from a far distance,—"I am suffering: shall we go out to the air?"

CHAPTER VI

"But more than loss about me clings."
JEAN INGELOW

"No! no, I am mad to think it! I must have been dreaming! what could there have been in that talk to have such an effect as I have conjured up? She pitied Franklin! yes, she pities every one whom she thinks suffering or wronged. Dear little tender heart! of course it was the room,—didn't she say she was ill? it must have been awful; the heat and the closeness got into my head,—that's it. Bad air is as bad as whiskey on a man's brain. What a fool I made of myself! not even answering her questions. What did she think of me? Well."

Surrey in despair pushed away the book over which he had been bending all the afternoon, seeing for every word Francesca, and on every page an image of her face. "I'll smoke myself into some sort of decent quiet, before I go

up town, at least"; and taking his huge meerschaum, set-
tling himself sedately, began his quieting operation with
appalling energy. The soft rings, gray and delicate, taking
curious and airy shapes, floated out and filled the room;
but they were not soothing shapes, nor ministering spirits
of comfort. They seemed filmy garments, and from their
midst faces beautiful, yet faint and dim, looked at him, all
of them like unto her face; but when he dropped his pipe
and bent forward, the wreaths of smoke fell into lines that
made the faces appear sad and bathed in tears, and the
images faded from his sight.

As the last one, with its visionary arms outstretched
towards him, receded from him, and disappeared, he
thought, "That is Francesca's spirit, bidding me an eternal
adieu"—and, with the foolish thought, in spite of its fool-
ishness, he shivered and stretched out his arms in return.

"Of a verity," he then cried, "if nature failed to make
me an idiot, I am doing my best to consummate that end,
and become one of free choice. What folly possesses me?
I will dissipate it at once,—I will see her in bodily shape,—
that will put an end to such fancies,"—starting up, and
beginning to pull on his gloves.

"No! no, that will not do,"—pulling them off again.
"She will think I am an uneasy ghost that pursues her. I must
wait till this evening, but ah, what an age till evening!"

Fortunately, all ages, even lovers' ages, have an end.
The evening came; he was at the Fifth Avenue,—his card
sent up,—his feet impatiently travelling to and fro upon

the parlor carpet,—his heart beating with happiness and expectancy. A shadow darkened the door; he flew to meet the substance,—not a sweet face and graceful form, but a servant, big and commonplace, bringing him his own card and the announcement, "The ladies is both out, sir."

"Impossible! take it up again."

He said "impossible" because Francesca had that morning told him she would be at home in the evening.

"All right, sir; but it's no use, for there's nobody there, I know"; and he vanished for a second attempt, unsuccessful as the first. Surrey went to the office, still determinedly incredulous.

"Are Mrs. Lancaster and Miss Ercildoune not in?"

"No, sir; both out. Keys here,"—showing them. "Left for one of the five-o'clock trains; rooms not given up; said they would be back in a few days."

"From what depot did they leave?"

"Don't know, sir. They didn't go in the coach; had a carriage, or I could tell you."

"But they left a note, perhaps,—or some message?"

"Nothing at all, sir; not a word, nor a scrap. Can I serve you in any way further?"

"Thanks! not at all. Good evening."

"Good evening, sir."

That was all. What did it mean?—to vanish without a sign! an engagement for the evening, and not a line left in explanation or excuse! It was not like her. There must be something wrong, some mystery. He tormented himself with a thousand fancies and fears over what, he confessed, was probably a mere accident; wisely determined to do so no longer,—but did, spite of such excellent resolutions and intent.

This took place on the evening of Saturday, the 13th of April, 1861. The events of the next few days doubtless augmented his anxiety and unhappiness. Sunday followed,—a day filled not with a Sabbath calm, but with the stillness felt in nature before some awful convulsion; the silence preceding earthquake, volcano, or blasting storm; a quiet broken from Maine to the Pacific slope when the next day shone, and men roused themselves from the sleep of a night to the duty of a day, from the sleep of generations, fast merging into death, at the trumpet-call to arms,—a cry which sounded through every State and every household in the land, which, more powerful than the old songs of Percy and Douglas, "brought children from their play, and old men from their chimney-corners," to emulate humanity in its strength and prime, and contest with it the opportunity to fight and die in a deathless cause.

A cry which said, "There are wrongs to be redressed already long enough endured,—wrongs against the flag of the nation, against the integrity of the Union, against the life of the republic; wrongs against the cause of order, of law, of good government, against right, and justice, and liberty, against humanity and the world; not merely in the present, but in the great future, its countless ages and its generations yet unborn."

To this cry there sounded one universal response, as men dropped their work at loom, or forge, or wheel, in counting-room, bank, and merchant's store, in pulpit, office, or platform, and with one accord rushed to arms, to save these rights so frightfully and arrogantly assailed.

One voice that went to swell this chorus was Surrey's; one hand quick to grasp rifle and cartridge-box, one soul eager to fling its body into the breach at this majestic call, was his. He felt to the full all the divine frenzy and passion of those first days of the war, days unequalled in the history of nations and of the world. All the elegant dilettanteism, the delicious idleness, the luxurious ease, fell away, and were as though they had never been. All the airy dreams of a renewed chivalrous age, of courage, of heroism, of sublime daring and self-sacrifice, took substance and shape, and were for him no longer visions of the night, but realities of the day.

Still, while flags waved, drums beat, and cannon thundered; while friends said, "Go!" the world stood ready to cheer him on, and fame and honor and greater things than these beckoned him to come; while he felt the whirl and excitement of it all,—his heart cried ceaselessly, "Only let me see her—once—if but for a moment, before I go!" It was so little he asked of fate, yet too much to be granted.

In vain he went every day, and many times a day, in the brief space left him, to her hotel. In vain he once more questioned clerk and servants; in vain haunted the house of his aunt, with the dim hope that Clara might hear from her, or that in some undefined way he might learn of her whereabouts, and so accomplish his desire.

But the days passed, too slowly for the ardent young patriot, all too rapidly for the unhappy lover. Friday came. Early in the day multitudes of people began to collect in the street, growing in numbers and enthusiasm as the hours wore on, till, in the afternoon, the splendid thoroughfare of New York from Fourth Street down to the Cortlandt Ferry—a stretch of miles—was a solid mass of humanity; thousands and tens of thousands, doubled, quadrupled, and multiplied again.

Through the morning this crowd in squads and companies traversed the streets, collected on the corners, congregating chiefly about the armory of their pet regiment, the Seventh, on Lafayette Square,—one great mass gazing unweariedly at its windows and walls, then moving on to be replaced by another of the like kind, which, having gone through the same performance, gave way in turn to yet others, eager to take its place.

So the fever burned; the excitement continued and augmented till, towards three o'clock in the afternoon, the mighty throng stood still, and waited. It was no ordinary multitude; the wealth, refinement, fashion, the greatness and goodness of a vast city were there, pressed close against its coarser and darker and homelier elements. Men and women stood alike in the crowd, dainty patrician and toil-stained laborer, all thrilled by a common emotion, all vivified—if in unequal degree—by the same sublime enthusiasm. Overhead, from every window and doorway and housetop, in every space and spot that could sustain one, on ropes, on staffs, in human hands, waved, and curled, and floated, flags that were in multitude like the swells of the sea; silk, and bunting, and painted calico, from the great banner spreading its folds with an indescribable majesty, to the tiny toy shaken in a baby hand. Under all this glad and gay and splendid show, the faces seemed, perhaps by contrast, not sad, but grave; not sorrowful, but intense, and luminously solemn.

Gradually the men of the Seventh marched out of their armory. Hands had been wrung, adieus said, last fond embraces and farewells given. The regiment formed in the open square, the crowd about it so dense as to seem stifling, the windows of its building filled with the sweetest and finest and fairest of faces,—the mothers, wives, and sweethearts of these young splendid fellows just ready to march away.

Surrey from his station gazed and gazed at the window where stood his mother, so well beloved, his relations and friends, many of them near and dear to him,—some of them with clear, bright eyes that turned from the forms of brothers in the ranks to seek his, and linger upon it wistfully and tenderly; yet looking at all these, even his mother, he looked beyond, as though in the empty space a face would appear, eyes would meet his, arms be stretched towards him, lips whisper a fond adieu, as he, breaking from the ranks, would take her to his embrace, and speak, at the same time, his love and farewell. A fruitless longing.

Four o'clock struck over the great city, and the line moved out of the square, through Fourth Street, to Broadway. Then began a march, which whoso witnessed, though but a little child, will remember to his dying day, the story of which he will repeat to his children, and his children's children, and, these dead, it will be read by eyes that shall shine centuries hence, as one of the most memorable scenes in the great struggle for freedom.

Hands were stretched forth to touch the cloth of their uniforms, and kissed when they were drawn back. Mothers held up their little children to gain inspiration for a lifetime. A roar of voices, coutinuous, unbroken, rent the skies; while, through the deafening cheers, men and women, with eyes blinded by tears, repeated, a million times, "God bless—God bless and keep them!" And so, down the magnificent avenue, through the countless, shouting multitude, through the whirlwind of enthusiasm and adoration, under the glorious sweep of flags, the grand regiment moved from the beginning of its march to its close,—till it was swept away towards the capital, around which were soon to roll such bloody waves of death.

Meanwhile, where was Miss Ercildoune? Surrey had thought her behavior strange the last morning they spent together. How much stranger, how unaccountable, indeed, would it have seemed to him, could he have seen her through the afternoon following!

"What is wrong with you? are you ill, Francesca?" her

aunt had inquired as she came in, pulling off her hat with
the air of one stifling, and throwing herself into a chair.

"Ill! O no!"—with a quick laugh,—"what could have
made you think so? I am quite well, thank you; but I will
go to my room for a little while and rest. I think I am
tired."

"Do, dear, for I want you to take a trip up the Hudson
this afternoon. I have to see some English people who are
living at a little village a score of miles out of town, and
then I must go on to Albany before I take you home. It
will be pleasant at Tanglewood over the Sabbath,—unless
you have some engagements to keep you here?"

"O Aunt Alice, how glad I am! I was going home this
afternoon without you. I thought you would come when
you were ready; but this will do just as well,—anything to
get out of town."

"Anything to get out of town? why, Francesca, is it so
hateful to you? 'Going home! and this do almost as well!'—
what does the child mean? is she the least little bit mad? I'm
afraid so. She evidently needs some fresh country air, and rest
from excitement. Go, dear, and take your nap, and refresh
yourself before five o'clock; that is the time we leave."

As the door closed between them, she shook her head
dubiously. "'Going home this afternoon!' what does that
signify? Has she been quarrelling with that young lover of
hers, or refusing him? I should not care to ask any questions till she herself speaks; but I fear me something is
wrong."

She would not have feared, but been certain, could she
have looked then and there into the next room. She would
have seen that the trouble was something deeper than she
dreamed. Francesca was sitting, her hands supporting an
aching head, her large eyes fixed mournfully and immovably upon something which she seemed to contemplate
with a relentless earnestness, as though forcing herself to a
distressing task. What was this something? An image, a
shadow in the air, which she had not evoked from the
empty atmosphere, but from the depths of her own nature
and soul,—the life and fate of a young girl. Herself! what
cause, then, for mournful scrutiny? She, so young, so brilliant, so beautiful, upon whom fate had so kindly smiled,
admired by many, tenderly and passionately loved by at
least one heart,—surely it was a delightful picture to contemplate,—this life and its future; a picture to bring smiles
to the lips, rather than tears to the eyes.

Though, in fact, there were none dimming hers,—hot,
dry eyes, full of fever and pain. What visions passed before
them? what shadows of the life she inspected darkened
them? what sunshine now and then fell upon it, reflecting
itself in them, as she leaned forward to scan these bright
spots, holding them in her gaze after other and gloomier
ones had taken their places, as one leans forth from
window or doorway to behold, long as possible, the vanishing form of some dear friend.

Looking at these, she cried out, "Fool! to have been so
happy, and not to have known what the happiness meant,

and that it was not for me,—never for me! to have walked
to the verge of an abyss,—to have plunged in, thinking the
path led to heaven. Heaven for me! ah,—I forgot,—I
forgot. I let an unconscious bliss seize me, possess me,
exclude memory and thought,—lived in it as though it
would endure forever."

She got up and moved restlessly to and fro across the
room, but presently came back to the seat she had aban-
doned, and to the inspection which, while it tortured her,
she yet evidently compelled herself to pursue.

"Come," she then said, "let us ask ourself some questions, constitute ourself confessor and penitent, and see
what the result will prove."

"Did you think fate would be more merciful to you
than to others?"

"No, I thought nothing about fate."

"Did you suppose that he loved you sufficiently to
destroy 'an invincible barrier?' "

"I did not think of his love. I remembered no barrier.
I only knew I was in heaven, and cared for naught
beyond."

"Do you see the barrier now?"

"I do,—I do."

"Did *he* help you to behold it; to discover, or to
remember it? did he, or did he not?"

"He did. Too true,—he did."

"Does he love you?"

"I—how should I know? his looks, his acts—I never

thought—O Willie, Willie!"—her voice going out in a little gasping sob.

"Come,—none of that. No sentiment,—face the facts. Think over all that was said, every word. Have you done so?"

"I have,—every word."

"Well?"

"Ah, stop torturing me. Do not ask me any more questions. I am going away,—flying like a coward. I will not tempt further suffering. And yet—once more—only once? could that do harm? Ah, God, my God, be merciful!" she cried, clasping her hands and lifting them above her bowed head. Then remembering, in the midst of her anguish, some words she had been reading that morning, she repeated them with a bitter emphasis,—"What can wringing of the hands do, that which is ordained to alter?" As she did so she tore asunder her clasped hands, to drop them clinched by her side,—the gesture of despair substituted for that of hope.

"It is not Heaven I am to besiege!" she exclaimed. "Will I never learn that? Its justice cannot overcome the injustice of man. My God!" she cried then, with a sudden, terrible energy, "our punishment should be light, our rest sure, our paradise safe, at the end, since we have to make now such awful atonement; since men compel us to endure the pangs of purgatory, the tortures of hell, here upon earth."

After that she sat for a long while silent, evidently

revolving a thousand thoughts of every shape and hue, judging from the myriads of lights and shadows that flitted over her face. At last, rousing herself, she perceived that she had no more time to spend in this sorrowful employment,—that she must prepare to go away from him, as her heart said, forever. "Forever!" it repeated. "This, then, is the close of it all,—the miserable end!" With that thought she shut her slender hand, and struck it down hard, the blood almost starting from the driven nails and bruised flesh, unheeding; though a little space thereafter she smiled, beholding it, and muttered, "So—the drop of savage blood is telling at last!"

Presently she was gone. It was a pleasant spot to which her aunt took her,—one of the pretty little villages scattered up and down the long sweep of the Hudson. Pleasant people they were too,—these English friends of Mrs. Lancaster,—who made her welcome, but did not intrude upon the solitude which they saw she desired.

Sabbath morning they all went to the little chapel, and left her, as she wished, alone. Being so alone, after hearing their adieus, she went up to her room and sat down to devote herself once again to sorrowful contemplation,— not because she would, but because she must.

Poor girl! the bright spring sunshine streamed over her where she sat;—not a cloud in the sky, not a dimming of mist or vapor on all the hills, and the broad river-sweep which, placid and beautiful, rolled along; the cattle far off on the brown fields rubbed their silky sides softly together,

and gazed through the clear atmosphere with a lazy content, as though they saw the waving of green grass, and
heard the rustle of wind in the thick boughs, so soon to
bear their leafy burden. Stillness everywhere,—the blessed
calm that even nature seems to feel on a sunny Sabbath
morn. Stillness scarcely broken by the voices, mellowed
and softened ere they reached her ear, chanting in the village church, to some sweet and solemn music, words
spoken in infinite tenderness long ago, and which, through
all the centuries, come with healing balm to many a sore
and saddened heart: "Come unto me," the voices sang,—
"come unto me, all ye that labor and are heavy laden, and
I will give you rest."

   "Ah, rest," she murmered while she listened,—"rest";
and with the repetition of the word the fever died out of
her eyes, leaving them filled with such a look, more pitiful
than any tears, as would have made a kind heart ache even
to look at them; while her figure, alert and proud no
longer, bent on the window ledge in such lonely and
weary fashion that a strong arm would have involuntarily
stretched out to shield it from any hardness or blow that
might threaten, though the owner thereof were a stranger.

   There was something indescribably appealing and
pathetic in her whole look and air. Outside the window
stood a slender little bird which had fluttered there, spent
and worn, and did not try to flit away any further. Too
early had it flown from its southern abode; too early aban-
doned the warm airs, the flowers and leafage, of a more

hospitable region, to find its way to a northern home; too early ventured into a rigorous clime; and now, shivering, faint, near to death, drooped its wings and hung its weary head, waiting for the end of its brief life to come.

Francesca, looking up with woeful eyes, beheld it, and, opening the window, softly took it in. "Poor birdie!" she whispered, striving to warm it in her gentle hand and against her delicate cheek,—"poor little wanderer!—didst thou think to find thy mate, and build thy tiny nest, and be a happy mother through the long bright summer-time? Ah, my pet, what a sad close is this to all these pleasant dreams!"

The frail little creature could not eat even the bits of crumbs which she put into its mouth, nor taste a drop of water. All her soothing presses failed to bring warmth and life to the tiny frame that presently stretched itself out, dead,—all its sweet songs sung, its brief, bright existence ended forever. "Ah, my little birdie, it is all over," whispered Francesca, as she laid it softly down, and unconsciously lifted her hand to her own head with a self-pitying gesture that was sorrowful to behold.

"Like me," she did not say; yet a penetrating eye looking at them—the slight bird lying dead, its brilliant plumage already dimmed, the young girl gazing at it— would perceive that alike these two were fitted for the warmth and sunshine, would perceive that both had been thwarted and defrauded of their fair inheritance, would perceive that one lay spent and dead in its early spring. What of the other?

"Aunt Alice," said Francesca a few days after that, "can you go to New York this afternoon or tomorrow morning?"

"Certainly, dear. I purposed returning to-day or early in the morning to see the Seventh march away. Of course you would like to be there."

"Yes." She spoke slowly, and with seeming indifference. It was because she could scarcely control her voice to speak at all. "I should like to be there."

Francesca knew, what her aunt did not, that Surrey was a member of the Seventh, and that he would march away with it to danger,—perhaps to death.

So they were there, in a window overlooking the great avenue,—Mrs. Lancaster, foreigner though she was, thrilled to the heart's core by the magnificent pageant; Francesca straining her eyes up the long street, through the vast sea of faces, to fasten them upon just one face that she knew would presently appear in the throng.

"Ah, heavens!" cried Mrs. Lancaster, "what a sight! look at those young men; they are the choice and fine of the city. See, see! there is Hunter, and Winthrop, and Pursuivant, and Mortimer, and Shaw, and Russell, and, yes—no—it is, over there—your friend, Surrey, himself. Did you know, Francesca?"

Francesca did not reply. Mrs. Lancaster turned to see her lying white and cold in her chair. Endurance had failed at last.

CHAPTER VII

"The plain, unvarnished tale of my whole course of love."

SHAKESPEARE

"WHAT a handsome girl that is who always waits on us!" Francesca had once said to Clara Russell, as they came out of Hyacinth's with some dainty laces in their hands.

"Very," Clara had answered.

The handsome girl was Sallie.

At another time Francesca, admiring some particular specimen of the pomps and vanities with which the store was crowded, was about carrying it away, but first experimented as to its fit.

"O dear!" she cried, in dismay, "it is too short, and"—rummaging through the box—"there is not another like it, and it is the only one I want."

"How provoking!" sympathized Clara.

"I could very easily alter that," said Sallie, who was behind the counter; "I make these up for the shop, and I'll be glad to fix this for you, if you like it so much."

"Thanks. You are very kind. Can you send it up to-morrow?"

"This evening, if you wish it."

"Very good; I shall be your debtor."

"Well!" exclaimed Clara, as they turned away, this is the first time in all my shopping I ever found a girl ready to put herself out to serve one. They usually act as if they were conferring the most overwhelming favor by conde-scending to wait upon you at all."

"Why, Clara, I'm sure I always find them civil."

"I know they seem devoted to you. I wonder why. Oh!"—laughing and looking at her friend with honest admiration,—"it must be because you are so pretty."

"Excellent,—how discerning you are!" smiled Francesca, in return.

If Clara had had a little more discernment, she would have discovered that what wrought this miracle was a friendly courtesy, that never failed to either equal or sub-ordinate.

Six weeks after the Seventh had marched out of New York, Francesca, sitting in her aunt's room, was roused from evidently painful thought by the entrance of a ser-vant, who announced, "If you please, a young woman to see you."

"Name?"

"She gave none, miss."

"Send her up."

Sallie came in. "Bird of Paradise" Francesca had called her more than once, she was so dashing and handsome; but the title would scarcely fit now, for she looked poor, and sad, and woefully dispirited.

"Ah, Miss Sallie, is it you? Good morning."

"Good morning, Miss Ercildoune." She stood, and looked as though she had something important to say. Presently Francesca had drawn it from her,—a little story of her own sorrows and troubles.

"The reason I have come to you, Miss Ercildoune, when you are so nearly a stranger, is because you have always been so kind and pleasant to me when I waited on you at the store, and I thought you'd anyway listen to what I have to say."

"Speak on, Sallie."

"I've been at Hyacinth's now, over four years, ever since I left school. It's a good place, and they paid me well, but I had to keep two people out of it, my little brother Frank and myself; Frank and I are orphans. And I'm very fond of dress; I may as well confess that at once. So the consequence is, I haven't saved a cent against a rainy day. "Well," blushing scarlet, "I had a lover,—the best heart that ever beat,—but I liked to flirt, and plague him a little, and make him jealous; and at last he got dreadfully so about a young gentleman,—a Mr. Snipe, who was very attentive

to me,—and talked to me about it in a way I didn't like.
That made me worse. I don't know what possessed me; but
after that I went out with Mr. Snipe a great deal more, to
the theatre and the like, and let him spend his money on
me, and get things for me, as freely as he chose. I didn't
mean any harm, indeed I didn't,—but I liked to go about
and have a good time; and then it made Jim show how
much he cared for me, which, you see, was a great thing
to me; and so this went on for a while, till Jim gave me a
real lecture, and I got angry and wouldn't listen to anything he had to say, and sent him away in a huff"—here
she choked—"to fight; to the war; and O dear! O dear!"
breaking down utterly, and hiding her face in her shawl,
"he'll be killed,—I know he will; and oh! what shall I do?
My heart will break, I am sure."

Francesca came and stood by her side, put her hand
gently on her shoulder, and stroked her beautiful hair.
"Poor girl!" she said, softly, "poor girl!" and then, so low
that even Sallie could not hear, "*You* suffer, too: do we all
suffer, then?"

Presently Sallie looked up, and continued: "Up to that
time, Mr. Snipe hadn't said anything to me, except that he
admired me very much, and that I was pretty, too pretty to
work so hard, and that I ought to live like a lady, and a
good deal more of that kind of talk that I was silly enough
to listen to; but when he found Jim was gone, first, he
made fun of him for 'being such a great fool as to go and
be shot at for nothing,' and then he—O Miss Ercildoune,

I can't tell you what he said; it makes me choke just to think of it. How dared he? what had I done that he should believe me such a thing as that? I don't know what words I used when I did find them, and I don't care, but they must have stung. I can't tell you how he looked, but it was dreadful; and he said, 'I'll bring down that proud spirit of yours yet, my lady. I'm not through with you,—don't think it,—not by a good deal'; and then he made me a fine bow, and laughed, and went out of the room.

"The next day Mr. Dodd—that's one of our firm— gave me a week's notice to quit: 'work was slack,' he said, 'and they didn't want so many girls.' But I'm just as sure as sure can be that Mr. Snipe's at the bottom of it, for I've been at the store, as I told you, four years and more, and they always reckoned me one of their best hands, and Mr. Dodd and Mr. Snipe are great friends. Since then I've done nothing but try to get work. I must have been into a thousand stores, but it's true work *is* slack; there's not a thing been doing since the war commenced, and I can't get any place. I've been to Miss Russell and some of the ladies who used to come to the store, to see if they'd give me some fine sewing; but they hadn't any for me, and I don't know what in the world to do, for I understand nothing very well but to sew, and to stand in a store. I've spent all my money, what little I had, and—and—I've even sold some of my clothes, and I can't go on this way much longer. I haven't a relative in the world; nor a home, except in a boarding-house; and the girls I know all treat me cool, as though I had done something bad, because I've lost my place, I suppose, and am poor.

"All along, at times, Mr. Snipe has been sending me things,—bouquets, and baskets of fruit, and sometimes a note, and, though I won't speak to him when I meet him on the street, he always smiles and bows as if he were intimate; and last night, when I was coming home, tired enough from my long search, he passed me and said, with such a look, 'You've gone down a peg or two, haven't you, Sallie? Come, I guess we'll be friends again before long.' You think it's queer I'm telling you all this. I can't help it; there's something about you that draws it all out of me. I came to ask you for work, and here I've been talking all this while about myself. You must excuse me; I don't think I would have said so much, if you hadn't looked so kind and so interested"; and so she had,—kind as kind could be, and interested as though the girl who talked had been her own sister.

"I am glad you came, Sallie, and glad that you told me all this, if it has been any relief to you. You may be sure I will do what I can for you, but I am afraid that will not be a great deal, here; for I am a stranger in New York, and know very few people. Perhaps—Would you go away from here?"

"Would I?—O wouldn't I? and be glad of the chance. I'd give anything to go where I couldn't get sight or sound of that horrid Snipe. Can't I go with you, Miss Ercildoune?"

"I have no counter behind which to station you," said Francesca, smiling.

"No, I know,—of course; but"—looking at the daintily arrayed figure—"you have plenty of elegant things to make, and I can do pretty much anything with my needle, if you'd like to trust me with some work. And then—I'm ashamed to ask so much of you, but a few words from you to your friends, I'm sure, would send me all that I could do, and more."

"You think so?" Miss Ercildoune inquired, with a curious intonation to her voice, and the strangest expression darkening her face. "Very well, it shall be tried."

Sallie was nonplussed by the tone and look, but she comprehended the closing words fully and with delight. "You will take me with you," she cried. "O, how good, how kind you are! how shall I ever be able to thank you?"

"Don't thank me at all," said Miss Ercildoune, "at least not now. Wait till I have done something to deserve your gratitude."

But Sallie was not to be silenced in any such fashion, and said her say with warmth and meaning; then, after some further talk about time and plans, went away carrying a bit of work which Miss Ercildoune had found, or made, for her, and for which she had paid in advance.

"God bless her!" thought Sallie; "how nice and how thoughtful she is! Most ladies, if they'd done anything for me, would have given me some money and made a beggar of me, and I should have felt as mean as dish-water. But now"—she patted her little bundle and walked down the street, elated and happy.

Francesca watched her out of the door with eyes that presently filled with tears. "Poor girl!" she whispered; "poor Sallie! her lover has gone to the wars with a shadow between them. Ah, that must not be; I must try to bring them together again, if he loves her dearly and truly. He might die,"—she shuddered at that,—"die, as other men die, in the heat and flame of battle. My God! my God! how shall I bear it? Dead! and without a word! Gone, and he will never know how well I love him! O Willie, Willie! my life, my love, my darling, come back, come back to me."

Vain cry!—he cannot hear. Vain lifting of an agonized face, beautiful in its agony!—he cannot see. Vain stretching forth of longing hands and empty arms!—he is not there to take them to his embrace. Carry thy burden as others have carried it before thee, and learn what multitudes, in times past and in time present, have learned,—the lesson of endurance when happiness is denied, and of patience and silence when joy has been withheld. Go thou thy way, sorrowful and suffering soul, alone; and if thy own heart bleeds, strive thou to soothe its pangs, by medicining the wounds and healing the hurts of another.

A few days thereafter, when Miss Ercildoune went over to Philadelphia, Sallie and Frank bore her company. She had become as thoroughly interested in them as though she had known and cared for them for a long while; and as she was one who was incapable of doing in an imperfect or partial way aught she attempted, and whose friendship never stopped short with pleasant sounding words, this interest had already bloomed beautifully, and was fast ripening into solid fruit.

She had written in advance to desire that certain preparations should be made for her *protégés*,—preparations which had been faithfully attended to; and thus, reaching a strange city, they felt themselves not strangers, since they had a home ready to receive them, and this excellent friend by their side.

The home consisted of two rooms, neat, cheerful, high up,—"the airier and healthier for that," as Sallie decided when she saw them.

"I believe everything is in order," said the good-natured-looking old lady, the mistress of the establishment. "My lodgers are all gentlemen who take their meals out, and I shall be glad of some company. Any one whom Friend Comstock recommends will be all right, I know."

As Mrs. Healey's style of designation indicated, Friend Comstock was a Quakeress, well known, greatly esteemed, an old friend of Miss Ercildoune, and of Miss Ercildoune's father. She it was to whom Francesca had written, and who had found this domicile for the wanderers, and who at the outset furnished Sallie with an abundance of fine and dainty sewing. Indeed, without giving the matter special thought, she was surprised to discover that, with one or two exceptions, the people Miss Ercildoune sent her were of the peaceful and quiet sect. This bird of brilliant plumage seemed ill assorted with the sober-hued flock.

She found in this same bird a helper in more ways than one. It was not alone that she gave her employment and paid her well, nor that she sent her others able and willing to do the same. She found Frankie a good school, and saw him properly installed. She never came to them empty-handed; through the long, hot summer-time she brought them fruit and flowers from her home out of town; and when she came not herself, if the carriage was in the city it stopped with these same delightful burdens. Sallie declared her an angel, and Frank, with his mouth stuffed full, stood ready to echo the assertion.

So the heated term wore away,—before it ended, telling heavily on Sallie. Her anxiety about Jim, her close confinement and constant work, the fever everywhere in the spiritual air through that first terrible summer of the war, bore her down.

"You need rest," said Miss Ercildoune to her one day, looking at her with kindly solicitude,—"rest, and change, and fresh air, and freedom from care. I can't give you the last, but I can the first if you will accept them. You need some country living."

"O Miss Ercildoune, will you let me do your work at your own home? I know it would do me good just to be under the same roof with you, and then I should have all the things you speak of combined and another one added. If you only will!"

This was not the plan Francesca had proposed to herself. She had intended sending Sallie away to some pleasant country or seaside place, till she was refreshed and ready to come to her work once more. Sallie did not know what to make of the expression of the face that watched her, nor of the exclamation, "Why not? let me try her." But she had not long to consider, for Miss Ercildoune added, "Be it so. I will send in for you to-morrow, and you shall stay till you are better and stronger, or—till you please to come home,"—the last words spoken in a bitter and sorrowful tone.

The next day Sallie found her way to the superb home of her employer. Superb it was, in every sense. Never before had she been in such a delightful region, never before realized how absolutely perfect breeding sets at ease all who come within the charm of its magic sphere,— employed, acquaintance, or friend.

There was a shadow, however, in this house,—a shadow, the premonition of which she had seen more than once on the face of its mistress ere she ever beheld her home; a shadow to which, for a few days, she had no clew, but which was suddenly explained by the arrival of the master of this beautiful habitation; a shadow from which most people would have fled as from the breath of a pestilence, or the shade of the tomb; nay, one from which, but a few short months before, Sallie herself would have sped with feet from which she would have shaken the very dust of the threshold when she was beyond its doors,—but not now. Now, as she beheld it, she sat still to survey it, with surprise that deepened into indignation and compassion, that many a time filled her eyes with tears, and brought an added expression of respect to her voice when she spoke to these people who seemed to have all the good things that this world can offer, upon whom fortune had expended her treasures, yet—

Whatever it was, Sallie came from that home with many an old senseless prejudice destroyed forever, with a new thought implanted in her soul, the blossoming of which was a noxious vapor in the nostrils of some who were compelled to inhale it, but as a sweet-smelling savor to more than one weary wayfarer, and to that God to whom the darkness and the light are alike, and who, we are told by His own word, is no respecter of persons.

"Poor, dear Miss Ercildoune!" half sobbed, half scolded Sallie, as she sat at her work, blooming and, fresh, the day after her return. "What a tangled thread it is, to be sure," jerking at her knotty needleful. "Well, I know what I'll do,—I'll treat her as if she was a queen born and crowned, just so long as I have anything to do with her,—so I will." And she did.

CHAPTER VIII

"For hearts of truest mettle
Absence doth join, and time doth settle."
ANONYMOUS

I T were a vain endeavor to attempt the telling of what
filled the heart and soul of Surrey, as he marched away
that day from New York, and through the days and weeks
and months that followed. Fired by a sublime enthusiasm
for his country; thirsting to drink of any cup her hand
might present, that thus he might display his absolute
devotion to her cause; burning with indignation at the
wrongs she had suffered; thrilled with an adoring love for
the idea she embodied; eager to make manifest this love at
whatever cost of pain and sorrow and suffering to himself,—through all this the man never once was steeped in
forgetfulness in the soldier; the divine passion of patriotism
never once dulled the ache, or satisfied the desire, or

answered the prayer, or filled the longing heart, that through the day marches and the night watches cried, and would not be appeased, for his darling.

"Surely," he thought as he went down Broadway, as he reflected, as he considered the matter a thousand times thereafter,—"surely I was a fool not to have spoken to her then; not to have seen her, have devised, have forced some way to reach her, not to have met her face to face, and told her all the love with which she had filled my heart and possessed my soul. And then to have been such a coward when I did write to her, to have so said a say which was nothing"; and he groaned impatiently as he thought of the scene in his room and the letter which was its final result.

How he had written once, and again, and yet again, letters short and long, letters short and burning, or lengthy and filled almost to the final line with delicate fancies and airy sentiment, ere he ventured to tell that of which all this was but the prelude; how, at the conclusion of each attempt, he had watched these luminous effusions blaze and burn as he regularly committed them to the flames; how he found it difficult to decide which he enjoyed the most,—writing them out, or seeing them burn; how at last he had put upon paper some such words as these:—

"After these delightful weeks and months of inter-course, I am to go away from you, then, without a single word of parting, or a solitary sentence of adieu. Need I tell you how this pains me? I have in vain besieged the house that has held you; in vain made a thousand inquiries, a thousand efforts to discover your retreat and to reach your side, that I might once more see your face and take your hand ere I went from the sight and touch of both, perchance forever. This I find may not be. The hour strikes, and in a little space I shall march away from the city to which my heart clings with infinite fondness, since it is filled with associations of you. I have again and again striven to write that which will be worthy the eyes that are to read, and striven in vain. 'Tis a fine art to which I do not pretend. Then, in homely phrase, good by. Give me thy spiritual hand, and keep me, if thou wilt, in thy gentle remembrance. Adieu! a kind adieu, my friend; may the brighter stars smile on thee, and the better angels guard thy footsteps wherever thou mayst wander, keep thy heart and spirit bright, and let thy thoughts turn kindly back to me, I pray, very, very often. And so, once more, farewell."

Remembering all this, thinking what he would do and say were the doing and saying yet possible in an untried future, the time sped by. He waited and waited in vain. He looked, yet was gratified by no sight for which his eyes longed. He hoped, till hope gave place to despondency and almost despair: not a word came to him, not a line of answer or remembrance. This long silence was all the more intolerable, since the time that intervened did but the more vividly stamp upon his memory the delights of the past, and color with softer and more exquisite tints the recollection of vanished hours,—hours spent in galloping gayly by her side in the early morning, or idly and deli-

ciously lounged away in picture-galleries or concert-
rooms, or in a conversation carried on in some curious and
subtle shape between two hearts and spirits with the help
of very few uttered words; hours in which he had whirled
her through many a fairy maze and turn of captivating
dance-music, or in some less heated and crowded room, or
cool conservatory, listened to the voice of the siren who
walked by his side, "while the sweet wind did gently kiss
the flowers and make no noise," and the strains of "flute,
violin, bassoon," and the sounds of the "dancers dancing in
tune," coming to them on the still air of night, seemed like
the sounds from another and a far-off world,—listened,
listened, listened, while his silver-tongued enchantress
builded castles in the air, or beguiled his thought,
enthralled his heart, his soul and fancy, through many a
golden hour.

Thinking of all this, his heart well found expression for
its feelings in the half-pleasing, half-sorrowful lines which
almost unconsciously repeated themselves again and again
in his brain:—

> "Still o'er those scenes my memory wakes,
> And fondly broods with miser care;
> Time but the impression deeper makes,
> As streams their channels deeper wear."

Thinking of all this, he took comfort in spite of his
trouble. "Perhaps," he said to himself, "he was mistaken.
Perhaps"—O happy thought!—"it was but make-believe

displeasure which had so tortured him. Perhaps—yes, he would believe it—she had never received his letter; they had been careless, they had failed to give it her or to send it aright. He would write her once again, in language which would relieve his heart, and which she must comprehend. He loved her; perhaps, ah, perhaps she loved him a little in return: he would believe so till he was undeceived, and be infinitely happy in the belief.

Is it not wondrous how even the tiniest grain of love will permeate the saddest and sorest recesses of the heart, and instantly cause it to pulsate with thoughts and emotions the sweetest and dearest in life? O Love, thou sweet, thou young and rose lipped cherubim, how does thy smile illuminate the universe! how does thy slightest touch electrify the soul! how gently and tenderly dost thou lead us up to heaven!

With Surrey, to decide was to act. The second letter, full of sweetest yet intensest love,—his heart laid bare to her,—was written; was sent, enclosed in one to his aunt. Tom was away in another section, fighting manfully for the dear old flag, or the precious missive would have been intrusted to his care. He sent it thus that it might reach her sooner. Now that he had a fresh hope, he could not wait to write for her address, and forward it himself to her hands; he must adopt the speediest method of putting it in her possession.

In a little space came answer from Mrs. Russell, enclosing the letter he had sent: a kindly epistle it was. He was a sort of idol with this same aunt, so she had put many things on paper that were steeped in gentleness and affection ere she said at the end, "I re-enclose your letter. I have seen Miss Ercildoune. She restores it to you; she implores you never to write her again,—to forget her. I add my entreaties to hers. She begs of me to beseech you not to try her by any further appeals, as she will but return them unopened." That was all.

What could it mean? He loved her so absolutely, he had such exalted faith in her kindness, her gentleness, her fairness and superiority,—in *her*,—that he could not believe she would so thrust back his love, purely and chivalrously offered, with something that seemed like ignominy, unless she had a sufficient reason—or one she deemed such—for treating so cruelly him and the offering he laid at her feet.

But she had spoken. It was for him, then, when she bade silence, to keep it; when she refused his gift, to refrain from thrusting it upon her attention and heart. But ah, the silence and the refraining! Ah, the time—the weary, sore, intolerable time—that followed! Summer, and autumn, and winter, and the seasons repeated once again, he tramped across the soil of Virginia, already wet with rebel and patriot blood; he felt the shame and agony of Bull Run; he was in the night struggle at Ball's Bluff, where those wondrous Harvard boys found it "sweet to die for their country," and discovered, for them, "death to be but one step onward in life." He lay in camp, chafing with impatience and indignation as the long months wore away, and the thousands of graves about Washington, filled by disease and inaction, made "all quiet along the Potomac." He went down to Yorktown; was in the sweat and fury of the seven days' fight; away in the far South, where fever and pestilence stood guard to seize those who were spared by the bullet and bayonet; and on many a field well lost or won. Through it all marching or fighting, sick, wounded thrice and again; praised, admired, heroic, promoted,— from private soldier to general,—through two years and more of such fiery experience, no part of the tender love was burned away, tarnished, or dimmed.

Sometimes, indeed, he even smiled at himself for the constant thought, and felt that he must certainly be demented on this one point at least, since it colored every impression of his life, and, in some shape, thrust itself upon him at the most unseemly and foreign times.

One evening, when the mail for the division came in, looking over the pile of letters, his eye was caught by one addressed to James Given. The name was familiar,—that of his father's old foreman, whom he knew to be somewhere in the army; doubtless the same man. Unquestionably, he thought, that was the reason he was so attracted to it; but why he should take up the delicate little missive, scan it again and again, hold it in his hand with the same touch with which he would have pressed a rare flower, and lay it down as reluctantly as he would have yielded a known and visible treasure,—that was the mystery. He had never seen

Francesca's writing, but he stood possessed, almost assured, of the belief that this letter was penned by her hand; and at last parted with it slowly and unwillingly, as though it were the dear hand of which he mused; then took himself to task for this boyish weakness and folly. Nevertheless, he went in pursuit of Jim, not to question him,—he was too thorough a gentleman for that,—but led on partly by his desire to see a familiar face, partly by this folly, as he called it with a sort of amused disdain.

Folly, however, it was not, save in such measure as the subtle telegraphings between spirit and spirit can be thus called. Unjustly so called they are, constantly; it being the habit of most people to denounce as heresy or ridicule as madness things too high for their sight or too deep for their comprehension. As these people would say, "oddly enough," or "by an extraordinary coincidence," this very letter was from Miss Ercildoune,—a letter which she wrote as she purposed, and as she well knew how to write, in behalf of Sallie. It was ostensibly on quite another theme; asking some information in regard to a comrade, but so cunningly devised and executed as to tell him in few words, and unsuspiciously, some news of Sallie,—news which she knew would delight his heart, and overthrow the little barrier which had stood between them, making both miserable, but which he would not, and she could not, clamber over or destroy. It did its work effectually, and made two hearts thoroughly happy,—this letter which had so strangely bewitched Surrey; which, in his heart, spite of the ridicule of his reason, he was so sure was hers; and which, indeed, was hers, though he knew not that till long afterward.

"So," he thought, as he went through the camp, "Given is here, and near. I shall be glad to see a face from home, whatever kind of a face it may be, and Given's is a good one; it will be a pleasant rememberance."

"Whither away?" called a voice behind him.

"To the 29th," he answered the questioner, one of his officers and friends, who, coming up, took his arm,—"in pursuit of a man."

"What's his name?"

"Given,—christened James. What are you laughing at? do you know him?"

"No, I don't know him, but I've heard some funny stories about him; he's a queer stick, I should think."

"Something in that way.—Helloa! Brooks, back again?" to a fine, frank-looking young fellow,—"and were you successful?"

"Yes, to both your questions. In addition I'll say, for your rejoicing, that I give in, cave, subside, have nothing more to say against your pet theory,—from this moment swear myself a rank abolitionist, or anything else you please, now and forever,—so help me all ye black gods and goddesses!"

"Phew! what's all this?" cried Whittlesly, from the other side of his Colonel; "what are you driving at? I'll defy anybody to make head or tail of that answer."

"Surrey understands."

"Not I; your riddle's too much for me."

"Didn't you go in pursuit of a dead man?" queried Whittlesly.

"Just that."

"Did the dead man convert you?"

"No, Colonel, not precisely. And yet yes, too; that is, I suppose I shouldn't have been converted if he hadn't died, and I gone in search of him."

"I believe it; you're such an obstinate case that you need one raised from the dead to have any effect on you."

"Obstinate! O, hear the pig-headed fellow talk! You're a beauty to discourse on that point, aren't you!"

"Surrey laughed, and stopped at the call of one of his men, who hailed him as he went by. Evidently a favorite here as in New York, in camp as at home; for in a moment he was surrounded by the men, who crowded about him, each with a question, or remark, to draw special attention to himself, and a word or smile from his commander. Whatever complaint they had to enter, or petition to make, or favor to beg, or wish to urge, whatever help they wanted or information they desired, was brought to him to solve or to grant, and—never being repulsed by their officer—they speedily knew and loved their friend. Thus it was that the two men standing at a little distance, watching the proceeding, were greatly amused at the motley drafts made upon his attention in the shape of tents, shoes, coats, letters to be sent or received, books borrowed and lent, a man sick, or a chicken captured. They brought their interests and cares to him,—these big, brown fellows,—as though they were children, and he a parent well beloved.

"One might think him the father of the regiment," said Brooks, with a smile.

"The mother, more like: it must be the woman element in him these fellows feel and love so."

"Perhaps; but it would have another effect on them, if, for instance, he didn't carry that sabre-slash on his hand. They've seen him under steel and fire, and know where he's led them."

"What is this you were joking about with him, a while ago?"

"What! about turning abolitionist?"

"Precisely."

"O, you know he's rampant on the slavery question. I believe it's the only thing he ever loses his temper over, and he has lost it with me more than once. I've always been a rank heretic with regard to Cuffee, and the result was, we disagreed."

"Yes, I know. But what connection has that with your expedition?"

"Just what I want to know," added Surrey, coming up at the moment.

"Ah! you're in time to hear the confession, are you?"

"'An honest confession—' You know what the wise man says."

"Come, don't flatter yourself we will think you so because you quote him. Be quiet, both of you, and let me go on to tell my tale."

"Attention!"

"Proceed!"

"Thus, then. You understand what my errand was?"

"Not exactly; Lieutenant Hunt was drowned somewhere, wasn't he?"

"Yes: fell overboard from a tug; the men on board tried to save him, and then to recover his body, and couldn't do either. Some of his people came down here in pursuit of it, and I was detailed with a squad to help them in their search.

"Well, the naval officers gave us every facility in their power; the river was dragged twice over, and the woods along-shore ransacked, hoping it might have been washed in and, maybe, buried; but there wasn't sight or trace of it. While we were hunting round we stumbled on a couple of darkies, who told us, after a bit of questioning, that darky number three, somewhere about, had found the body of a Federal officer on the river bank, and buried it. On that hint we acted, posted over to the fellow's shanty, and found, not him, but his wife, who was ready enough to tell us all she knew. She showed us some traps of the buried officer, among them a pair of spurs, which his brother recognized directly. When she was quite sure that we were all correct, and that the thing had fallen into the right hands, she fished out of some safe corner his wallet, with fifty-seven dollars in it. I confess I stared, for they were slaves, both of them, and evidently poor as Job's turkey, and it has always been one of my theories that a nigger invariably steals when he gets a chance. However, I wasn't going to give in at that."

"Of course you weren't," said the Colonel. "Did you ever read about the man who was told that the facts did not sustain his theory, and of his sublime answer? 'Very well,' said he, 'so much the worse for the facts!' "

"Come, Colonel, you talk too much. How am I ever to get on with my narrative, if you keep interrupting me in this style? Be quiet."

"Word of command. Quiet. Quiet it is. Continue."

"No, I said, of course they expect some reward,— that's it."

"What an ass you must be!" broke in Whittlesly.

"Hadn't you sense enough to see they could keep the whole of it, and nobody the wiser? and of course they couldn't have supposed any one was coming after it,— could they?

"How am I to know what they thought? If you don't stop your comments, I'll stop the story; take your choice."

"All right: go ahead."

"While I was considering the case, in came the master of the mansion,—a thin, stooped, tired-looking little fellow,—'Sam,' he told us, was his name; then proceeded to narrate how he had found the body, and knew the uniform, and was kind and tender with it because of its dress, 'for you see, sah, we darkies is all Union folks'; how he had brought it up in the night, for fear of his Secesh master, and made a coffin for it, and buried it decently. After that he took us out to a little spot of fresh earth, covered with leaves and twigs, and, digging down, we came to a rough pine box made as well as the poor fellow knew how to put it together. Opening it, we found all that was left of poor Hunt, respectably clad in a coarse, clean white garment which Sam's wife had made as nicely as she could out of her one pair of sheets. 'It wa'n't much,' said the good soul, with tears in her eyes, 'it wa'n't much we's could do for him, but I washed him, and dressed him, peart as I could, and Sam and me, we buried him. We wished, both on us, that we could have done heaps more for him, but we did all that we could,'—which, indeed, was plain enough to be seen.

"Before we went away, Sam brought from a little hole, which he burrowed in the floor of his cabin, a something, done up in dirty old rags; and when we opened it, what under the heavens do you suppose we found? You'll never guess. Three hundred dollars in bank-bills, and some important papers, which he had taken and hid,—concealed them even from his wife, because, he said, the guerillas often came round, and they might frighten her into giving them up if she knew they were there.

"I collapsed at that, and stood with open mouth, watching for the next proceeding. I knew there was to be some more of it, and there was. Hunt's brother offered back half the money; *offered* it! why, he tried to force it on the fellow, and couldn't. His master wouldn't let him buy himself and his wife,—I suspect, out of sheer cussedness,—and he hadn't any other use for money, he said. Besides, he didn't want to take, and wouldn't take, anything that looked like pay for doing aught for a 'Linkum sojer,' alive or dead.

"'They'se going to make us all free, sometime,' he said, 'that's enough. Don't look like it, jest yet, I knows; but I lives in faith; it'll come byumby.' When the fellow said that, I declare to you, Surrey, I felt like hiding my face. At last I began to comprehend what your indignation meant against the order forbidding slaves coming into our lines, and commanding their return when they succeed in entering. Just then we all seemed to me meaner than dirt."

"As we are; and, as dirt, deserve to be trampled underfoot, beaten, defeated, till we're ready to stand up and fight like men in this struggle."

"Amen to that, Colonel," added Whittlesly.

"Well, I'm pretty nearly ready to say so myself," finished Brooks, half reluctantly.

CHAPTER IX

"The best-laid schemes o' mice and men
Gang aft agley."
BURNS

THEY didn't find Jim in the camp of his regiment, so went up to head-quarters to institute inquiries. "Given?" a little thought and investigation. "Oh! Given is out on picket duty."

"Whereabouts?"

The direction indicated. "Thanks! we'll find him." Having commenced the search, Surrey was determined to end it ere he turned back, and his two friends bore him company. As they came down the road, they saw in the distance a great stalwart fellow, red-shirted and conspicuous, evidently absorbed in some singular task,—what they did not perceive, till, coming to closer quarters, they discovered, perched by his side, a tin cup filled with soapsuds, a pipe in his mouth, and that by the help of the two he was regaling himself with the pastime of blowing bubbles.

"I'll wager that's Jim," said Surrey, before he saw his face.

"It's like him, certainly: from what I've heard of him, I think he would die outright if he couldn't amuse himself in some shape."

"Why, the fellow must be a curiosity worth coming here to see."

"Pretty nearly."

Surrey walked on a little in advance, and tapped him on the shoulder. Down came the pipe, up went the hand in a respectful military salute, but before it was finished he saw who was before him.

"Wow!" he exclaimed, "if it ain't Mr. Willie Surrey. My! ain't I glad to see you? How *do* you do? The sight of you is as good as a month's pay."

"Come, Given, don't stun me with compliments," cried Surrey, laughing and putting out his hand to grasp the big, red paw that came to meet it, and shake it heartily. "If I'd known you were over here, I'd have found you before, though my regiment hasn't been down here long."

Jim at that looked sharply at the "eagles," and then over the alert, graceful person, finishing his inspection with an approving nod, and the emphatic declaration, "Well, if I know what's what, and I rayther reckon I do, you're about the right figger for an officer, and on the whole I'd sooner pull off my cap to you than any other fellow I've seen round,"—bringing his hand once more to the salute.

"Why, Jim, you have turned courtier; army life is spoiling you," protested the inspected one; protesting,—yet pleased, as any one might have been, at the evidently sincere admiration.

"Nary time," Jim strenuously denied; and, these little courtesies being ended, they talked about enlistment, and home, and camp, and a score of things that interested officer and man alike. In the midst of the confab a dust was seen up the road, coming nearer, and presently out of it appeared a family carriage somewhat dilapidated and worse for wear, but still quite magnificent; enthroned on the back seat a fullblown F. F. V. with rather more than the ordinary measure of superciliousness belonging to his race; driven, of course, by his colored servant. Jim made for the middle of the road, and, holding his bayonet in such wise as to threaten at one charge horse, negro, and chivalry, roared out, "Tickets!"

At such an extraordinary and unceremonious demand the knight flushed angrily, frowned, made an expressive gesture with his lips and his nose which suggestively indicated that there was something offensive in the air between the wind and his gentility, ending the pantomime by finding a pass and handing it over to his "nigger," then—not deigning to speak—motioned him and it to the threatening figure. As this black man came forward, Brooks, looking at him a moment, cried excitedly, "By Jove! it's Sam."

"No? Hunt's Sam?"

"Yes, the very same; and I suppose that's his cantankerous old master."

Surrey ran forward to Jim, for the three had fallen back when the carriage came near, and said a few sentences to him quickly and earnestly.

"All right, Colonel! just as you please," he replied. "You leave it to me; I'll fix him." Then, turning to Sam, who stood waiting, demanded, "Well, have you got it?"

"Yes, massa."

"Fork over,"—and looking at it a moment pronounced "All right! Move on!" elucidating the remark by a jerk at the coat-collar of the unsuspecting Sam, which sent him whirling up the road at a fine but uncomfortable rate of speed.

"Now, sir, what do *you* want?" addressing the astounded chevalier, who sat speechlessly observant of this unlooked-for proceeding.

"Want?" cried the irate Virginian, his anger loosening his tongue, "want? I want to go on, of course; that was my pass."

"Was it now? I want to know! that's singular! Why didn't you offer it yourself then?"

"Because I thought my nigger a fitter person to parley with a Lincoln vandal," loftily responded his eminence.

"That's kind of you, I'm sure. Sorry I can't oblige you in return,—very; but you'll just have to turn tail and drive back again. That bit of paper says 'Pass the bearer,' and the bearer's already passed. You can't get two men through this picket on one man's pass, not if one is a nigger and t'other a skunk; so, sir, face about, march!"

This was an unprepared-for dilemma. Mr. V. looked at the face of the "Lincoln vandal," but saw there no sign of relenting; then into the distance whither he was anxiously desirous to tend; glanced reflectively at the bayonet in the centre and the narrow space on either side the road; and finally called to his black man to come back.

Sam approached with reluctance, and fell back with alacrity when the glittering steel was brandished towards his own breast.

"Where's your pass, sirrah?" demanded Jim, with asperity.

"Here, massa," said the chattel, presenting the same one which had already been examined.

"Won't do," said Jim. "Can't come that game over this child. That passes you *to* Fairfax,—can't get any one *from* Fairfax on that ticket. Come," flourishing the shooting-stick once more, "move along"; which Sam proceeded to do with extraordinary readiness.

"Now, sir," turning to the again speechless chevalier, "if you stay here any longer, I shall take you under arrest to head-quarters: consequently, you'd better accept the advice of a disinterested friend, and make tracks, lively."

By this time the scion of a latter-day chivalry seemed to comprehend the situation, seized his lines, wheeled about, and went off at a spanking trot over the "sacred *clonky metaphor, over done*

soil,"—Jim shouting after him, "I say, Mr. F. F. V., if you meet any 'Lincoln vandals,' just give them my respects, will you?" to which as the knight gave no answer, we are left in doubt to this day whether Given's commission was ever executed.

"There! my mind's relieved on that point," announced Jim, wiping his face with one hand and shaking the other after the retreating dust. "Mean old scoot! I'll teach him to insult one of our boys,—'Lincoln vandals' indeed! I'd like to have whanged him!" with a final shake and a final explosion, cooling off as rapidly as he had heated, and continuing the interrupted conversation with recovered temper and *sang froid*.

He was delighted at meeting Surrey, and Surrey was equally glad to see once more his old favorite, for Jim and he had been great friends when he was a little boy and had watched the big boy at work in his father's foundry,—a favoritism which, spite of years and changes, and wide distinctions of social position, had never altered nor cooled, and which showed itself now in many a pleasant shape and fashion so long as they were near together.

They aided and abetted one another in more ways than one. Jim at Surrey's request, and by a plan of his proposing, succeeded in getting Sam's wife away from her home,— not from any liking for the expedition, or interest in either of the "niggers," as he stoutly asserted, but solely to please the Colonel. If that, indeed, were his only purpose, he succeeded to a charm, for when Surrey saw the two re-

united, safe from the awful clutch of slavery, supplied with
ample means for the journey and the settlement thereafter,
and on their way to a good Northern home, he was more
than pleased,—he was rejoiced, and said, "Thank God!"
with all his heart, and reverently, as he watched them away.

Before the summer ended Jim was down with what he
called "a scratch"; a pretty ugly wound, the surgeon
thought it, and the Colonel remembered and looked after
him with unflagging interest and zeal. Many a book and
paper, many a cooling drink and bit of fruit delicious to the
parched throat and fevered lips, found their way to the little
table by his side. Surrey was never too busy by reason of his
duties, or among his own sick and wounded men, to find
time for a chat, or a scrap of reading, or to write a letter for
the prostrate and helpless fellow, who suffered without
complaining, as, indeed, they did all about him, only
relieving himself now and then by a suppressed growl.

And so, with occasional episodes of individual interest,
with marches and fightings, with extremes of heat and
cold, of triumph and defeat, the long months wore away.
These men were soldiers, each in his place in the great war
with the record of which all the world is familiar, a tale
written in blood, and flame, and tears,—terrible, yet
heroic; ghastly, yet sublime. As soldiers in such a conflict,
they did their duty and noble endeavor,—Jim, a nameless
private in the ranks,—Surrey, not braver perchance, but so
conspicuous with all the elements which fit for splendid
command, so fortunate in opportunities for their display,

so eminent in seizing them and using them to their fullest extent, regardless of danger and death, as to make his name known and honored by all who watched the progress of the fight, read its record with interest, and knew its heroes and leaders with pride and love.

In the winter of '63 Jim's regiment was ordered away to South Carolina; and he who at parting looked with keen regret on the face of the man who had been so faithful and well tried a friend, would have looked upon it with something deeper and sadder, could he at the same time have gazed a little way into the future, and seen what it held in store for him.

Four months after he marched away, Surrey's brigade was in that awful fight and carnage of Chancellorsville, where men fought like gods to counteract the blunders, and retrieve the disaster, induced by a stunned and helpless brain. There was he stricken down, at the head of his command, covered with dust and smoke; twice wounded, yet refusing to leave the field,—his head bound with a handkerchief, his eyes blazing like stars beneath its stained folds, his voice cheering on his men; three horses shot under him; on foot then; contending for every inch of the ground he was compelled to yield; giving way only as he was forced at the point of the bayonet; his men eager to emulate him, to follow him into the jaws of death, to fall by his side,—thus was he prostrated; not dead, as they thought and feared when they seized him and bore him at last from the field, but insensible, bleeding with frightful abundance, his right arm shattered to fragments; not dead, yet at death's door—and looking in.

May blossoms had dropped, and June harvests were ripe on all the fields, ere he could take advantage of the unsolicited leave, and go home. Home—for which his heart longed!

He was not, however, in too great haste to stop by the way, to pause in Washington, and do what he had sooner intended to accomplish,—solicit, as a special favor to himself, as an honor justly won by the man for whom he entreated it, a promotion for Jim. "It is impossible now," he was informed, "but the case should be noted and remembered. If anything could certainly secure the man an advance, it was the advocacy of General Surrey"; and so, not quite content, but still satisfied that Jim's time was in the near future, he went on his way.

As the cars approached Philadelphia his heart beat so fast that it almost stifled him, and he leaned against the window heavily for air and support. It was useless to reason with himself, vain to call good judgment to his counsels and summon wisdom to his aid. This was her home. Somewhere in this city to which he was so rapidly hastening, she was moving up and down, had her being, was living and loving. After these long years his eyes so ached to see her, his heart was so hungry for her presence, that it seemed to him as though the sheer longing would call her out of her retreat, on to the streets through which he must pass, across his path, into the sight of his eyes and reach of his hand. He had thought that he felt all this before. He found, as the space diminished between them,—as, perchance, she was but a stone's throw from his side,—that the pain, and the longing, and the intolerable desire to behold her once again, increased a hundred-fold.

Eager as he had been a little while before to reach his home, he was content to remain quietly here now. He laughed at himself as he stepped into a carriage, and, tired as he was,—for his amputated arm, not yet thoroughly healed, made him weak and worn,—drove through all the afternoon and evening, across miles and miles of heated, wearisome stones, possessed by the idea that somewhere, somehow, he should see her, he would find her before his quest was done.

After that last painful rebuff, he did not dare to go to her home, could he find it, till he had secured from her, in some fashion, a word or sign. "This," he said, "is certainly doubly absurd, since she does not live in the city; but she is here to-day, I know,—she must be here"; and persisted in his endeavor,—persisted, naturally, in vain; and went to bed, at last, exhausted; determined that to-morrow should find him on his journey farther north, whatever wish might plead for delay, yet with a final cry for her from the depths of his soul, as he stretched out his solitary arm, ere sinking to restless sleep, and dreams of battle and death— sleep unrefreshing, and dreams ill-omened; as he thought, again and again, rousing himself from their hold, and looking out to the night, impatient for the break of day.

When day broke he was unable to rise with its dawn. The effect of all this tension on his already overtaxed nerves was to induce a fever in the unhealed arm, which, though not painful, was yet sufficient to hold him close prisoner for several days; a delay which chafed him, and which filled his family at home with an intolerable anxiety, not that they knew its cause,—*that* would have been a relief,—but that they conjectured another, to them infinitely worse than sickness or suffering, bad and sorrowful as were these.

CHAPTER X

"Gentlemen, let not prejudice prepossess you."
IZAAK WALTON

CAR No. 14, Fifth Street line, Philadelphia, was crowded. Travelling bags, shawls, and dusters marked that people were making for the 11 A.M. New York train, Kensington depot. One pleasant-looking old gentleman whose face shone under a broad brim, and whose cleanly drabs were brought into distasteful proximity with the garments of a drunken coal-heaver, after a vain effort to edge away, relieved his mind by turning to his neighbor with the statement, "Consistency is a jewel."

"Undoubtedly true, Mr. Greenleaf," answered the neighbor, "but what caused the remark?"

"That,"—looking with mild disgust at the dirty and ragged leg sitting by his own. "Here's this filthy fellow, a nuisance to everybody near him, can ride in these cars, and a nice, respectable colored person can't. So I couldn't help thinking, and saying, that consistency is a jewel."

"Well, it's a shame,—that's a fact; but of course nobody can interfere if the companies don't choose to let them ride; it's their concern, not ours."

"There's a fine specimen now, out there on the sidewalk." The fine specimen was a large, powerfully made man, black as ebony, dressed in army blouse and trousers, one leg gone,—evidently very tired, for he leaned heavily on his crutches. The conductor, a kindly-faced young fellow, pulled the strap, and helped him on to the platform with a peremptory "Move up front, there!" to the people standing inside.

"Why!" exclaimed the old Friend,—"do my eyes deceive me?" Then getting up, and taking the man by the arm, he seated him in his own place: "Thou art less able to stand than I."

Tears rushed to his eyes as he said, "Thank you, sir! you are too kind." Evidently he was weak, and as evidently unaccustomed to find any one "too kind."

"Thee has on the army blue; has thee been fighting any?"

"Yes, sir!" he answered, promptly.

"I didn't know black men were in the army; yet thee has lost a leg. Where did that go?"

"At Newbern, sir."

"At Newbern,—ah! long ago? and how did it happen?"

"Fourteenth of March, sir. There was a land fight, and the gunboats came up to the rescue. Some of us black men were upon board a little schooner that carried one gun. 'Twasn't a great deal we could do with that, but we did the best we could; and got well peppered in return. This is what it did for me,"—looking down at the stump.

"I guess thee is sorry now that thee didn't keep out of it, isn't thee?"

"No, sir; no indeed, sir. If I had five hundred legs and fifty lives, I'd be glad to give them all in such a war as this."

Here somebody got out; the old Friend sat down; and the coal-heaver, roused by the stir, lifted himself from his drunken sleep, and, looking round, saw who was beside him.

A vile oath, an angry stare from his bloodshot eyes.

"Ye ———, what are ye doin' here? out wid ye, quick!"

"What's the matter?" queried the conductor, who was collecting somebody's fare.

"The matther, is it? matther enough! what's this nasty nagur doin' here? Put him out, can't ye?"

The conductor took no notice.

"Conductor!" spoke up a well-dressed man, with the air and manner of a gentleman, "what does that card say?"

The conductor looked at the card indicated, upon which was printed "Colored people not allowed in this car," legible enough to require less study than he saw fit to give it. "Well!" he said.

"Well," was the answer,—"your duty is plain. Put that fellow out."

The conductor hesitated,—looked round the car. Nobody spoke.

"I'm sorry, my man! I hoped there would be no objection when I let you in; but our orders are strict, and, as the passengers ain't willing, you'll have to get off,"—jerking angrily at the bell.

As the car slackened speed, a young officer, whom nobody noticed, got on.

There was a moment's pause as the black man gathered up his crutches, and raised himself painfully. "Stop!" cried a thrilling and passionate voice,—"stand still! Of what stuff are you made to sit here and see a man, mangled and maimed in *your* cause and for *your* defence, insulted and outraged at the bidding of a drunken boor and a cowardly traitor?" The voice, the beautiful face, the intensity burning through both, electrified every soul to which she appealed. Hands were stretched out to draw back the crippled soldier; eyes that a moment before were turned away looked kindly at him; a Babel of voices broke out, "No, no," "let him stay," "it's a shame," "let him alone, conductor," "we ain't so bad as that," with more of the same kind; those who chose not to join in the chorus discreetly held their peace, and made no attempt to sing out of time and tune.

The car started again. The *gentleman*, furious at the turn of the tide, cried out, "Ho, ho! here's a pretty

preacher of the gospel of equality! why, ladies and gentlemen, this high-flyer, who presumes to lecture us, is
nothing but a"— *how does he know??*

The sentence was cut short in mid-career, the insolent
sneer dashed out of his face,—face and form prone on the
floor of the car,—while over him bent and blazed the
young officer, whose entrance, a little while before,
nobody had heeded.

Spurning the prostrate body at his feet, he turned to
Francesca, for it was she, and stretched out his hand,—his
left hand,—his only one. It was time; all the heat, and passion, and color, had died out, and she stood there shivering, a look of suffering in her face.

"Miss Ercildoune! you are ill,—you need the air,—
allow me!" drawing her hand through his arm, and taking
her out with infinite deference and care.

"Thank you! a moment's faintness,—it is over now," as
they reached the sidewalk.

"No, no, you are too ill to walk,—let me get you a carriage."

Hailing one that was passing by, he put her in, his hand
lingering on hers, lingering on the folds of her dress as he
bent to arrange it; his eyes clinging to her face with a passionate, woeful tenderness. "It is two years since I saw you,
since I have heard from you," he said, his voice hoarse with
the effort to speak quietly.

"Yes," she answered, "it is two years." Stooping her
head to write upon a card, her lips moved as if they said

something,—something that seemed like "I must! only once!" but of course that could not be. "It is my address," she then said, putting the card in his hand. "I shall be happy to see you in my own home."

"This afternoon?" eagerly.

She hesitated. "Whenever you may call. I thank you again,—and good morning."

Meanwhile the car had moved on its course: outwardly, peaceful enough; inwardly, full of commotion. The conservative gentleman, gathering himself up from his prone estate, white with passion and chagrin, saw about him everywhere looks of scorn, and smiles of derision and contempt, and fled incontinently from the sight.

His coal-heaving *confrère*, left to do battle alone, came to the charge valiant and unterrified. Another outbreak of blasphemy and obscenity were the weapons of assault; the ladies looked shocked, the gentlemen indignant and disgusted.

"Friend," called the non-resistant broad-brim, beckoning peremptorily to the conductor,—"friend, come here."

The conductor came.

"If colored persons are not permitted to ride, I suppose it is equally against the rules of the company to allow nuisances in their cars. Isn't it?"

"You are right, sir," assented the conductor, upon whose face a smile of comprehension began to beam.

"Well, I don't know what thee thinks, or what these

other people think, but I know of no worse nuisance than a filthy, blasphemous drunkard. There he sits,—remove him."

There was a perfect shout of laughter and delight; and before the irate "citizen" comprehended what was intended, or could throw himself into a pugilistic attitude, he was seized, *sans* ceremony, and ignominiously pushed and hustled from the car; the people therein, black soldier and all, drawing a long breath of relief, and going on their way rejoicing. Everybody's eyes were brighter; hearts beat faster, blood moved more quickly; everybody felt a sense of elation, and a kindness towards their neighbor and all the world. A cruel and senseless prejudice had been lost in an impulse, generous and just; and for a moment the sentiment which exalted their humanity, vivified and gladdened their souls.

CHAPTER XI

"The future seemed barred
By the corpse of a dead hope."
OWEN MEREDITH

So, then, after these long years he had seen her again. Having seen her, he wondered how he had lived without her. If the wearisome months seemed endless in passing, the morning hours were an eternity. "This afternoon?" he had said. "Be it so," she had answered. He did not dare to go till then.

Thinking over the scene of the morning, he scarcely dared go at all. She had not offered her hand; she had expressed no pleasure, either by look or word, at meeting him again. He had forced her to say, "Come": she could do no less when he had just interfered to save her insult, and had begged the boon.

"Insult!" his arm ached to strike another blow, as he

remembered the sentence it had cut short. Of course the fellow had been drinking, but outrage of her was intolerable, whatever madness prompted it. The very sun must shine more brightly, and the wind blow softly, when she passed by. Ah me! were the whole world what an ardent lover prays for his mistress, there were no need of death to enjoy the bliss of heaven.

What could he say? what do? how find words to speak the measured feelings of a friend? how control the beatings of his heart, the passion of his soul, that no sign should escape to wound or offend her? She had bade him to silence: was he sufficiently master of himself to strike the lighter keys without sounding some deep chords that would jar upon her ear?

He tried to picture the scene of their second meeting. He repeated again and again her formal title, Miss Ercildoune, that he might familiarize his tongue and his ear to the sound, and not be on the instant betrayed into calling the name which he so often uttered in his thoughts. He said over some civil, kindly words of greeting, and endeavored to call up, and arrange in order, a theme upon which he should converse. "I shall not dare to be silent," he thought, "for if I am, my silence will tell the tale; and if that do not, she will hear it from the throbbings of my heart. I don't know though,"—he laughed a little, as he spoke aloud,—bitterly it would have been, had his voice been capable of bitterness,—"perhaps she will think the organism of the poor thing has become diseased in camp and fightings,"—putting his hand up to his throat and holding the swollen veins, where the blood was beating furiously.

Presently he went down stairs and out to the street, in pursuit of some cut flowers which he found in a little cellar, a stone's throw from his hotel,—a fresh, damp little cellar, which smelt, he could not help thinking, like a grave. Coming out to the sunshine, he shook himself with disgust. "Faugh!" he thought, "what sick fancies and sentimental nonsense possess me? I am growing unwholesome. My dreams of the other night have come back to torment me in the day. These must put them to flight.

The fancy which had sent him in pursuit of these flowers he confessed to be a childish one, but none the less soothing for that. He had remembered that the first day he beheld her a nosegay had decorated his button-hole; a fair, sweet-scented thing which seemed, in some subtle way, like her. He wanted now just such another,—some mignonette, and geranium, and a single tea-rosebud. Here they were,—the very counterparts of those which he had worn on a brighter and happier day. How like they were! how changed was he! In some moods he would have smiled at this bit of girlish folly as he fastened the little thing over his heart; now, something sounded in his throat that was pitifully like a sob. Don't smile at him! he was so young; so impassioned, yet gentle; and then he loved so utterly with the whole of his great, sore heart.

By and by the time came to go, and eager, yet fearful,

he went. It was a fresh, beautiful day in early June; and
when the city, with its heat, and dust, and noise, was left
behind, and all the leafy greenness—the soothing quiet of
country sights and country sounds—met his ear and eye, a
curious peace took possession of his soul. It was less the
whisper of hope than the calm of assured reality. For the
moment, unreasonable as it seemed, something made him
blissfully sure of her love, spite of the rebuffs and coldness
she had compelled him to endure.

"This is the place, sir!" suddenly called his driver, stopping the horses in front of a stately avenue of trees, and
jumping down to open the gates.

"You need not drive in; you may wait here."

This, then, was her home. He took in the exquisite
beauty of the place with a keen pleasure. It was right that
all things sweet and fine should be about her; he had before
known that they were, but it delighted him to see them
with his own eyes. Walking slowly towards the house,—
slowly, for he was both impelled and retarded by the con-
flicting feelings that mastered him,—he heard her voice at
a little distance, singing; and directly she came out of a by-
path, and faced him. He need not have feared the meeting;
at least, any display of emotion; she gave no opportunity
for any such thing.

A frankly extended hand,—an easy "Good afternoon,
Mr. Surrey!" That was all. It was a cool, beautiful room
into which she ushered him; a room filled with an atmosphere of peace, but which was anything but peaceful to

him. He was restless, nervous; eager and excited, or absent and still. He determined to master his emotion, and give no outward sign of the tempest raging within.

At the instant of this conclusion his eye was caught by an exquisite portrait miniature upon an easel near him. Bending over it, taking it into his hands, his eyes went to and fro from the pictured face to the human one, tracing the likeness in each. Marking his interest, Francesca said, "It is my mother."

"If the eyes were dark, this would be your veritable image."

"Or, if mine were blue, I should be a portrait of mamma, which would be better."

"Better?"

"Yes." She was looking at the picture with weary eyes, which he could not see. "I had rather be the shadow of her than the reality of myself: an absurd fancy!" she added, with a smile, suddenly remembering herself.

"I would it were true!" he exclaimed.

She looked a surprised inquiry. His thought was, "for then I should steal you, and wear you always on my heart." But of course he could speak no such lover's nonsense; so he said, "Because of the fitness of things; you wished to be a shadow, which is immaterial, and hence of the substance of angels."

Truly he was improving. His effort to betray no love had led him into a ridiculous compliment. "What an idiot she will think me to say anything so silly!" he reflected;

while Francesca was thinking, "He has ceased to love me, or he would not resort to flattery. It is well!" but the pang that shot through her heart belied the closing thought, and, glancing at him, the first was denied by the unconscious expression of his eyes. Seeing that, she directly took alarm, and commenced to talk upon a score of indifferent themes.

He had never seen her in such a mood: gay, witty, brilliant,—full of a restless sparkle and fire; she would not speak an earnest word, nor hear one. She flung about bon-mots, and chatted airy persiflage till his heart ached. At another time, in another condition, he would have been delighted, dazzled, at this strange display; but not now.

In some careless fashion the war had been alluded to, and she spoke of Chancellorsville. "It was there you were last wounded?"

"Yes," he answered, not even looking down at the empty sleeve.

"It was there you lost your arm?"

"Yes," he answered again, "I am sorry it was my sword-arm."

"It was frightful,"—holding her breath. "Do you know you were reported mortally wounded? worse?"

"I have heard that I was sent up with the slain," he replied, half-smiling.

"It is true. I looked for your name in the columns of 'wounded' and 'missing,' and read it at last in the list of 'killed.' "

"For the sake of old times, I trust you were a little sorry to so read it," he said, sadly, for the tone hurt him.

"Sorry? yes, I was sorry. Who, indeed, of your friends would not be?"

"Who, indeed?" he repeated: "I am afraid the one whose regret I should most desire would sorrow the least."

"It is very like," she answered, with seeming carelessness,—"disappointment is the rule of life."

This would not do. He was getting upon dangerous ground. He would change the theme, and prevent any farther speech till he was better master of it. He begged for some music. She sat down at once and played for him; then sang at his desire. Rich as she was in the gifts of nature, her voice was the chief,—thrilling, flexible, with a sympathetic quality that in singing pathetic music brought tears, though the hearer understood not a word of the language in which she sang. In the old time he had never wearied listening, and now he besought her to repeat for him some of the dear, familiar songs. If these held for her any associations, he did not know it; she gave no outward sign,— sang to him as sweetly and calmly as to the veriest stranger. What else had he expected? Nothing; yet, with the unreasonableness of a lover, was disappointed that nothing appeared.

Taking up a piece at random, without pausing to remember the words, he said, spreading it before her, "May I tax you a little farther? I am greedy, I know, but then how can I help it?"

It was the song of the Princess.

She hesitated a moment, and half closed the book. Had he been standing where he could see her face, he would have been shocked by its pallor. It was over directly: she recovered herself, and, opening the music with a resolute air, began to sing:—

"Ask me no more: the moon may draw the sea;
    The cloud may stoop from heaven and take the shape,
    With fold to fold, of mountain and of cape;
But, O too fond, when have I answered thee?
        Ask me no more.

"Ask me no more: what answer should I give?
    I love not hollow cheek or faded eye;
    Yet, O my friend, I will not have thee die!
Ask me no more, lest I should bid thee live:
        Ask me no more."

She sang thus far with a clear, untrembling voice,—so clear and untrembling as to be almost metallic,—the restraint she had put upon herself making it unnatural. At the commencement she had estimated her strength, and said, "It is sufficient!" but she had overtaxed it, as she found in singing the last verse:—

"Ask me no more: thy fate and mine are sealed;
    I strove against the stream and all in vain;
    Let the great river take me to the main;

No more, dear love, for at a touch I yield:
Ask me no more."

All the longing, the passion, the prayer of which a human soul is capable found expression in her voice. It broke through the affected coldness and calm, as the ocean breaks through its puny barriers when, after wind and tempest, all its mighty floods are out. Surrey had changed his place, and stood fronting her. As the last word fell, she looked at him, and the two faces saw in each but a reflection of the same passion and pain: pallid, with eyes burning from an inward fire,—swayed by the same emotion,—she bent forward as he, stretching forth his arms, in a stifling voice cried, "Come!" L⇒ *uh. sloppy.*

Bent, but for an instant; then, by a superhuman effort, turned from him, and put out her hand with a gesture of dissent, though she could not control her voice to speak a word.

At that he came close to her, not touching her hand or even her dress, but looking into her face with imploring eyes, and whispering, "Francesca, my darling, speak to me! say that you love me! one word! You are breaking my heart!"

Not a word.

"Francesca!"

She had mastered her voice. "Go!" she then said, beseechingly. "Oh, why did you ask me? why did I let you come?"

"No, no," he answered. "I cannot go,—not till you answer me."

"Ah!" she entreated, "do not ask! I can give no such answer as you desire. It is all wrong,—all a mistake. You do not comprehend."

"Make me, then."

She was silent.

"Forgive me. I am rude: I cannot help it. I will not go unless you say, 'I do not love you.' Nothing but this shall drive me away."

Francesca's training in her childhood had been by a Catholic governess; she never quite lost its effect. Now she raised her hand to a little gold cross that hung at her neck, her fingers closing on it with a despairing clasp. "Ah, Christ, have pity!" her heart cried. "Blessed Mother of God, forgive me! have mercy upon me!"

Her face was frightfully pale, but her voice did not tremble as she gave him her hand, and said gently, "Go, then, my friend. I do not love you."

He took her hand, held it close for a moment, and then, without another look or word, put it tenderly down, and was gone.

So absorbed was he in painful thought that, passing down the long avenue with bent head, he did not notice, nor even see, a gentleman who, coming from the opposite direction, looked at him at first carelessly, and then searchingly, as he went by.

This gentleman, a man in the prime of life, handsome,

stately, and evidently at home here, scrutinized the stranger with a singular intensity,—made a movement as though he would speak to him,—and then, drawing back, went with hasty steps towards the house.

Had Willie looked up, beheld this face and its expression, returned the scrutiny of the one, and comprehended the meaning of the other, while memory recalled a picture once held in his hands, some things now obscured would have been revealed to him, and a problem been solved. As it was, he saw nothing, moved mechanically onward to the carriage, seated himself and said, "Home!"

This young man was neither presumptuous nor vain. He had been once repulsed and but now utterly rejected. He had no reason to hope, and yet—perhaps it was his poetical and imaginative temperament—he could not resign himself to despair.

Suddenly he started with an exclamation that was almost a cry. What was it? He remembered that, more than two years ago, on the last day he had been with her, he had begged the copy of a duet which they sometimes sang. It was in manuscript, and he desired to have it written out by her own hand. He had before petitioned, and she promised it; and when he thus again spoke of it, she laughed, and said, "What a memory it is, to be sure! I shall have to tie a bit of string on my finger to refresh it." *did he go back??*
clumsily written – this is
"Is that efficacious?" he had asked. *still flashback*

"Doubtless," she had replied, searching in her pocket for a scrap of anything that would serve.

"Will this do?" he then queried, bringing forth a coil of gold wire which he had been commissioned to buy for some fanciful work of his mother.

"Finely," she declared; "it is durable, it will give me a wide margin, it will be long in wearing out."

"Nay, then, you must have something more fragile," he had objected.

At that they both laughed, as he twisted a fragment of it on the little finger of her right hand. "There it is to stay," he asserted, "till your promise is redeemed." That was the last time he had seen her till to-day.

Now, sitting, thinking of the interview just passed, suddenly he remembered, as one often recalls the vision of something seemingly unnoticed at the time, that, upon her right hand, the little finger of the right hand, there was a delicate ring,—a mere thread,—in fact, a wire of gold; the very one himself had tied there two years ago.

In an instant, by one of those inexplicable connections of the brain or soul, he found himself living over an experience of his college youth.

He had been spending the day in Boston with a dear friend, some score of years his senior; a man of the rarest culture, and of a most sweet and gentle nature withal; and when evening came they had drifted naturally to the theatre,—the fool's paradise it may be sometimes, but to them on that occasion a real paradise.

He remembered well the play. It was Scott's *Bride of Lammermoor*. He had never read it, but, before the curtain rose, his friend had unfolded the story in so kind and skilful a manner as to have imbued him as fully with the spirit of the tale as though he had studied the book.

What he chiefly recalled in the play was the scene in which Ravenswood comes back to Emily long after they had been plighted,—long after he had supposed her faith-less,—long after he had been tossed on a sea of troubles, touching the seeming decay in her affections. Just as she is about to be enveloped in the toils which were spread for her,—just as she is about to surrender herself to the hated nuptials, and submit to the embrace of one whom she loathed more than she dreaded death,—Ravenswood, the man whom Heaven had made for her, presents himself.

What followed was quiet, yet intensely dramatic. Ravenswood, wrought to the verge of despair, bursts upon the scene at the critical moment, detaches Emily from her party, and leads her slowly forward. He is unutterably sad. He questions her very tenderly; asks her whether she is not enforced; whether she is taking this step of her own free will and accord; whether she has indeed dismissed the dear, old fond love for him from her heart forever? He must hear it from her own lips. When timidly and feebly informed that such is indeed the case, he requests her to return a cer-tain memento,—a silver trinket which had been given her as the symbol of his love on the occasion of their betrothal. Raising her hand to her throat she essays to draw it from her bosom. Her fingers rest upon the chain which binds it to her neck, but the o'erfraught heart is still,—the

troubled, but unconscious head droops upon his
shoulder,—he lifts the chain from its resting-place, and
withdraws the token from her heart.

Supporting her with one hand and holding this badge
of a lost love with the other, he says, looking down upon
her with a face of anguish, and in a voice of despair, *"And
she could wear it thus!"*

As this scene rose and lived before him, Surrey
exclaimed, "Surely that must have been the perfection of
art, to have produced an effect so lasting and profound,—
'and she could wear it thus!'—ah," he said, as in response
to some unexpressed thought, "but Emily loved
Ravenswood. Why—?" Evidently he was endeavoring to
answer a question that baffled him.

CHAPTER XII

"And down on aching heart and brain
Blow after blow unbroken falls."

BOKER

" A letter for you, sir," said the clerk, as Surrey stopped at the desk for his key. It was a bulky epistle, addressed in his aunt Russell's hand, and he carried it off, wondering what she could have to say at such length.

He was in no mood to read or to enjoy; but, nevertheless, tore open the cover, finding within it a double letter. Taking the envelope of one from the folds of the other, his eye fell first upon his mother's writing; a short note and a puzzling one.

"MY DEAR WILLIE:—

"I have tried to write you a letter, but cannot. I never wounded you if I could avoid it, and I do not wish to begin now. Augusta and I had a talk about you yesterday which crazed me with anxiety. She told me it was my place to write you what ought to be said under these trying circumstances, for we are sure you have remained in Philadelphia to see Miss Ercildoune. At first I said I would, and then my heart failed me. I was sure, too, that she could write, as she always does, much better than I; so I begged her to say all that was necessary, and I would send her this note to enclose with her letter. Read it, I entreat you, and then hasten, I pray you, hasten to us at once.

"Take care of your arm, do not hurt yourself by any excitement; and, with dear love from your father, which he would send did he know I was writing, believe me always your devoted

"MOTHER."

"'Trying circumstances!'—'Miss Ercildoune!'—what does it mean?" he cried, bewildered. "Come, let us see."

The letter which he now opened was an old and much-fingered one, written—as he saw at the first glance—by his aunt to his mother. Why it was sent to him he could not conjecture; and, without attempting to so do, at once plunged into its pages:—

"CONTINENTAL HOTEL,

PHILADELPHIA, JUNE 27, 1861

"MY DEAR LAURA:—

"I can readily understand with what astonishment you will read this letter, from the amazement I have experienced in collecting its details. I will not weary you with any personal narration, but tell my tale at once.

"Miss Ercildoune, as you know, was my daughter's intimate at school,—a school, the admittance to which was of itself a guarantee of respectability. Of course I knew nothing of her family, nor of her,—save as Clara wrote me of her beauty and her accomplishments, and, above all, of her style,—till I met Mrs. Lancaster. Of her it is needless for me to speak. As you know, she is irreproachable, and her position is of the best. Consequently when Clara wrote me that her friend was to come to New York to her aunt, and begged to entertain her for a while, I added my request to her entreaty, and Miss Ercildoune came. Ill-fated visit! would it had never been made!

"It is useless now to deny her gifts and graces. They are, reluctantly I confess, so rare and so conspicuous—have so many times been seen, and known, and praised by us all,—that it would put me in the most foolish of attitudes should I attempt to reconsider a verdict so frequently pronounced, or to eat my own words, uttered a thousand times.

"It is also, I presume, useless to deny that we were well pleased—nay, delighted—with Willie's evident sentiment

for her. Indeed, so thoroughly did she charm me, that, had
I not seen how absolutely his heart was enlisted in her pursuit, she is the very girl whom I should have selected,
could I have so done, as a wife for Tom and a daughter for
myself.

"I knew full well how deep was this feeling for her
when he marched away, on that day so full of supreme
splendor and pain, unable to see her and to say adieu. His
eyes, his face, his manner, his very voice, marked his rest-
lessness, his longing, and disappointment. I was positively
angry with the girl for thwarting and hurting him so, and,
whatever her excuse might be, for her absence at such a
time. How constantly are we quarrelling with our best
fates!

"She remained in New York, as you know, for some
weeks after the 19th; in fact, has been at home but for a
little while. Once or twice, so provoked with her was I for
disappointing our pet, I could not resist the temptation of
saying some words about him which, if she cared for him,
I knew would wound her: and, indeed, they did,—
wounded her so deeply, as was manifest in her manner and
her face, that I had not the heart to repeat the experiment.

"One week ago I had a letter from Willie, enclosing
another to her, and an entreaty, as he had written one
which he was sure had miscarried, that I would see that
this reached her hands in safety. So anxious was I to fulfil
his request in its word and its spirit, and so certain that I
could further his cause,—for I was sure this letter was a

love-letter,—that I did not forward it by post, but, being compelled to come to Burlington, I determined to go on to Philadelphia, drive out to her home, and myself deliver the missive into her very hands. A most fortunate conclusion, as you will presently decide.

"Last evening I reached the city,—rested, slept here,— and this morning was driven to her father's place. For all our sakes, I was somewhat anxious, under the circumstances, that this should be quite the thing; and I confess myself, on the instant of its sight, more than satisfied. It is really superb!—the grounds extensive, and laid out with the most absolute taste. The house, large and substantial, looks very like an English mansion; with a certain quaint style and antique elegance, refreshing to contemplate, after the crude newness and ostentatious vulgarity of almost everything one sees here in America. It is within as it is without. Although a great many lovely things are scattered about of recent make, the wood-work and the heavy furniture are aristocratic from their very age, and in their way, literally perfection.

"Miss Ercildoune met me with not quite her usual grace and ease. She was, no doubt, surprised at my unexpected appearance, and—I then thought, as a consequence—slightly embarrassed. I soon afterwards discovered the constraint in her manner sprang from another cause.

"I had reached the house just at lunch-time, and she would take me out to the table to eat something with her.

I had hoped to see her father, and was disappointed when she informed me he was in the city. All I saw charmed me. The appointments of the table were like those of the house: everything exquisitely fine, and the silver massive and old,—not a new piece among it,—and marked with a monogram and crest.

"I write you all this that you may the more thoroughly appreciate my absolute horror at the final *denouement*, and share my astonishment at the presumption of these people in daring to maintain such style.

"I had given her Willie's letter before we left the parlor, with a significant word and smile, and was piqued to see that she did not blush,—in fact, became excessively white as she glanced at the writing, and with an unsteady hand put it into her pocket. After lunch she made no motion to look at it, and as I had my own reasons for desiring her to peruse it, I said, 'Miss Francesca, will you not read your letter? that I may know if there is any later news from our soldier.'

"She hesitated a moment, and then said, with what I thought an unnatural manner, 'Certainly, if you so desire,' and, taking it out, broke the seal. 'Allow me,' she added, going towards a window,—as though she desired more light, but in reality, I knew, to turn her back upon me,— forgetting that a mirror, hanging opposite, would reveal her face with distinctness to my gaze.

"It was pale to ghastliness, with a drawn, haggard look about the mouth and eyes that shocked as much as it amazed me; and before commencing to read she crushed the letter in her hands, pressing it to her heart with a gesture which was less of a caress than of a spasm.

"However, as she read, all this changed; and before she finished said, 'Ah, Willie, it is clear your cause needs no advocate.' Positively, I did not know a human countenance could express such happiness; there was something in it absolutely dazzling. And evidently entirely forgetful of me, she raised the paper to her mouth, and kissed it again and again, pressing her lips upon it with such clinging and passionate fondness as would have imbued it with life were that possible."

Here Willie flung down his aunt's epistle and tore from his pocket this self-same letter. He had kept it,—carried it about with him,—for two reasons: because it was *hers*, he said,—this avowal of his love was hers, whether she refused it or no, and he had no right to destroy her property; and because, as he had nothing else she had worn or touched, he cherished this sacredly since it had been in her dear hands.

Now he took it into his clasp as tenderly as though it were Francesca's face, and kissed it with the self-same clinging and passionate fondness as this of which he had just read. Here had her lips rested,—here; he felt their fragrance and softness thrilling him under the cold, dead paper, and pressed it to his heart while he continued to read:—

"Before she turned, I walked to another window,—

wishing to give her time to recover calmness, or at least self-control, and was at once absorbed in contemplating a gentleman whom I felt assured to be Mr. Ercildoune. He stood with his back to me, apparently giving some order to the coachman: thus I could not see his face, but I never before was so impressed with, so to speak, the personality of a man. His physique was grand, and his air and bearing magnificent, and I watched him with admiration as he walked slowly away. I presume he passed the window at which she was standing, for she called, 'Papa!' 'In a moment, dear,' he answered, and in a moment entered, and was presented; and I, raising my eyes to his face,—ah, how can I tell you what sight they beheld!

"Self-possessed as I think I am, and as I certainly ought to be, I started back with an involuntary exclamation, a mingling doubtless of incredulity and disgust. This man, who stood before me with all the ease and self-assertion of a gentleman, was—you will never believe it, I fear—*a mulatto*!

"Whatever effect my manner had on him was not perceptible. He had not seated himself, and, with a smile that was actually satirical, he bowed, uttered a few words of greeting, and went out of the room.

"'How dared you?' I then cried, for astonishment had given place to rage, 'how dared you deceive me—deceive us all—so? how dared you palm yourself off as white and respectable, and thus be admitted to Mr. Hale's school and to the society and companionship of his pupils?' I could scarcely control myself when I thought of how shamefully we had all been cozened.

"'Pardon me, madam,' she answered with effrontery,— effrontery under the circumstances,—'you forget yourself, and what is due from one lady to another.' (Did you ever hear of such presumption!) 'I practised no deceit upon Professor Hale. He knew papa well,—was his intimate friend at college, in England,—and was perfectly aware who was Mr. Ercildoune's daughter when she was admitted to his school. For myself, I had no confessions to make, and made none. I was your daughter's friend; as such, went to her house, and invited her here. I trust you have seen in me nothing unbecoming a gentlewoman, as, *up to this time*, I have beheld in you naught save the attributes of a lady. If we are to have any farther conversation, it must be conducted on the old plan, and not the extraordinary one you have just adopted; else I shall be compelled, in self-respect, to leave you alone in my own parlor.'

"Imagine if you can the effect of this speech upon me. I assure you I was composed enough outwardly, if not inwardly, ere she ended her sentence. Having finished, I said, 'Pardon me, Miss Ercildoune, for any words which may have offended your dignity. I will confine myself for the rest of our interview to your own rules!'

"'It is well,' she responded. I had spoken satirically, and expected to see her shrink under it, but she answered with perfect coolness and *sang froid*. I continued, 'You will not deny that you are a negro, at least a mulatto.'

"'Pardon me, madam,' she replied; 'my father is a mulatto, my mother was an Englishwoman. Thus, to give you accurate information upon the subject, I am a quadroon.'

"'Quadroon be it!' I answered, angrily again, I fear. 'Quadroon, mulatto, or negro, it is all one. I have no desire to split hairs of definition. You could not be more obnoxious were you black as Erebus. I have no farther words to pass upon the past or the present, but something to say of the future. You hold in your hands a letter—a love-letter, I am sure—a declaration, as I fear—from my nephew, Mr. Surrey. You will oblige me by at once sitting down, writing a peremptory and unqualified refusal to his proposal, if he has made you one,—a refusal that will admit of no hope and no double interpretation,—and give it into my keeping before I leave this room.'

"When I first alluded to Willie's letter she had crimsoned, but before I closed she was so white I should have thought her fainting, but for the fire in her eyes. However, she spoke up clear enough when she said, 'And what, madam, if I deny your right to dictate any action whatever to me, however insignificant, and utterly refuse to obey your command?'

"'At your peril do so,' I exclaimed. 'Refuse, and I will write the whole shameful story, with my own comments; and you may judge for yourself of the effect it will produce.'

"At that she smiled,—an indescribable sort of smile,— and shut her fingers on the letter she held,—I could not help thinking as though it were a human hand. 'Very well, madam, write it. He has already told me'—

"'That he loves you,' I broke in. 'Do you think he would continue to do so if he knew what you are?'

"'He knows me as well now,' she answered, 'as he will after reading any letter of yours.'

"'Incredible!' I exclaimed. 'When he wrote you that, he did not know, he could not have known, your birth, your race, the taint in your blood. I will never believe it.'

"'No,' she said, 'I did not say he did. I said he knew *me*; so well, I think, judging from this,'—clasping his letter with the same curious pressure I had before noticed,— 'that you could scarcely enlighten him farther. He knows my heart, and soul, and brain,—as I said, he knows *me*.'

"'O, yes,' I answered,—or rather sneered, for I was uncontrollably indignant through all this,—'if you mean *that*, very likely. I am not talking lovers' metaphysics, but practical common-sense. He does not know the one thing at present essential for him to know; and he will abandon you, spurn you,—his love turned to scorn, his passion to contempt,—when he reads what I shall write him if you refuse to do what I demand!'

"I expected to see her cower before me. Conceive, then, if you can, my sensations when she cried, 'Stop, madam! Say what you will to me; insult, outrage me, if you please, and have not the good breeding and dignity to forbear; but do not presume to so slander him. Do not presume to accuse him, who is all nobility and greatness of soul, of a sentiment so base, a prejudice so infamous. Study him, madam, know him better, ere you attempt to be his mouth-piece.'

"As she uttered these words, a horrible foreboding seized me, or, to speak more truthfully, I so felt the certainty of what she spoke, that a shudder of terror ran over me. I thought of him, of his character, of his principles, of his insane sense of honor, of his terrible will under all that soft exterior,—the hand of steel under the silken glove; I saw that if I persisted and she still refused to yield I should lose all. On the instant I changed my attack.

"'It is true,' I said, 'having asked you to become his wife, he will marry you; he will redeem his pledge though it ruin his life and blast his career, to say nothing of the effect an unending series of outrages and mortifications will have upon his temper and his heart. A pretty love, truly, yours must be,—whatever his is,—to condemn him to so terrible an ordeal, so frightful a fate.'

"She shivered at that, and I went on,—blaming my folly in not remembering, being a woman, that it was with a woman and her weakness I had to deal.

"'He is young,' I continued; 'he has probably a long life before him. Rich, handsome, brilliant,—a magnificent career opening to him,—position, ease, troops of friends,—you will ruthlessly ruin all this. Married to you, white as you are, the peculiarity of your birth would in some way be speedily known. His father would disinherit him (it was not necessary to tell her he has a fortune in his own right), his family disown him, his friends abandon him, society close its doors upon him, business refuse to seek him, honor and riches elude his grasp. If you do not know the strength of this prejudice, which you call infamous, pre-eminently in the circle to which he belongs, I cannot tell it you. Taking all this from him, what will you give him in return? Ruining his life, can your affection make amends? Blasting his career, will your love fill the gap? Do you flatter yourself by the supposition that you can be father, mother, relatives, friends, society, wealth, position, honor, career,—all,—to him? Your people are cursed in America, and they transfer their curse to any one mad enough, or generous enough (that was a diplomatic turn), to connect his fate with yours.'

"Before I was through, I saw that I had carried my point. All the fine airs went out of my lady, and she looked broken and humbled enough. I might have said less, but I ached to say more to the insolent.

"'Enough, madam,' she gasped, 'stop.' And then said, more to herself than to me, 'I could give heaven for him,'—the rest I rather guessed from the motion of her lips than from any sound,—'but I cannot ask him to give the world for me.'

"'Will you write the letter?' I asked.

"'No.'—She said the word with evident effort, and then, still more slowly, 'I will give you a message. Say "I implore you never to write me again,—to forget me. I beseech of you not to try me by any farther appeals, as I shall but return them unopened.'" I wrote down the words as she spoke them. 'This is well,' I said when she finished; 'but it is not enough. I must have the letter.'

"'The letter?' she said. 'What need of a letter? surely that is sufficient.'

"'I do not mean your letter. I mean his,—the one which you hold in your hands.'

"'This?' she queried, looking down on it,—'this?'

"I thought the repetition senseless and affected, but I answered, 'Yes,—that. He will not believe you are in earnest if you keep his avowal of love. You must give him up entirely. If you let me send that back, with your words, he shall never—at least from me—have clew or reason for your conduct. That will close the whole affair.'

"'Close the whole affair,' she repeated after me, mechanically,—'close the whole affair.'

"I was getting heartily tired of this, and had no desire to listen to an echo conversation; so, without answering, I stretched out my hand for it. She held it towards me, then drew it back and raised it to her heart with the same gesture I had marked when she first opened it,—a gesture as I said, of that, which was less of a caress than a spasm. Indeed, I think now that it was wholly physical and involuntary. Then she handed it to me, and, motioning towards the door, said, 'Go!'

"I rose, and, infamous as I thought her past deceit, wearied as I was with the interview, small claim as she had upon me for the slightest consideration, I said 'You have done well, Miss Ercildoune! I commend you for your sensible decision, and for your ability, if late, to appreciate the situation. I wish you all success in life, I am sure; and, permit me to add, a future union with one of your own race, if that will bring you happiness.'

"Heavens! what a face and what eyes she turned upon me as, rising, she once more pointed to the door, and cried, 'Go!' And indeed I went,—the girl actually frightened me.

"When I got on to the lawn, I missed my bag and parasol, and had to return for them. I opened the door with some slight trepidation, but had no need for fear. She was lying prostrate upon the floor, as I saw on coming near, in a dead faint. She had evidently fallen so suddenly and with such force as to have hurt herself; her head had struck against an ornament of the bookcase, near which she had been standing; and a little stream of blood was trickling from her temple. It made me sick to behold it. As I looked at her where she lay, I could not but pity her a little, and think what a merciful fate it would be for her, and such as she, if they could all die,—and so put an end to what, I presume, though I never before thought of it, is really a very hard existence.

"It was no time, however, to sentimentalize. I rang for a servant, and, having waited till one came, took my leave.

"Of course all this is very shocking and painful, but I am glad I came. The matter is ended now in a satisfactory manner. I think it has been well done. Let us both keep

our counsel, and the affair will soon become a memory
with us, as it is nothing with every one else.

"Always your loving sister,

"AUGUSTA."

It is better to be silent upon some themes than to say
too little. Words would fail to express the emotions with
which Willie read this history: let silence and imagination
tell the tale.

Flinging down the paper with a passionate cry, he saw
yet another letter,—the one in which these had been
enfolded,—a letter written to him, and by Mrs. Russell.
As by a flash, he perceived that there had been some
blunder here, by which he was the gainer; and, partly at
least, comprehended it.

These two, mother and aunt, fearing the old fire had
not yet burned to ashes,—nay, from their knowledge of
him, sure of it,—hearing naught of his illness, for he did
not care to distress them by any account thereof, were satisfied that he had either met, or was remaining to compass
a meeting, with Miss Ercildoune. His mother had not the
courage, or the baseness, to write such a letter as that to
which Mrs. Russell urged her,—a letter which should
degrade his love in his own eyes, and recall him from an
unworthy pursuit. "Very well!" Mrs. Russell had then said,
"It will be better from you; it will look more like unwar-
ranted interference from me; but I will write, and you shall
send an accompanying line. Let me have it tomorrow."

The next morning Mrs. Surrey was not well enough to drive out, and thus sent her note by a servant, enclosing with it the letter of June 27th,—thinking that her sister might want it for reference. When it reached Mrs. Russell, it was almost mail-time, and with the simple thought, "So,—Laura has written it, after all," she enclosed it in her own, and sent it off, post-haste; not even looking at the unsealed envelope, as Mrs. Surrey had taken for granted she would, and thus failing to know of its double contents.

Thus the very letter which they would have compassed land and sea to have prevented coming under his eyes, unwisely yet most fortunately kept in existence, was sent by themselves to his hands.

Without pausing to read a line of that which his aunt had written him, he tore it into fragments, flung it into the empty grate; and, bounding down the stairs and on to the street, plunged into a carriage and was whirled away, all too slowly, to the home he had left but a little space before with such widely, such painfully different emotions.

CHAPTER XIII

"I could not love thee, dear, so much,
Loved I not honor more."
LOVELACE

J UST after Surrey, for the third time, had passed through
the avenue of trees, two men appeared in it, earnestly
conversing. One, the older, was the same who had met
Willie as he was going out, and had examined him with such
curious interest. The other, in feature, form, and bearing,
was so absolutely the counterpart of his companion that it
was easy to recognize in them father and son,—a father and
son whom it would be hard to match. "The finest type of the
Anglo-Saxon race I have seen from America," was the verdict pronounced upon Mr. Ercildoune, when he was a
young man studying abroad, by an enthusiastic and nation-
ally ignorant Englishman; "but then, sir," he added, "what
very dark complexions you Americans have! Is it universal?"

"By no means, sir," was Mr. Ercildoune's reply. "There are some exceedingly fine ones among my countrymen. I come from the South: that is a bad climate for the tint of the skin."

"Is it so?" exclaimed John Bull,—"worse than the North?"

"Very much worse, sir, in more ways than one."

Perhaps Robert Ercildoune was a trifle fairer than his father, but there was still perceptible the shade which marked him as effectually an outcast from the freedom of American society, and the rights of American citizenship, as though it had been the badge of crime or the strait jacket of a madman. Something of this was manifested in the conversation in which the two were engaged.

"It is folly, Robert, for you to carry your refinement and culture into the ranks as a common soldier, to fight and to die, without thanks. You are made of too good stuff to serve simply as food for powder."

"Better men than I, father, have gone there, and are there to-day; men in every way superior to me."

"Perhaps,—yes, if you will have it so. But what are they? white men, fighting for their own country and flag, for their own rights of manhood and citizenship, for a present for themselves and a future for their children, for honor and fame. What is there for you?"

"For one thing, just that of which you spoke. Perhaps not a present for me, but certainly a future for those that come after."

"A future! How are you to know? what warrant or guarantee have you for any such future? Do you judge by the past? by the signs of to-day? I tell you this American nation will resort to any means—will pledge anything, by word or implication—to secure the end for which it fights; and will break its pledges just so soon as it can, and with whomsoever it can with impunity. You, and your children, and your children's children after you, will go to the wall unless it has need of you in the arena."

"I do not think so. This whole nation is learning, through pain and loss, the lesson of justice; of expediency, doubtless, but still of justice; and I do not think it will be forgotten when the war is ended. This is our time to wipe off a thousand stigmas of contempt and reproach: this"—

"Who is responsible for them? ourselves? What cast them there? our own actions? I trow not. Mark the facts. I pay taxes to support the public schools, and am compelled to have my children educated at home. I pay taxes to support the government, and am denied any representation or any voice in regard to the manner in which these taxes shall be expended. I hail a car on the street, and am laughed to scorn by the conductor,—or, admitted, at the order of the passengers am ignominiously expelled. I offer my money at the door of any place of public amusement, and it is flung back to me with an oath. I enter a train to New York, and am banished to the rear seat or the 'negro car.' I go to a hotel, open for the accommodation of the public, and am denied access; or am requested to keep my room, and not show myself in parlor, office, or at table. I come within a church, to worship the good God who is no respecter of persons, and am shown out of the door by one of his insolent creatures. I carry my intelligence to the polls on election morning, and am elbowed aside by an American boor or a foreign drunkard, and, with opprobrious epithets by law officers and rabble, am driven away. All this in the North; all this without excuse of slavery and of the feeling it engenders; all this from arrogant hatred and devilish malignity. At last, the country which has disowned me, the government which has never recognized save to outrage me, the flag which has refused to cover or to protect me, are in direct need and utmost extremity. Then do they cry for me and mine to come up to their help ere they perish. At least, they hold forth a bribe to secure me? at least, if they make no apology for the past, they offer compensation for the future? at least, they bid high for the services they desire? Not at all!

"They say to one man, 'Here is twelve hundred dollars bounty with which to begin; here is sixteen dollars a month for pay; here is the law passed, and the money pledged, to secure you in comfort for the rest of life, if wounded or disabled, or help for your family, if killed. Here is every door set wide for you to rise, from post to post; money yours, advancement yours, honor, and fame, and glory yours; the love of a grateful country, the applause of an admiring world.'

"They say to another man,—you, or me, or Sam out there in the field,—'There is no bounty for you, not a cent; there is pay for you, twelve dollars a month, the hire of a servant; there is no pension for you, or your family, if you be sent back from the front, wounded or dead; if you are taken prisoner you can be murdered with impunity, or be sold as a slave, without interference on our part. Fight like a lion! do acts of courage and splendor! and you shall never rise above the rank of a private soldier. For you there is neither money nor honor, rights secured, nor fame gained. Dying, you fall into a nameless grave: living, you come back to your old estate of insult and wrong. If you refuse these tempting offers, we brand you cowards. If, under these infamous restraints and disadvantages, you fail to equal the white troops by your side, you are written down—inferiors. If you equal them, you are still inferiors. If you perform miracles, and surpass them, you are, in a measure, worthy commendation at last; we consent to see in you human beings, fit for mention and admiration,— not as types of your color and of what you intrinsically are, but as exceptions; made such by the habit of association, and the force of surrounding circumstances.'

"These are the terms the American people offer you, these the terms which you stoop to accept, these the proofs that they are learning a lesson of justice! So be it! there is need. Let them learn it to the full! let this war go on 'until the cities be wasted without inhabitant, and the houses without man, and the land be utterly destroyed.' Do not you interfere. Leave them to the teachings and the judgments of God."

Ercildoune had spoken with such impassioned feeling, with such fire in his eyes, such terrible earnestness in his voice, that Robert could not, if he would, interrupt him; and, in the silence, found no words for the instant at his command. Ere he summoned them they saw some one approaching.

"A fine looking fellow! fighting has been no child's play for him," said Robert, looking, as he spoke, at the empty sleeve.

Mr. Ercildoune advanced to meet the stranger, and Surrey beheld the same face upon whose pictured semblance he had once gazed with such intense feelings, first of jealousy, and then of relief and admiration; the same splendor of life, and beauty, and vitality. Surrey knew him at once, knew that it was Francesca's father, and went up to him with extended hand. Mr. Ercildoune took the proffered hand, and shook it warmly. "I am happy to meet you, Mr. Surrey."

"You know me?" said he with surprise. "I thought to present myself."

"I have seen your picture."

"And I yours. They must have held the mirror up to nature, for the originals to be so easily known. But may I ask where you saw mine? *yours* was in Miss Ercildoune's possession."

"As was yours," was answered after a moment's hesitation,—Surrey thought, with visible reluctance. His heart flew into his throat. "She has my picture,—she has spoken of me," he said to himself. "I wonder what her father will think,—what he will do. Come, I will to the point immediately."

"Mr. Ercildoune," said he, aloud, "you know something of me? of my position and prospects?"

"A great deal."

"I trust, nothing disparaging or ignoble."

"I know nothing for which any one could desire oblivion."

"Thanks. Let me speak to you, then, of a matter which should have been long since proposed to you had I been permitted the opportunity. I love your daughter. I cannot speak about that, but you will understand all that I wish to say. I have twice—once by letter, once by speech—let her know this and my desire to call her wife. She has twice refused,—absolutely. You think this should cut off all hope?"

Ercildoune had been watching him closely. "If she does not love you," he answered, at the pause.

"I do not know. I went away from here a little while ago with her peremptory command not to return. I should not have dared disobey it had I not learned—thought—in fact, but for some circumstances—I beg your pardon—I do not know what I am saying. I believed if I saw her once more I could change her determination,—could induce her to give me another response,—and came with that hope."

"Which has failed?"

"Which has thus far failed that she will not at all see me; will hold no communication with me. I should be a ruffian did I force myself on her thus without excuse or reason. My own love would be no apology did I not think, did I not dare to hope, that it is not aversion to me that induces her to act as she has done. Believing so, may I beg a favor of you? may I entreat that you will induce her to see me, if only for a little while?"

Ercildoune smiled a sad, bitter smile, as he answered, "Mr. Surrey, if my daughter does not love you, it would be hopeless for you or for me to assail her refusal. If she does, she has doubtless rejected you for a reason which you can read by simply looking into my face. No words of mine can destroy or do that away."

"There is nothing to destroy; there is nothing to do away. Thank you for speaking of it, and making the way easy. There is nothing in all the wide world between us,— there can be nothing between us,—if she loves me; nothing to keep us apart save her indifference or lack of regard for me. I want to say so to her if she will give me the chance. Will you not help me to it?"

"You comprehend all that I mean?"

"I do. It is, as I have said, nothing. That love would not be worth the telling that considered extraneous circumstances, and not the object itself."

"You have counted all the consequences? I think not. How, indeed, should you be able? Come with me a moment." The two went up to the house, across the wide veranda, into a room half library, half lounging-room, which, from a score of evidences strewn around, was plainly the special resort of the master. Over the mantel hung the life-size portrait of an excessively beautiful woman. A fine, *spirituelle* face, with proud lines around the mouth and delicate nostrils, but with a tender, appealing look in the eyes, that claimed gentle treatment. This face said, "I was made for sunshine and balmy airs, but, if darkness and storm assail, I can walk through them unflinching, though the progress be short; I can die, and give no sign." Willie went hastily up to this, and stood, absorbed, before it. "Francesca is very like her mother," said Ercildoune, coming to his side. It was his own thought, but he made no answer.

"I will tell you something of her and myself; a very little story; you can draw the moral. My father, who was a Virginian, sent my brother and me to England when we were mere boys, to be trained and educated. After his fashion, doubtless, he loved us; for he saw that we had every advantage that wealth, and taste, and care could provide; and though he never sent for us, nor came to us, in all the years after we left his house,—and though we had no legal claim upon him,—he acknowledged us his children, and left us the entire proceeds of his immense estates, unincumbered. We were so young when we went abroad, had been so tenderly treated at home, had seen and known so absolutely nothing of the society about us, that we were ignorant as Arabs of the state of feeling and prejudice in

America against such as we, who carried any trace of negro blood. Our treatment in England did but increase this oblivion.

"We graduated at Oxford; my brother, who was two years older than I, waiting upon me that we might go together through Europe; and together we had three of the happiest years of life. On the Continent I met *her*. You see what she is; you know Francesca: it is useless for me to attempt to describe her. I loved her,—she loved me,—it was confessed. In a little while I called her wife; I would, if I could, tell you of the time that followed: I cannot. We had a beautiful home, youth, health, riches, friends, happiness, two noble boys. At last an evil fate brought us to America. I was to look after some business affairs which, my agent said, needed personal supervision. My brother, whose health had failed, was advised to try a sea-voyage, and change of scene and climate. My wife was enthusiastic about the glorious Republic,—the great, free America,— the land of my birth. We came, carrying with us letters from friends in England, that were an open sesame to the most jealously barred doors. They flew wide at our approach, but to be shut with speed when my face was seen; hands were cordially extended, and drawn back as from a loathsome contact when mine went to meet them. In brief, we were outlawed, ostracised, sacrificed on the altar of this devilish American prejudice,—wholly American, for it is found nowhere else in the world,—I for my color, she for connecting her fate with mine.

"I was so held as to be unable to return at once, and she would not leave me. Then my brother drooped more and more. His disease needed the brightest and most cheerful influences. The social and moral atmosphere stifled him. He died; and we, with grief intensified by bitterness, laid him in the soil of his own country as though it had been that of the stranger and enemy.

"At this time the anti-slavery movement was provoking profound thought and feeling in America. I at once identified myself with it; not because I was connected with the hated and despised race, but because I loathed all forms of tyranny, and fought against them with what measure of strength I possessed. Doubtless this made me a more conspicuous mark for the shafts of malice and cruelty, and as I could nowhere be hurt as through her, malignity exhausted its devices there. She was hooted at when she appeared with me on the streets; she was inundated with infamous letters; she was dragged before a court of *justice* upon the plea that she had defied the law of the state against amalgamation, forbidding the marriage of white and colored; though at the time it was known that she was English, that we were married in England and by English law. One night, in the midst of the riots which in 1838 disgraced this city, our house was surrounded by a mob, burned over us; and I, with a few faithful friends, barely succeeded in carrying her to a place of safety,—uncovered, save by her delicate night-robe and a shawl, hastily caught up as we hurried her away. The yelling fiends, the burning

house, the awful horror of fright and danger, the shock to
her health and strength, the storm,—for the night was a
wild and tempestuous one, which drenched her to the
skin,—from all these she might have recovered, had not
her boy, her first-born, been carried into her, bruised and
dead,—dead, through an accident of burning rafters and
falling stones; an accident, they said; yet as really murdered
as though they had wilfully and brutally stricken him
down.

*1st is
dead*

"After that I saw that she, too, would die, were she not
taken back to our old home. The preparations were hastily
made; we turned our faces towards England; we hoped to
reach it at least before another pair of eyes saw the light,
but hoped in vain. There on the broad sea Francesca was
born. There her mother died. There was she buried."

*in leaving
had Francesca
x mom died.
when was ??
Robert born*

It was with extreme difficulty Ercildoune had con-
trolled his face and voice, through the last of this distressing recital, and with the final word he bowed his forehead on the picture-frame,—convulsed with agony,—
while voiceless sobs, like spasms, shook his form. Surrey
realized that no words were to be said here, and stood by,
awed and silent. What hand, however tender, could be laid
on such a wound as this?

Presently he looked up, and continued: "I came back
here, because, I said, here was my place. I had wealth, education, a thousand advantages which are denied the masses
of people who are, like me, of mixed race. I came here to
identify my fate with theirs; to work with and for them; to

fight, till I died, against the cruel and merciless prejudice which grinds them down. I have a son, who has just entered the service of this country, perhaps to die under its flag. I have a daughter,"—Willie flushed and started forward;—"I asked you when I began this recital, if you had counted all the consequences. You know my story; you see with what fate you link yours; reflect! Francesca carries no mark of her birth; her father or brother could not come inside her home without shocking society by the scandal, were not the story earlier known. The man whom you struck down this morning is one of our neighbors; you saw and heard his brutal assault: are you ready to face more of the like kind? Better than you I know what sentence will be passed upon you,—what measure awarded. It is for your own sake I say these things; consider them. I have finished."

Surrey had made to speak a half score of times, and as often checked himself,—partly that he should not interrupt his companion; partly that he might be master of his emotions, and say what he had to utter without heat or excitement.

"Mr. Ercildoune," he now said, "listen to me. I should despise myself were I guilty of the wicked and vulgar prejudice universal in America. I should be beneath contempt did I submit or consent to it. Two years ago I loved Miss Ercildoune without knowing aught of her birth. She is the same now as then; should I love her the less? If anything hard or cruel is in her fate that love can soften, it shall be done. If any painful burdens have been thrown upon her life, I can carry, if not the whole, then a part of them. If I cannot put her into a safe shelter where no ill will befall her, I can at least take her into my arms and go with her through the world. It will be easier for us, I think,—I hope,—to face any fate if we are together. Ah, sir, do not prevent it; do not deny me this happiness. Be my ambassador, since she will not let me speak for myself, and plead my own cause."

In his earnestness he had come close to Mr. Ercildoune, putting out his one hand with a gesture of entreaty, with a tone in his voice, and a look in his face, irresistible to hear and behold. Ercildoune took the hand, and held it in a close, firm grasp. Some strong emotion shook him. The expression, a combination of sadness and scorn, which commonly held possession of his eyes, went out of them, leaving them radiant. "No," he said, "I will say nothing for you. I would not for worlds spoil your plea; prevent her hearing, from your own mouth, what you have to say. I will send her to you,"—and, going to a door, gave the order to a servant, "Desire Miss Francesca to come to the parlor." Then, motioning Surrey to the room, he went away, buried in thought.

Standing in the parlor, for he was too restless to sit, he tried to plan how he should meet her; to think of a sentence which at the outset should disarm her indignation at being thus thrust upon him, and convey in some measure the thought of which his heart was full, without trespassing on her reserve, or telling her of the letter which he had read. Then another fear seized him; it was two years since he had written,—two years since that painful and terrible scene had been enacted in the very room where he stood,—two years since she had confessed by deed and look that she loved him. Might she not have changed? might she not have struggled for the mastery of this feeling with only too certain success? might she not have learned to regard him with esteem, perchance,—with friendship,—sentiment,—anything but that which he desired or would claim at her hands? Silence and absence and time are pitiless destructives. Might they not? aye, might they not? He paced to and fro, with quick, restless tread, at the thought. All his love and his longing cried out against such a cruel supposition. He stopped by the side of the bookcase against which she had fallen in that merciless and suffering struggle, and put his hand down on the little projection, which he knew had once cut and wounded her, with a strong, passionate clasp, as though it were herself he held. Just then he heard a step,—her step, yet how unlike!—coming down the stairs. Where he stood he could see her as she crossed the hall, coming unconsciously to meet him. All the brightness and airy grace seemed to have been drawn quite out of her. The alert, slender figure drooped as if it carried some palpable weight, and moved with a step slow and unsteady as that of sickness or age. Her face was pathetic in its sad pallor, and blue, sorrowful circles were drawn under the deep eyes, heavy and dim

with the shedding of unnumbered tears. It almost broke
his heart to look at her. A feeling, pitiful as a mother
would have for her suffering baby, took possession of his
soul,—a longing to shield and protect her. Tears blinded
him; a great sob swelled in his throat; he made a step forward as she came into the room. "Papa," she said, without
looking up, "you wanted me?" There was no response.
"Papa!" In an instant an arm enfolded her; a presence,
tender and strong, bent above her; a voice, husky with
crowding emotions, yet sweet with all the sweetness of
love, breathed, "My darling! my darling!" as *his* fair, sunny
hair swept her face.

Even then she remembered another scene, remembered her promise; even then she thought of him, of his
future, and struggled to release herself from his embrace.

What did he say? what could he say? Where were the
arguments he had planned, the entreaties he had purposed?
where the words with which he was to tell his tale, combat
her refusal, win her to a willing and happy assent? All gone.

There was nothing but his heart and its caresses to
speak for him. Silent, with the ineffable stillness he kissed
her eyes, her mouth, held her to his breast with a passionate fondness,—a tender, yet masterful hold, which
said, "Nothing shall separate us now." She felt it, recognized it, yielded without power to longer contend, clasped
her arms about his neck, met his eyes, and dropped her
face upon his heart with a long, tremulous sigh which
confessed that heaven was won.

CHAPTER XIV

"The golden hours, on angel wings,
Flew o'er me and my dearie."
BURNS

THE evening that followed was of the brightest and happiest; even the adieus spoken to the soldier who was just leaving his home did not sadden it. They were in such a state of exaltation as to see everything with courageous and hopeful eyes, and sent Robert off with the feeling that all these horrible realities they had known so long were but bogies to frighten foolish children, and that he would come back to them wearing, at the very least, the stars of a major-general. Whatever sombre and painful thoughts filled Ercildoune's heart he held there, that no gloom might fall from him upon these fresh young lives, nor sadden the cheery expectancy of his son.

Surrey, having carried the first line of defence, prepared

for a vigorous assault upon the second. Like all eager lovers, his primary anxiety was to hear "Yes"; afterwards, the day. To that end he was pleading with every resource that love and impatience could lend; but Francesca shook her head, and smiled, and said that was a long way off,—that was not to be thought of, at least till the war was over, and her soldier safe at home; but he insisted that this was the flimsiest, and poorest of excuses; nay, that it was the very reverse of the true and sensible idea, which was of course wholly on his side. He had these few weeks at home, and then must away once more to chances of battle and death. He did not say this till he had exhausted every other entreaty; but at last, gathering her close to him with his one loving arm,— "how fortunate," he had before said, "that it is the left arm, because if it were the other I could not hold you so near my heart!"—so holding her, he glanced down at the empty sleeve, and whispered, "My darling! who knows? I have been wounded so often, and am now only a piece of a fellow to come to you. It may be something more next time, and then I shall never call you wife. It would make no difference hereafter, I know: we belong to each other for time and eternity. But then I should like to feel that we were something more to one another than even betrothed lovers, before the end comes, if come it does, untimely. Be generous, dearie, and say yes."

He did not give utterance to another fear, which was that by some device she might again be taken away from him; that some cruel plan might be put in execution to separate them once more. He would not take the risk; he would bind her to him so securely that no device, however cunning,—no plan, however hard and shrewd,—could again divide them.

She hesitated long; was long entreated; but the result was sure, since her own heart seconded every prayer he uttered. At last she consented; but insisted that he should go home at once, see the mother and father who were waiting for him with such anxious hearts, give to them— as was their due—at least a part of the time, and then, when her hasty bride-preparations were made, come back and take her wholly to himself. Thus it was arranged, and he left her.

Into the mysteries which followed—the mysteries of hemming and stitching, of tucking and trimming, ruffling, embroidering, of all the hurry and delicious confusion of an elegant yet hasty bridal trousseau—let us not attempt to investigate.

Doubtless through those days, through this sweet and happy whirl of emotion, Francesca had many anxious and painful hours: hours in which she looked at the future— for him more than for herself—with sorrowful anticipations and forebodings. But with each evening came a letter, written in the morning by his dear hand; a letter so full of happy, hopeful love, of resolute, manly spirit, that her cares and anxieties all took flight, and were but as a tale that is told, or as a dream of darkness when the sun shines upon a blessed reality.

He wrote her that he had told his parents of his wishes and plans; and that, as he had known before, they were opposed, and opposed most bitterly; but he was sure that time would soften, and knowledge destroy this prejudice utterly. He wrote as he believed. They were so fond of him, so devoted to him who was their only child, that he was assured they would not and could not cast him off, nor hate that which he loved. He did not know that his father, who had never before been guilty of a base action,—his mother, who was fine to daintiness,—were both so warped by this senseless and cruel feeling—having seen Francesca and known all her beautiful and noble elements of personal character—as to have written her a letter which only a losel should have penned and an outcast read. She did not tell him. Being satisfied that they two belonged to one another; that if they were separated it would be as the tearing asunder of a perfect whole, leaving the parts rent and bleeding,—she would not listen to any voice that attempted, nor heed any hand that strove to drive an entering wedge, or to divide them. Why, then, should she trouble him by the knowledge that this effort had again been made, and by those he trusted and honored. Let it pass. The future must decide what the future must be, meanwhile, they were to live in a happy present.

He learned of it, however, before he left his home. Finding that neither persuasions, threats, nor prayers could move him,—that he would be true to honor and love,— they told him of what they had done; laid bare the whole intensity of their feeling; and putting her on the one side, placing themselves on the other, said, "Choose,—this wife, or those who have loved you for a lifetime. Cleave to her, and your father disowns you, your mother renounces, your home shuts its doors upon you, never to open. With the world and its judgment we have nothing to do; that is between it and you; but no judgment of indifferent strangers shall be more severe than ours."

A painful position; a cruel alternative; but not for an instant did he hesitate. Taking the two hands of father and mother into his solitary one, he said,—"Father, I have always found you a gentleman; mother, you have shown all the graces of the Christian character which you profess; yet in this you are supporting the most dishonorable senti-ment, the most infidel unbelief, with which the age is shamed. You are defying the dictates of justice and the teachings of God. When you ask me to rank myself on your side, I cannot do it. Were my heart less wholly enlisted in this matter, my reason and sense of right would rebel. Here, then, for the present at least, we must say farewell." And so, with many a heart-ache and many a pang, he went away.

As true love always grows with passing time, so his increased with the days, and intensified by the cruel heat which was poured upon it. He realized the torture to which, in a thousand ways, this darling of his heart had for a lifetime been subjected; and his tenderness and love—in which was an element of indignation and pathos—deepened with every fresh revelation of the passing hours. When he came back to her he had few words to speak, and no airy grace of sentence or caress to bestow; he followed her about in a curious, shadow-like way, with such a strain on his heart as made him many a time lift his hand to it, as if to check physical pain. For her, she was as one who had found a beloved master, able and willing to lighten all her burdens; a physician, whose slightest touch brought balm and healing to every aching wound. And so these two when the time came, spite of the absence of friends who should have been there, spite of warnings and denunciations and evil prophecies, stood up and said to those who listened what their hearts had long before confessed, that they were one for time and eternity; then, hand in hand, went out into the world.

For the present it was a pleasant enough world to them. Surrey had a lovely little place on the Hudson to which he would carry her, and pleased himself by fitting it up with every convenience and beauty that taste could devise and wealth supply.

How happy they were there! To be sure, nobody came to see them, but then they wished to see nobody; so every one was well satisfied. The delicious lovers' life of two years before was renewed, but with how much richer and deeper delights and blissfulness! They galloped on many a pleasant morning across miles and miles of country, down rocky slopes, and through wild and romantic glens. They drove lazily, on summer noons, through leafy fastnesses and cool forest paths; or sat idly by some little stream on the fresh, green moss, with a line dancing on the crystal water, amusing themselves by the fiction that it was fishing upon which they were intent, and not the dear delight of watching one another's faces reflected from the placid stream. They spent hours at home, reading bits of poems, or singing scraps of love-songs, talking a little, and then falling away into silence; or she sat perched on his knee or the elbow of his chair, smoothing his sunny hair, stroking his long, silky mustache, or looking into his answering eyes, till the world lapsed quite away from them, and they thought themselves in heaven.

An idle, happy time! a time to make a worker sigh only to behold, and a Benthamite lift his hands in deprecation and despair. A time which would not last, because it could not, any more than apple-blossoms and May flowers, but which was sweet and fragrant past all describing while it endured.

Some *kindly* disposed person sent Surrey a city paper with an item marked in such wise as to make him understand its unpleasant import without the reading. "Come," he said, "we will have none of this; this owl does not belong to our sunshine,"—and so destroyed and forgot it. Others, however, saw that which he scorned to read. He had not been into the city since he called at his father's house, and walked into the reception room of his aunt, and been refused interview or speech at either place. "Very well," he thought, "I will go from this painful inhospitality and coldness to my Paradise"; and he went, and remained.

The only letter he wrote was to his old friend and favorite cousin, Tom Russell,—who was away somewhere in the far South, and from whom he had not heard for many a day,—and hoped that he, at least, would not disappoint him; would not disappoint the hearty trust he had in his breadth of nature and manly sensibility.

And so, with clouds doubtless in the sky, but which they did not see,—the sun shone so bright for them; and some discords in the minor keys which they did not heed,—the major music was so sweet and intoxicating,— the brief, glad hours wore away, and the time for parting, with hasty steps, had almost reached and faced them. Meanwhile, what was occurring to others, in other scenes and among other surroundings?

CHAPTER XV

"There are some deeds so grand
That their mighty doers stand
Ennobled, in a moment, more than kings."
BOKER

IT was towards the evening of a blazing July day on Morris Island. The mail had just come in and been distributed. Jim, with some papers and a precious missive from Sallie in one hand, his supper in the other, betook himself to a cool spot by the river,—if, indeed, any spot could be called cool in that fiery sand,—and proceeded to devour the letter with wonderful avidity while the "grub," properly enough, stood unnoticed and uncared for. Presently he stopped, rubbed his eyes, and re-read a paragraph in the epistle before him, then re-rubbed, and read it again; and then, laying it down, gave utterance to a long whistle, expressive of unbounded astonishment, if not incredulity.

The whistle was answered by its counterpart, and Jim, looking up, beheld his captain,—Coolidge by name,—a fast, bright New York boy, standing at a little distance, and staring with amazed eyes at a paper he held in his bands. Glancing from this to Jim, encountering his look, he burst out laughing and came towards him.

"Helloa, Given!" he called: Jim was a favorite with him, as indeed with pretty much every one with whom he came in contact, officers and men,—"you, too, seem put out. I wonder if you've read anything as queer as that," handing him the paper and striking his finger down on an item; "read it." Jim read:—

"MISCEGENATION. DISGRACEFUL FREAK IN HIGH LIFE. FRUIT OF AN ABOLITION WAR.—We are credibly informed that a young man belonging to one of the first families in the city, Mr. W. A. S.,—we spare his name for the sake of his relatives,—who has been engaged since its outset in this fratricidal war, has just given evidence of its legitimate effect by taking to his bosom a nigger wench as *his wife*. Of course he is disowned by his family, and spurned by his friends, even radical fanaticism not being yet ready for such a dose as this. However—" Jim did not finish the homily of which this was the presage, but, throwing the paper on the ground, indignantly drove his heel through it, tearing and soiling it, and then viciously kicked it into the river.

Said the Captain when this operation was completed, having watched it with curious eyes, "Well, my man, are you aware of the fact that that is *my* paper?"

"Don't care if it is. What in thunder did you bring the damned Copperhead sheet to me for, if you didn't want it smashed? Ain't you ashamed of yourself having such a thing round? How'd you feel if you were picked up dead by a reb, with that stuff in your pocket? Say now!"

Coolidge laughed,—he was always ready to laugh: that was probably why the men liked him so well, and stood in awe of him not a bit. "Feel? horridly, of course. Bad enough, being dead, to yet speak, and tell 'em that paper didn't represent my politics: 'd that do?"

Jim shook his head dubiously.

"What are you making such a devil of a row for, I'd like to know? it's too hot to get excited. 'Tain't likely you know anything about Willie Surrey."

"O ho! it is Mr. Will, then, is it? Know him,—don't I, though? Like a book. Known him ever since he was knee-height of a grasshopper. I'd like to have that fellow"—shaking his fist toward the floating paper—"within arm's reach. Wouldn't I pummel him some? O no, of course not,—not at all. Only, if he wants a sound skin, I'd advise him, as a friend, to be scarce when I'm round, because it'd very likely be damaged."

"You think it's all a Copperhead lie, then! I should have thought so, at first, only I know Surrey's capable of doing any Quixotic thing if he once gets his mind fixed on it."

"I know what I know," Jim answered, slowly folding and unfolding Sallie's letter, which he still held in his hand. "I know all about that young lady he's been marrying.

She's young, and she's handsome—handsome as a picture—and rich, and as good as an angel; that's about what she is, if Sallie Howard and I know B from a bull's foot."

"Who is Sallie Howard?" queried the Captain.

"She? O,"—very red in the face,—"she's a friend of mine, and she's Miss Ercildoune's seamstress."

"Ercildoune? good name! Is she the *lady* upon whom Surrey has been bestowing his—?"

"Yes, she is; and here's her photograph. Sallie begged it of her, and sent it to me, once after she had done a kind thing by both of us. Looks like a 'nigger wench,' don't she?"

The Captain seized the picture, and, having once fastened his eyes upon it, seemed incapable of removing them. "This? this her?" he cried. "Great Cæsar! I should think Surrey would have the fellow out at twenty paces in no time. Heavens, what a beauty!"

Jim grinned sardonically: "She *is* rather pretty, now,— ain't she?"

"Pretty! ugh, what an expression! pretty, indeed! I never saw anything so beautiful. But what a sad face it is!"

"Sad! well, 'tain't much wonder. I guess her life's been sad enough, in spite of her youth, and her beauty, and her riches, and all the rest."

"Why, how should that be?"

"Suppose you take another squint at that face."

"Well."

"See anything peculiar about it?"

"Nothing except its beauty."

"Not about the eyes?"

"No,—only I believe it is they that make the face so sorrowful."

"Very like. You generally see just such big mournful-looking eyes in the faces of people that are called—octoroons."

"What?" cried the Captain, dropping the picture in his surprise.

"Just so," Jim answered, picking it up and dusting it carefully before restoring it to its place in his pocket-book.

"So, then, it is part true, after all."

"True!" exclaimed Jim, angrily,—"don't make an ass of yourself, Captain."

"Why, Given, didn't you say yourself that she was an octoroon, or some such thing?"

"Suppose I did,—what then?"

"I should say, then, that Surrey has disgraced himself forever. He has not only outraged his family and his friends, and scandalized society, but he has run against nature itself. It's very plain God Almighty never intended the two races to come together."

"O, he didn't, hey? Had a special despatch from him, that you know all about it? I've heard just such talk before from people who seemed to be pretty well posted about his intentions,—in this particular matter,—though I generally noticed they weren't chaps who were very intimate with him in any other way."

The Captain laughed. "Thank you, Jim, for the compliment; but come, you aren't going to say that nature hasn't placed a barrier between these people and us? an instinct that repels an Anglo-Saxon from a negro always and everywhere?"

"Ho, ho! that's good! why, Captain, if you keep on, you'll make me talk myself into a regular abolitionist. Instinct, hey? I'd like to know, then, where all the mulattoes, and the quadroons, and the octoroons come from,—the yellow-skins and brown-skins and skins so nigh white you can't tell 'em with your spectacles on! The darkies must have bleached out amazingly here in America, for you'd have to hunt with a long pole and a telescope to boot to find a straight-out black one anywhere round,—leastwise that's my observation."

"That was slavery."

"Yes 'twas,—and then the damned rascals talk about the amalgamationists, and all that, up North. 'T wan't the abolitionists; 'twas the slaveholders and their friends that made a race of half-breeds all over the country; but, slavery or no slavery, they showed nature hadn't put any barriers between them,—and it seems to me an enough sight decenter and more respectable plan to marry fair and square than to sell your own children and the mother that bore them. Come, now, ain't it?"

"Well, yes, if you come to that, I suppose it is!"

"You *suppose* it is! See here,—I've found out something since I've been down here, and have had time to think; 'tain't the living together that troubles squeamish stomachs; it's the marrying. That's what's the matter!"

"Just about!" assented the Captain, with an amused look, "and here's a case in point. Surrey ought to have been shot for marrying one of that degraded race."

"Bah! he married one of his own race, if I know how to calculate."

"There, Jim, don't be a fool! If she's got any negro blood in her veins she's a nigger, and all your talk won't make her anything else."

"I say, Captain, I've heard that some of your ancestors were Indians: is that so?"

"Yes: my great-grandmother was an Indian chief's daughter,—so they say; and you might as well claim royalty when you have the chance."

"Bless me! your great-grandmother, eh? Come, now, what do you call yourself,—an Injun?"

"No, I don't. I call myself an Anglo-Saxon."

"What, not call yourself an Injun,—when your great-grandmother was one? Here's a pretty go!"

"Nonsense! 'tisn't likely that filtered Indian blood can take precedence and mastery of all the Anglo-Saxon material it's run through since then."

"Hurray! now you've said it. Lookee here, Captain. You say the Anglo-Saxon's the master race of the world."

"Of course I do."

"Of course you do,—being a sensible fellow. So do I; and you say the negro blood is mighty poor stuff, and the race a long way behind ours."

"Of course, again."

"Now, Captain, just take a sober squint at your own logic. You back Anglo-Saxon against the field; very well! here's Miss Ercildoune, we'll say, one eighth negro, seven eighths Anglo-Saxon. You make that one eighth stronger than all the other seven eighths: you make that little bit of negro master of all the lot of Anglo-Saxon. Now I have such a good opinion of my own race that if it were t'other way about, I'd think the one eighth Saxon strong enough to beat the seven eighths nigger. That's sound, isn't it? consequently, I call anybody that's got any mixture at all, and that knows anything, and keeps a clean face,—and ain't a rebel, nor yet a Copperhead,—I call him, if it's a him, and her, if it's a she, one of us. And I mean to say to any such from henceforth, 'Here's your chance,—go in, and win, if you can,—and anybody be damn'd that stops you!' "

"Blow away, Jim," laughed the Captain, "I like to hear you; and it's good talk if you don't mean it."

"I'll be blamed if I don't."

"Come, you're talking now,—you're saying a lot more than you'll live up to,—you know that as well as I. People always do when they're gassing."

"Well, blow or no blow, it's truth, whether I live up to it or not." And he, evidently with not all the steam worked off, began to gather sticks and build a fire to fry his bit of pork and warm the cold coffee.

Just then they heard the plash of oars keeping time to the cadence of a plantation hymn, which came floating solemn and clear through the night:—

"My brudder sittin' on de tree ob life,
An' he yearde when Jordan roll.
Roll Jordan, roll Jordan, roll Jordan, roll,
   Roll Jordan, roll!"

They both paused to listen as the refrain was again and again repeated.

"There's nigger for you," broke out Jim, "what 'n thunder'd they mean by such gibberish as that?"

The Captain laughed. "Come, Given, don't quarrel with what's above your comprehension. Doubtless there's a spiritual meaning hidden away somewhere, which your unsanctified ears can't interpret."

"Spiritual fiddlestick!"

"Worse and worse! what a heathen you're demonstrating yourself! Violins are no part of the heavenly chorus."

"Much you know about it! Hark,—they're at it again"; and again the voices and break of oars came through the night:—

"O march, de angel march! O march, de angel march!
O my soul arise in heaven, Lord, for to yearde when
   Jordan roll!
      Roll Jordan, roll Jordan, roll Jordan, roll."

"Well, I confess that's a little bit above my comprehension,—that is. Spiritual or something else. Lazy vermin! they'll paddle round in them boats, or lie about in the sun,

and hoot all day and all night about 'de good Lord' and 'de
day ob jubilee,'—and think God Almighty is going to
interfere in their special behalf, and do big things for them
generally."

"It's a fact; they do all seem to be waiting for something."

"Well, I reckon they needn't wait any longer. The day
of miracles is gone by, for such as them, anyway. They ain't
worth the salt that feeds them, so far as I can discover."

Through the wash of the waters they could hear from
the voices, as they sang, that their possessors were evidently
drawing nearer.

"Sense or not," said the Captain, "I never listen to them
without a queer feeling. What they sing is generally
ridiculous enough, but their voices are the most pathetic
things in the world."

Here the hymn stopped; a boat was pulled up, and
presently they saw two men coming from the sands and
into the light of their fire,—ragged, dirty; one shabby old
garment—a pair of tow pantaloons—on each; bareheaded,
barefooted,—great, clumsy feet, stupid and heavy-looking
heads; slouching walk, stooping shoulders; something eager
yet deprecating in their black faces.

"Look at 'em, Captain; now you just take a fair look at
'em; and then say that Mr. Surrey's wife belongs to the
same family,—own kith and kin,—you ca–a–n't do it."

"Faugh! for heaven's sake, shut up! of course, when it
comes to this, I can't say anything of the kind."

"'Nuff said. You see, I believe in Mr. Surrey, and what's more, I believe in Miss Ercildoune,—have reason to; and when I hear anybody mixing her up with these onry, good-for-nothing niggers, it's more'n I can stand, so don't let's have any more of it"; and turning with an air which said that subject was ended, Jim took up his forgotten coffee, pulled apart some brands and put the big tin cup on the coals, and then bent over it absorbed, sniffing the savory steam which presently came up from it. Meanwhile the two men were skulking about among the trees, watching, yet not coming near,—"at their usual work of waiting," as the Captain said.

"Proper enough, too, let 'em wait. Waiting's their business. Now," taking off his tin and looking towards them, "what d'ye s'pose those anemiles want? Pity the boat hadn't tipped over before they got here. Camp's overrun now with just such scoots. Here, you!" he called.

The men came near. "Where'd you come from?"

One of them pointed back to the boat, seen dimly on the sand.

"Was that you howling a while ago, 'Roll Jordan,' or something?"

"Yes, massa."

"And where did you come from?—no, you needn't look back there again,—I mean, where did you and the boat too come from?"

"Come from Mass' George Wingate's place, massa."

"Far from here?"

"Big way, massa."

"What brought you here? what did you come for?"

"If you please, massa, 'cause the Linkum sojers was yere, an' de big guns, an' we yearde dat all our people's free when dey gets yere."

"Free! what'll such fellows as you do with freedom, hey?"

The two looked at their interrogator, then at one another, opened their mouths as to speak, and shut them hopelessly,—unable to put into words that which was struggling in their darkened brains,—and then with a laugh, a laugh that sounded woefully like a sob, answered, "Dunno, massa."

"What fools!" cried Jim, angrily; but the Captain, who was watching them keenly, thought of a line he had once read, "There is a laughter sadder than tears." "True enough,—poor devils!" he added to himself.

"Are you hungry?" Jim proceeded.

"I hope massa don't think we's come yere for to git suthin' to eat," said the smaller of the two, a little, thin, haggard-looking fellow,—"we's no beggars. Some ob de darkies is, but we's not dem kind,—Jim an' me,—we's willin' to work, ain't we, Jim?"

"Jim!" soliloquized Given,—"my name, hey? we'll take a squint at this fellow."

The squint showed two impoverished-looking wretches, with a starved look in their eyes, which he did not comprehend, and a starved look in their faces and forms, which he did.

"Come, now, are you hungry?" he queried once more.

"If ye please, massa," began the little one who was spokesman,—'little folks always are gas-bags,' Jim was fond of saying from his six feet of height,—"if ye please, massa, we's had nothin' to eat but berries an' roots an' sich like truck for long while."

"Well, why by the devil haven't you had something else then? what've you been doing with yourselves for 'long while'? what d'ye mean, coming here starved to death, making a fellow sick to look at you? Hold your gab, and eat up that pork," pushing over his tin plate, "'n' that bread," sending it after, "'n' that hard tack,—'tain't very good, but it's better'n roots, I reckon, or berries either,—'n' gobble up that coffee, double-quick, mind; and don't you open your heads to talk till the grub's gone, slick and clean. Ugh!" he said to the Captain,—"sight o' them fellows just took my appetite away; couldn't eat to save my soul; lucky they came to devour the rations; pity to throw them away." The Captain smiled,—he knew Jim. "Poor cusses!" he added presently, "eat like cannibals, don't they? hope they enjoy it. Had enough?" seeing they had devoured everything put before them.

"Thankee, massa. Yes, massa. Bery kind, massa. Had quite 'nuff."

"Well, now, you, sir!" looking at the little one,—"by the way, what's your name?"

"'Bijah, if ye please, massa."

"'Bijah? Abijah, hey? well, I don't please; however, it's

none of my name. Well, 'Bijah, how came you two to be
looking like a couple of animated skeletons? that's the next
question."

"Yes, massa."

"I say, how came you to be starved? Hai'n't they
nothing but roots and berries up your way? Mass' George
Wingate must have a jolly time, feasting, in that case.
Come, what's your story? Out with the whole pack of lies
at once."

"I hope massa thinks we wouldn't tell nuffin but de
truf," said Jim, who had not before spoken save to say,
"Thankee,"—"cause if he don't bleeve us, ain't no use in
talkin'."

"You shut up! I ain't conversing with you, rawbones!
Speak when you're spoken to! Come, 'Bijah, fire away."

"Bery good, massa. Ye see I'se Mass' George Wingate's
boy. Mass' George he lives in de back country, good long
way from de coast,—over a hundred miles, Jim calklates,—
an' Jim's smart at calklating; well, Mass' George he's not
berry good to his people; never was, an' he's been wuss'n
ever since the Linkum sojers cum round his way, 'cause it's
made feed scurce ye see, an' a lot of de boys dey tuck to
runnin' away,—so what wid one ting an' anoder, his temper
got spiled, an' he was mighty hard on us all de time.

"At las' I got tired of bein' cuffed an' knocked round,
an' den I yearde dat if our people, any of dem, got to de
Fedral lines dey was free, so I said, 'Cum, 'Bijah,—
freedom's wuth tryin' for'; an' one dark night I did up some

hoe-cake an' a piece of pork an' started. I trabbeled hard's I could all night,—'bout fifteen mile, I reckon,—an' den as 'twas gittin' toward mornin' I hid away in a swamp. Ye see I felt drefful bad, for I could year way off, but plain enuff, de bayin' of de hounds, an' I knew dat de men an' de guns an' de dogs was all after me; but de day passed an' dey did n't come. So de next night I started off agen, an' run an' walked hard all night, an' towards mornin' I went up to a little house standen off from de road, thinking it was a nigger house, an' jest as I got up to it out walked a white woman scarin' me awfully, an' de fust ting she axed me was what I wanted."

"Tight slave!" interrupted Jim,—"what d' ye do then?"

"Well, massa, ye see I saw mighty quick I was in for a lie anyhow, so I said, 'Is massa at home?' 'Yes,' says she,— an' sure nuff, he cum right out. 'Hello, nigger!' he said when he seed me, 'whar you cum from? so I tells him from Pocotaligo, an' before he could ax any more queshuns, I went on an' tole him we cotched fifty Yankees down dere yesterday, an' massa he was so tickled dat he let me go to Barnwells to see my family, an' den I said I'd got off de track an' was dead beat an' drefful hungry, an' would he please to sell me suthin to eat. At dat de woman streaked right into de house, an' got me some bread an' meat, an' tole me to eat it up an' not talk about payin','—'we don't charge good, faithful niggers nothin',' she said,—so I thanked her an' eat it all up, an' den, when de man had tole me how to go, I went right long till I got out ob sight ob de little house, an' den I got into de woods, an' turned right round de oder way an' made tracks fast as I could in dat direcshun."

"Ho! ho! you're about what I call a 'cute nigger," laughed Jim. "Come, go on,—this gets interesting."

"Well, directly I yearde de dogs. Dere was a pond little way off; so I tuck to it, an' waded out till I could just touch my toes an' keep my nose above water so's to breathe. Presently dey all cum down, an' I yearde Mass' George say, 'I'll hunt dat nigger till I find him if takes a month. I'se goin' to make a zample of him,'—so I shook some at dat, for I know'd what Mass' George's zamples was. Arter while one ob de men says, 'He ain't yere,—he'd shown hisself before dis, if he was,' an' I spose I would, for I was pretty nearly choked, only I said to myself when I went in, 'I'll go to de bottom before I'll come up to be tuck,' so I jest held on by my toes an' waited.

"I didn't dare to cum out when dey rode away to try a new scent, an' when I did I jest skulked round de edge ob de pond, ready to take to it agen if I yearde dem, an' when night cum I started off an' run an' walked agen hard's I could, an' den at day-dawn I tuck to anoder pond, an' went on a log dat was stickin' in de water, and broke down some rushes an' bushes enuf to lie down on an' cover me up, an' den I slept all day, for I was drefful tired an' most starved too. Next evenin' when it got dark, I went on agen, an' trabblin through de woods I seed a little light, an' sartin dis time dat it was a darkey's cabin, I made for it, an' it was. It was his'n,"—pointing to the big fellow who stood beside him, and who nodded his head in assent.

"I had a palaver before he'd let me in, but when I was in I seed what de matter was. He had a sojer dere, a Linkum sojer, bad wounded, what he'd found in de woods,—he was a runaway hisself, ye see, like me,—an' he'd tuck him to dis ole cabin an 'd been nussin him on for good while. When I seed dat I felt drefful bad, for I knowed dey was a huntin for me yet, an' I tought if de dogs got on de trail dey'd get to dis cabin, sure: an' den dey'd both be tuck. So I up an' tole dem, an' de sojer he says, 'Come, Jim, you've done quite enuff fur me, my boy. If you're in danger now, be off with you fast as you can,—an' God reward you, for I never can, for all you've done for me.'

" 'No,' says Jim, 'Capen, ye needn't talk in dat way, for I'se not goin to budge widout you. You got wounded fur me an' my people, an' now I'll stick by you an' face any thing fur you if it's Death hisself!' That's just what Jim said; an' de sojer he put his hand up to his face, an' I seed it tremble bad,—he was weak, you see,—an' some big tears cum out troo his fingers onto de back ob it.

"Den Jim says, 'Dis isn't a safe place for any on us, an' we'll have to take to our heels agen, an' so de sooner we's off de better.' So he did up some vittels,—all he had dere,— an, gave 'em to me to tote,—an' den before de Capen could sneeze he had him up on his back, an' we was off.

"It was pretty hard work I kin tell you, strong as Jim was, an' we'd have to stop an' rest putty ofen; an' den, Jim an' I, we'd tote him atween us on some boughs; an' den we had to lie by, some days, all day,—an' we trabbled putty slow, cause we'd lost our bearing an' was in a secesh country, we knowed,—an' we had nudin but berries an' sich to eat, an' got nigh starved.

"One night we cum onto half a dozen fellows skulkin' in de woods, an' at fust dey made fight, but d'rectly dey know'd we was friends, fur dey was some more Linkum sojers, an' dey'd lost dere way, or ruther, dey know'd where dey was, but dey didn't know how to git way from dere. Dey was 'scaped pris'ners, dey told us; when I yearde where 'twas I know'd de way to de coast, an' said I'd show 'em de way if dey'd cum long wid us, so dey did; an' we got 'long all right till we got to de ribber up by Mass' Rhett's place."

"Yes, I know where it is," said the Captain.

"Den what to do was de puzzle. De country was all full ob secesh pickets, an' dere was de ribber, an' we had no boat,—so Jim, he says, 'I know what to do; fust I'll hide you yere,' an' he did all safe in de woods; 'an' den I'll git ye suthin to eat from de niggers round,' an' he did dat too, do he couldn't git much, for fear he'd be seen; an' den we, he and I, made some ropes out ob de tall grass like dat we'd ofen made fur mats, an' tied dem together wid some oder grass, an' stuck a board in, an' den made fur de Yankee camp, an' yere we is."

"Yes," said the black man Jim, here,—breaking silence,—"we'll show you de way back if you kin go up in a boat dey can rest in, fur dey's most all clean done out, an' de capen's wound is awful bad yit."

"This captain,—what's his name?" inquired Coolidge.

"His name is here," said Jim, carefully drawing forth a paper from his rags,—"he has on dis some figgers an' a map of de country he took before he got wounded, an' some words he writ wid a bit of burnt stick just before we cum away,—an' he giv it to me, an' tole me to bring it to camp, fur fear something might happen to him while we was away."

"My God!" cried Coolidge when he had opened the paper, and with hasty eyes scanned its contents, "it's Tom Russell; I know him well. This must be sent up to head-quarters, and I'll get an order, and a boat, and some men, to go for them at once." All of which was promptly done.

"See here! I speak to be one of the fellows what goes," Jim emphatically announced.

"All right. I reckon we'll both go, Given, if the General will let us,—and I think he will,"—which was a safe guess and a true one. The boat was soon ready and manned. 'Bijah, too weak to pull an oar, was left behind; and Jim, really not fit to do aught save guide them, still insisted on taking his share of work. They found the place at last, and the men; and taking them on board,—Russell having to be moved slowly and carefully,—they began to pull for home.

The tide was going out, and the river low: that, with the heavy laden boat, made their progress lingering; a fact which distressed them all, as they knew the night to be almost spent, and that the shores were so lined with batteries, open and masked, and the country about so scoured by rebels, as to make it almost sure death to them if they were not beyond the lines before the morning broke.

The water was steadily and perceptibly ebbing,—the rowing growing more and more insecure,—the danger becoming imminent.

"Ease her off, there! ease her off!" cried the Captain,— as a harsh, gravelly sound smote on his ear, and at the same moment a shot whizzed past them, showing that they were discovered,—"ease her off, there! or we're stuck!"

The warning came too late,—indeed, could not have been obeyed, had it come earlier. The boat struck; her bottom grating hard on the wet sand.

"Great God! she's on a bar," cried Coolidge, "and the tide's running out, fast."

"Yes, and them damned rebs are safe enough from *our* fire," said one of the men.

A few scattering shot fell about them.

"They're going to make their mark on us, anyway," put in another.

"And we can't send 'em anything in return, blast 'em!" growled a third.

"That's the worst of it," broke out a fourth, "to be shot at like a rat in a hole."

All said in a breath, and the balls by this time falling thick and fast,—a fiery, awful rain of death. The men were no cowards, and the captain was brave enough; but what could they do? To stand up was but to make figure-heads at which the concealed enemy could fire with ghastly certainty; to fire in return was to waste their ammunition in the air. The men flung themselves face foremost on the deck, silent and watchful.

Through it all Jim had been sitting crouched over his oar. He, unarmed, could not have fought had the chance offered; breaking out, once and again, into the solemn-sounding chant which he had been singing when he came up in his boat the evening before:—

"O my soul arise in heaven, Lord, for to yearde when Jordan roll,
    Roll Jordan, roll Jordan, roll Jordan, roll,"—

the words falling in with the sound of the water as it lapsed from them.

"Stop that infernal noise, will you?" cried one of the men, impatiently. The noise stopped.

"Hush, Harry,—don't swear!" expostulated another, beside whom was lying a man mortally wounded. "This is awful! 'tain't like going in fair and square, on your chance."

"That's so,—it's enough to make a fellow pray," was the answer.

Here Russell, putting up his hand, took hold of Jim's brawny black one with a gesture gentle as a woman's. It hurt him to hear his faithful friend even spoken to harshly.

All this, while the hideous shower of death was dropping about them; the water was ebbing, ebbing,—falling and running out fast to sea, leaving them higher and drier on the sands; the gray dawn was steadily brightening into day.

At this fearful pass a sublime scene was enacted. "Sirs!" said a voice,—it was Jim's voice, and in it sounded something so earnest and strange, that the men involuntarily turned their heads to look at him. Then this man stood up,—a black man,—a little while before a slave,—the great muscles swollen and gnarled with unpaid toil, the marks of the lash and the branding-iron yet plain upon his person, the shadows of a life-time of wrongs and sufferings looking out of his eyes. "Sirs!" he said, simply, "somebody's got to die to get us out of dis, and it may as well be me,"—plunged overboard, put his toil-hardened shoulders to the boat; a struggle, a gasp, a mighty wrench,—pushed it off clear; then fell, face foremost, pierced by a dozen bullets. Free at last!

CHAPTER XVI

"Ye died to live."
BOKER

THE next day Jim was recounting this scene to some men in camp, describing it with feeling and earnestness, and winding up the narration by the declaration, "and the first man that says a nigger ain't as good as a white man, and a damn'd sight better'n those graybacks over yonder, well"—

"Well, suppose he does?"—interrupted one of the men.

"O, nothing, Billy Dodge,—only he and I'll have a few words to pass on the subject, that's all"; doubling up his fist and examining the big cords and muscles on it with curious and well-satisfied interest.

"See here, Billy!" put in one of his comrades, "don't you go to having any argument with Jim,—he's a dabster with his tongue, Jim is."

"Yes, and a devil with his fist," growled a sullen-looking fellow.

"Just so,"—assented Jim,—"when a blackguard's round to feel it."

"Well, Given, do you like the darkies well enough to take off your cap to them?" queried a sergeant standing near.

"What are you driving at now, hey?"

"O, not much; but you'll have to play second fiddle to them to-night. The General thinks they're as good as the rest of us, and a little bit better, and has sent over for the Fifty-fourth to lead the charge this evening. What have you got to say to that?"

"Bull, for them! that's what I've got to say. Any objection?" looking round him.

"Nary objec!" "They deserve it!" "They fought like tigers over on James Island!" "I hope they'll pepper the rebs well!"—"It ought to be a free fight, and no quarter, with them!" "Yes, for they get none if they're taken!" "Go in, Fifty-fourth!" These and the like exclamations broke from the men on all sides, with absolute heartiness and good will.

"It seems to me," sneered a dapper little officer who had been looking and listening, "that the niggers have plenty of advocates here."

Two or three of the men looked at Jim. "You may bet your pile on that, Major!" said he, with becoming gravity; "we love our friends, and we hate our enemies, and it's the dark-complected fellows that are the first down this way."

"Pretty-looking set of friends!"

"Well, they ain't much to look at, that's a fact; but I never heard of anybody saying you was to turn a cold shoulder on a helper because he was homely, except,"— this as the Major was walking away, "except a secesh, or a fool, or one of little Mac's staff officers."

"Homely? what are you gassing about?" objected a little fellow from Massachusetts; "the Fifty-fourth is as fine-looking a set of men as shoulder rifles anywhere in the army."

"Jack's sensitive about the credit of his State," chaffed a big Ohioan. "He wants to crack up these fellows, seeing they're his comrades. I say, Johnny, are all the white men down your way such little shavers as you?"

"For a fellow that's all legs and no brains, you talk too much," answered Johnny. "Have any of you seen the Fifty-fourth?"

"I haven't." "Nor I." "Yes, I saw them at Port Royal." "And I." "And I."

"Well, the Twenty-third was at Beaufort while they were there, and I used to go over to their camp and talk with them. I never saw fellows so in earnest; they seemed ready to die on the instant, if they could help their people, or walk into the slaveholders any, first. They were just full of it; and yet it seemed absurd to call 'em a black regiment; they were pretty much all colors, and some of 'em as white as I am."

"Lord," said Jim, "that's not saying much, you've got a smutty face."

The men laughed, Jack with the rest, as he dabbed at his heated, powder-stained countenance. "Come," said he, "that's no fair,—they're as white as I am, then, when I've just scrubbed; and some of them are first-raters, too; none of your rag, tag, and bobtail. There's one I remember, a man from Philadelphia, who walks round like a prince. He's a gentleman, every inch,—and he's rich,—and about the handsomest-looking specimen of humanity I've set eyes upon for an age."

"Rich, is he? how do you know he's rich?"

"I was over one night with Captain Ware, and he and this man got to talking about the pay for the Fifty-fourth. The government promised them regular pay, you see, and then when it got 'em refused to stick to its agreement, and they would take no less, so they haven't seen a dime since they enlisted; and it's a darned mean piece of business, that's my opinion of the matter, and I don't care who knows it," looking round belligerently.

"Come, Bantam, don't crow so loud," interrupted the big Ohioan; "nobody's going to fight you on that statement; it's a shame, and no mistake. But what about your paragon?"

"I'll tell you. The Captain was trying to convince him that they had better take what they could get till they got the whole, and that, after all, it was but a paltry difference. 'But,' said the man, 'it's not the money, though plenty of us are poor enough to make that an item. It's the badge of disgrace, the stigma attached, the dishonor to the government. If it were only two cents we wouldn't submit to it, for the difference would be made because we are colored, and we're not going to help degrade our own people, not if we starve for it. Besides, it's *our* flag, and *our* government now, and we've got to defend the honor of both against any assailants, North or South,—whether they're Republican Congressmen or rebel soldiers.' The Captain looked puzzled at that, and asked what he meant. 'Why,' said he, 'the United States government enlisted us as soldiers. Being such, we don't intend to disgrace the service by accepting the pay of servants.' "

"That's the kind of talk," bawled Jim from a fencerail upon which he was balancing. "I'd like to have a shake of that fellow's paw. What's his name, d'ye know?"

"Ercildoune."

"Hey?"

"Ercildoune."

"Jemime! Ercildoune,—from Philadelphia, you say?"

"Yes,—do you know him?"

"Well, no,—I don't exactly know him, but I think I know something about him. His pa's rich as a nob, if it's the one I mean,"—and then finished *sotto voce*, "it's Mrs. Surrey's brother, sure as a gun!"

"Well, he ought to be rich, if he ain't. As we, that's the Captain and me, were walking away, the Captain said to one of the officers of the Fifty-fourth who'd been listening to the talk, 'It's easy for that man to preach self-denial for a principle. He's rich, I've heard. It don't hurt him any; but it's rather selfish to hold some of the rest up to his standard; and I presume that such a man as he has no end of influence with them!'

" 'As he should,' said his officer. 'Ercildoune has brains enough to stock a regiment, and refinement, and genius, and cultivation that would assure him the highest position in society or professional life anywhere out of America. He won't leave it though; for in spite of its wrongs to him he sees its greatness and goodness,—says that it is *his*, and that it is to be saved, it and all its benefits, for Americans,—no matter what the color of their skin,—of whom he is one. He sees plain enough that this war is going to break the slave's chain, and ultimately the stronger chain of prejudice that binds his people to the grindstone, and he's full of enthusiasm for it, accordingly; though I'm free to confess, the magnanimity of these colored men from the North who fight, on faith, for the government, is to me something amazing.' "

" 'Why,' said the Captain,—'why, any more from the North than from the South?' "

"Why? the blacks down here can at least fight their ex-masters, and pay off some old scores; but for a man from the North who is free already, and so has nothing to gain in that way,—whose rights as a man and a citizen are denied,—for such a man to enlist and to fight, without bounty, pay, honor, or promotion,—without the promise of gaining anything whatever for himself,—condemned to a thankless task on the one side,—to a merciless death or even worse fate on the other,—facing all this because he has faith that the great republic will ultimately be redeemed; that some hands will gather in the harvest of this bloody sowing, though he be lying dead under it,—I tell you, the more I see of these men, the more I know of them, the more am I filled with admiration and astonishment.

"Now here's this one of whom we are talking, Ercildoune, born with a silver spoon in his mouth: instead of eating with it, in peace and elegance, in some European home, look at him here. You said something about his lack of self-sacrifice. He's doing what he is from a principle; and beyond that, it's no wonder the men care for him: he has spent a small fortune on the most needy of them since they enlisted,—finding out which of them have families, or any one dependent on them, and helping them in the finest and most delicate way possible. There are others like him here, and it's a fortunate circumstance, for there's not a man but would suffer, himself,—and, what's more, let his family suffer at home,—before he'd give up the idea for which they are contending now."

" 'Well, good luck to them!' said the Captain as we came away; and so say I," finished Jack.

"And I,"—"And I," responded some of the men. "We must see this man when they come over here."

"I'll bet you a shilling," said Jim, pulling out a bit of currency, "that he'll make his mark to-night."

"Lend us the change, Given, and I'll take you up," said one of the men.

The others laughed. "He don't mean it," said Jim: which, indeed, he didn't. Nobody seemed inclined to run any risks by betting on the other side of so likely a proposition.

This talk took place late in the afternoon, near the head-quarters of the commanding General; and the men directly scattered to prepare for the work of the evening: some to clean a bayonet, or furbish up a rifle; others to chat and laugh over the chances and to lay plans for the morrow,—the morrow which was for them never to dawn on earth; and yet others to sit down in their tents and write letters to the dear ones at home, making what might, they knew, be a final-farewell,—for the fight impending was to be a fierce one,—or to read a chapter in a little book carried from some quiet fireside, balancing accounts perchance, in anticipation of the call of the Great Captain to come up higher.

Through the whole afternoon there had been a tremendous cannonading of the fort from the gunboats and the land forces: the smooth, regular engineer lines were broken, and the fresh-sodded embankments torn and roughened by the unceasing rain of shot and shell.

About six o'clock there came moving up the island, over the burning sands and under the burning sky, a stalwart, splendid-appearing set of men, who looked equal to any daring, and capable of any heroism; men whom nothing could daunt and few things subdue. Now, weary, travel-stained, with the mire and the rain of a two days' tramp; weakened by the incessant strain and lack of food, having taken nothing for forty-eight hours save some crackers and cold coffee; with gaps in their ranks made by the death of comrades who had fallen in battle but a little time before,—under all these disadvantages, it was plain to be seen of what stuff these men were made, and for what work they were ready.

As this regiment, the famous Fifty-fourth, came up the island to take its place at the head of the storming party in the assault on Wagner, it was cheered from all sides by the white soldiers, who recognized and honored the heroism which it had already shown, and of which it was soon to give such new and sublime proof.

The evening, or rather the afternoon, was a lurid and sultry one. Great masses of clouds, heavy and black, were piled in the western sky, fringed here and there by an angry red, and torn by vivid streams of lightning. Not a breath of wind shook the leaves or stirred the high, rank grass by the water-side; a portentous and awful stillness filled the air,—the stillness felt by nature before a devastating storm. Quiet, with the like awful and portentous calm, the black regiment, headed by its young, fair-haired, knightly colonel, marched to its destined place and action.

When within about six hundred yards of the fort it was halted at the head of the regiments already stationed, and the line of battle formed. The prospect was such as might daunt the courage of old and well-tried veterans, but these soldiers of a few weeks seemed but impatient to take the odds, and to make light of impossibilities. A slightly rising

ground, raked by a murderous fire, to within a little distance of the battery; a ditch holding three feet of water; a
straight lift of parapet, thirty feet high; an impregnable
position, held by a desperate and invincible foe.

Here the men were addressed in a few brief and
burning words by their heroic commander. Here they
were besought to glorify their whole race by the lustre of
their deeds; here their faces shone with a look which said,
"Though men, we are ready to do deeds, to achieve tri-
umphs, worthy the gods!" here the word of command was
given:—

"We are ordered and expected to take Battery Wagner
at the point of the bayonet. Are you ready?"

"Ay, ay, sir! ready!" was the answer.

And the order went pealing down the line, "Ready!
Close ranks! Charge bayonets! Forward! Double-quick,
march!"—and away they went, under a scattering fire, in
one compact line till within one hundred feet of the fort,
when the storm of death broke upon them. Every gun
belched forth its great shot and shell; every rifle whizzed
out its sharp-singing, death-freighted messenger. The men
wavered not for an instant;—forward,—forward they
went; plunged into the ditch; waded through the deep
water, no longer of muddy hue, but stained crimson with
their blood; and commenced to climb the parapet. The
foremost line fell, and then the next, and the next. The
ground was strewn with the wrecks of humanity, scattered
prostrate, silent, where they fell,—or rolling under the

very feet of the living comrades who swept onward to fill their places. On, over the piled-up mounds of dead and dying, of wounded and slain, to the mouth of the battery; seizing the guns; bayoneting the gunners at their posts; planting their flag and struggling around it; their leader on the walls, sword in hand, his blue eyes blazing, his fair face aflame, his clear voice calling out, "Forward, my brave boys!"—then plunging into the hell of battle before him. Forward it was. They followed him, gathered about him, gained an angle of the fort, and fought where he fell, around his prostrate body, over his peaceful heart,— shielding its dead silence by their living, pulsating ones,— till they, too, were stricken down; then hacked, hewn, battered, mangled, heroic, yet overcome, the remnant was beaten back.

Ably sustained by their supporters, Anglo-African and Anglo-Saxon vied together to carry off the palm of courage and glory. All the world knows the last fought with heroism sublime: all the world forgets this and them in contemplating the deeds and the death of their compatriots. Said Napoleon at Austerlitz to a young Russian officer, overwhelmed with shame at yielding his sword, "Young man, be consoled: those who are conquered by my soldiers may still have titles to glory." To say that on that memorable night the last were surpassed by the first is still to leave ample margin on which to write in glowing characters the record of their deeds.

As the men were clambering up the parapet their color-sergeant was shot dead, the colors trailing stained and wet in the dust beside him. Ercildoune, who was just behind, sprang forward, seized the staff from his dying hand, and mounted with it upward. A ball struck his right arm, yet ere it could fall shattered by his side, his left hand caught the flag and carried it onward. Even in the mad sweep of assault and death the men around him found breath and time to hurrah, and those behind him pressed more gallantly forward to follow such a lead. He kept in his place, the colors flying,—though faint with loss of blood and wrung with agony,—up the slippery steep; up to the walls of the fort; on the wall itself, planting the flag where the men made that brief, splendid stand, and melted away like snow before furnace-heat. Here a bayonet thrust met him and brought him down, a great wound in his brave breast, but he did not yield; dropping to his knees, pressing his unbroken arm upon the gaping wound,—bracing himself against a dead comrade,—the colors still flew; an inspiration to the men about him; a defiance to the foe.

At last when the shattered ranks fell back, sullenly and slowly retreating, it was seen by those who watched him,—men lying for three hundred rods around in every form of wounded suffering,—that he was painfully working his way downward, still holding aloft the flag, bent evidently on saving it, and saving it as flag had rarely, if ever, been saved before.

Some of the men had crawled, some had been carried, some hastily caught up and helped by comrades to a sheltered tent out of range of the fire; a hospital tent, they called it, if anything could bear that name which was but a place where men could lie to suffer and expire, without a bandage, a surgeon, or even a drop of cooling water to moisten parched and dying lips. Among these was Jim. He had a small field-glass in his pocket, and forgot or ignored his pain in his eager interest of watching through this the progress of the man and the flag, and reporting accounts to his no less eager companions. Black soldiers and white were alike mad with excitement over the deed; and fear lest the colors which had not yet dipped should at last bite the ground.

Now and then he paused at some impediment: it was where the dead and dying were piled so thickly as to compel him to make a detour. Now and then he rested a moment to press his arm tighter against his torn and open breast. The rain fell in such torrents, the evening shadows were gathering so thickly, that they could scarcely trace his course, long before it was ended.

Slowly, painfully, he dragged himself onward,—step by step down the hill, inch by inch across the ground,—to the door of the hospital; and then, while dying eyes brightened,—dying hands and even shattered stumps were thrown into the air,—in brief, while dying men held back their souls from the eternities to cheer him,—gasped out, "I did—but do—my duty, boys,—and the dear—old flag—never once—touched the ground,"—and then, away from the reach and sight of its foes, in the midst of its defenders, who loved and were dying for it, the flag at last fell.

* * * * * *

Meanwhile, other troops had gone up to the encounter; other regiments strove to win what these men had failed to gain; and through the night, and the storm, and the terrific reception, did their gallant endeavor—in vain.

* * * * * *

The next day a flag of truce went up to beg the body of the heroic young chief who had so led that marvellous assault. It came back without him. A ditch, deep and wide, had been dug; his body, and those of twenty-two of his men found dead upon and about him, flung into it in one common heap and the word sent back was, "We have buried him with his niggers."

It was well done. The fair, sweet face and gallant breast lie peacefully enough under their stately monument of ebony.

It was well done. What more fitting close of such a life,—what fate more welcome to him who had fought with them, had loved, and believed in them, had led them to death,—than to lie with them when they died?

It was well done. Slavery buried these men, black and white, together,—black and white in a common grave. Let Liberty see to it, then, that black and white be raised together in a life better than the old.

CHAPTER XVII

*"Spirits are not finely touched
But to fine issues."*
SHAKESPEARE

SURREY was to depart for his command on Monday
night, and as there were various matters which
demanded his attention in town ere leaving, he drove
Francesca to the city on the preceding Sunday,—a soft
clear summer evening, full of pleasant sights and sounds.
They scarcely spoke as, hand in hand, they sat drinking in
the scene whilst the old gray, for they wished no high-
stepping prancers for this ride, jogged on the even tenor of
his way. Above them, the blue of the sky never before
seemed so deep and tender, while in it floated fleecy
clouds of delicate amber, rose, and gold, like gossamer
robes of happy spirits invisible to human eyes. The leaves
and grass just stirred in the breeze, making a slight, musical

murmur, and across them fell long shadows cast by the westering sun. A sentiment so sweet and pleasurable as to be tinged with pain, took possession of these young, susceptible souls, as the influences of the time closed about them. In our happiest moments, our moments of utmost exaltation, it is always thus:—when earth most nearly approaches the beatitudes of heaven, and the spirit stretches forward with a vain longing for the far off, which seems but a little way beyond; the unattained and dim, which for a space come near.

"Darling!" said Surrey softly, "does it not seem easy now to die?"

"Yes, Willie," she whispered, "I feel as though it would be stepping over a very little stream to some new and beautiful shore."

Doubtless, when a pure and great soul is close to eternity, ministering angels draw nigh to one soon to be of their number, and cast something of the peace and glory of their presence on the spirit yet held by its cerements of clay.

At last the ride and the evening had an end. The country and its dear delights were mere memories,—fresh, it is true, but memories still, and no longer realities,—in the luxurious rooms of their hotel.

Evidently Surrey had something to say, which he hesitated and feared to utter. Again and again, when Francesca was talking of his plans and purposes, trusting and hoping that he might see no hard service, nor be called upon for any exposing duty, "not yet awhile," she prayed, at least,—

again and again he made as if to speak, and then, ere she could notice the movement, shook his head with a gesture of silence, or—she seeing it, and asking what it was he had to say—found ready utterance for some other thought, and whispered to himself, "not yet; not quite yet. Let her rest in peace a little space longer."

They sat talking far into the night, this last night that they could spend together in so long a time,—how long, God, with whom are hid the secrets of the future, could alone tell. They talked of what had passed, which was ended,—and of what was to come, which was not sure but full of hope,—but of both with a feeling that quickened their heart-throbs, and brought happy tears to their eyes.

Twice or thrice a sound from some far distance, undecided, yet full of a solemn melody, came through the open window, borne to their ears on the still air of night,— something so undefined as not consciously to arrest their attention, yet still penetrating their nerves and affecting some fine, inner sense of feeling, for both shivered as though a chill wind had blown across them, and Surrey— half ashamed of the confession—said, "I don't know what possesses me, but I hear dead marches as plainly as though I were following a soldier's funeral."

Francesca at that grew white, crept closer to his breast, and spread out her arms as if to defend him by that slight shield from some impending danger; then both laughed at these foolish and superstitious fancies, and went on with their cheerful and tender talk.

Whatever the sound was, it grew plainer and came nearer; and, pausing to listen, they discovered it was a mighty swell of human voices and the marching of many feet.

"A regiment going through," said they, and ran to the window to see if it passed their way, looking for it up the long street, which lay solemn and still in the moonlight. On either side the palace-like houses stood stately and dark, like giant sentinels guarding the magnificent avenue, from whence was banished every sight and sound of the busy life of day; not a noise, not a footfall, not a solitary soul abroad, not a wave nor a vestige of the great restless sea of humanity which a little space before surged through it, and which, in a little while to come, would rise and swell to its full, and then ebb, and fall, and drop away once more into silence and nothingness.

Through this white stillness there came marching a regiment of men, without fife or drum, moving to the music of a refrain which lifted and fell on the quiet air. It was the Battle Hymn of the Republic,—and the two listeners presently distinguished the words,—

"In the beauty of the lilies Christ was born across the sea,
With a glory in his bosom that transfigures you and me;
As he died to make men holy, let us die to make men free,
                    While God is marching on."

The effect of this; the thousand voices which sang; the marching of twice one thousand feet; the majesty of the words; the deserted street; the clear moonlight streaming over the men, reflected from their gleaming bayonets, brightening the faded blue of their uniforms, illumining their faces which, one and all, seemed to wear—and probably *did* wear—a look more solemn and earnest than that of common life and feeling,—the combined effect of it all was something indescribably impressive:—inspiring, yet solemn.

They stood watching and listening till the pageant had vanished, and then turned back into their room, Francesca taking up the refrain and singing the line,

> "As he died to make men holy, let us die to make men free,
>
>   While God is marching on."

Surrey's face brightened at the rapt expression of hers. "Sing it again, dearie!" he said. She sang it again. "Do you mean it?" he asked then. "Can you sing it, and mean it with all your heart, for me?"

She looked at him with an expression of anxiety and pain. "What are you asking, Willie?"

He sat down; taking her upon his knee, and with the old fond gesture, holding her head to his heart,—"I should have told you before, dearie, but I did not wish to throw any shadow on the happy days we have been spending together; they were few and brief enough without marring them; and I was certain of the effect it would have upon you, by your incessant anxiety for Robert."

She drew a long, gasping sigh, and started away from his hold: "O Willie, you are not going to—"

His arm drew her back to her resting-place. "I do not return to my command, darling. I am to raise a black brigade."

"Freedmen?"

"Yes, dearie."

"O Willie,—and that act just passed!"

"It is true; yet, after all, it is but one risk more."

"One? O Willie, it is a thousand. You had that many chances of escape where you were; you might be wounded and captured a score of times, and come home safe at last; but this!"

"I know."

"To go into every battle with the sentence of death hanging over you; to know that if you are anywhere captured, anyhow made prisoner, you are condemned to die,—O Willie, I can't bear it; I can't bear it! I shall die, or go mad, to carry such a thought all the time."

For answer he only held her close, with his face resting upon her hair, and in the stillness they could hear each other's heart beat.

"It is God's service," he said, at last.

"I know."

"It will end slavery and the war more effectually than aught else."

"I know."

"It will make these freedmen, wherever they fight, free

men. It will give them and their people a sense of dignity and power that might otherwise take generations to secure."

"I know."

"And I. Both feeling and knowing this, who so fit to yield and to do for such a cause? If those who see do not advance, the blind will never walk."

Silence for a space again fell between them. Francesca moved in his arm.

"Dearie." She looked up. "I want to do no half service. I go into this heart and soul, but I do not wish to go alone. It will be so much to me to know that you are quite willing, and bade me go. Think what it is."

She did. For an instant all sacrifices appeared easy, all burdens light. She could send him out to death unfaltering. One of those sublime moods in which martyrdom seems glorious filled and possessed her. She took away her clinging arms from his neck, and said, "Go,—whether it be for life or for death; whether you come back to me or go up to God; I am willing—glad—to yield you to such a cause."

It was finished. There was nothing more to be said. Both had climbed the mount of sacrifice, and sat still with God.

After a while the cool gray dawn stole into their room. The night had passed in this communion, and another day come.

There were many "last things" which claimed Surrey's attention; and he, wishing to get through them early so as to have the afternoon and evening undisturbed with Francesca, plunged into a stinging bath to refresh him for the day, breakfasted, and was gone.

He attended to his business, came across many an old acquaintance and friend, some of whom greeted him coldly; a few cut him dead; whilst others put out their hands with cordial frankness, and one or two congratulated him heartily upon his new condition and happiness. These last gave him fresh courage for the task which he had set himself. If friends regarded the matter thus, surely they—his father and mother—would relent, when he came to say what might be a final adieu.

He ran up the steps, rang the bell, and, speaking a pleasant word to the old servant, went directly to his mother's room. His father had not yet gone down town; thus he found them together. They started at seeing him, and his mother, forgetting for the instant all her pride, chagrin, and anger, had her arms about his neck, with the cry, "O Willie, Willie," which came from the depths of her heart; then seeing her husband's face, and recovering herself, sat down cold and still.

It was a painful interview. He could not leave without seeing them once more; he longed for a loving good by; but after that first outburst he almost wished he had not forced the meeting. He did not speak of his wife, nor did they; but a barrier as of adamant was raised between them, and he felt as though congealing in the breath of an iceberg. At length he rose to go.

"Father!" he said then, "perhaps you will care to know that I do not return to my old command, but have been commissioned to raise a brigade from the freedmen."

Both father and mother knew the awful peril of this service, and both cried, half in suffering, half in anger, "This is your wife's work!" while his father added, with a passionate exclamation, "It is right, quite right, that you should identify yourself with her people. Well, go your way. You have made your bed; lie in it."

The blood flushed into Surrey's face. He opened his lips, and shut them again. At last he said, "Father, will you never forego this cruel prejudice?"

"Never!" answered his mother, quickly. "Never!" repeated his father, with bitter emphasis. "It is a feeling that will never die out, and ought never to die out, so long as any of the race remain in America. She belongs to it, that is enough."

Surrey urged no further; but with few words, constrained on their part,—though under its covering of pride the mother's heart was bleeding for him,—sad and earnest on his, the farewell was spoken, and they watched him out of the room. How and when would they see him again?

There was one other call upon his time. The day was wearing into the afternoon, but he would not neglect it. This was to see his old *protégé*, Abram Franklin, in whom he had never lost interest, and for whose welfare he had cared, though he had not seen him in more than two years. He knew that Abram was ill, had been so for a long time, and wished to see him and speak to him a few friendly and cheering words,—sure, from what the boy's own hand had written, that this would be his last opportunity upon earth to so do.

Thus he went on from his father's stately palace up Fifth Avenue, turned into the quiet side street, and knocked at the little green door. Mrs. Franklin came to open it, her handsome face thinner and sadder than of old. She caught Surrey's hand between both of hers with a delighted cry: "Is it you, Mr. Willie? How glad I am to see you! How glad Abram will be! How good of you to come!" And, holding his hand as she used when he was a boy, she led him up stairs to the sick-room. This room was even cosier than the two below; its curtains and paper cheerfuller; its furniture of quainter and more hospitable aspect; its windows letting in more light and air; everything clean and homely, and pleasant for weary, suffering eyes to look upon.

Abram was propped up in bed, his dark, intelligent face worn to a shadow, fiery spots breaking through the tawny hue upon cheeks and lips, his eyes bright with fever. Surrey saw, as he came and sat beside him, that for him earthly sorrow and toil were almost ended.

He had brought some fruit and flowers, and a little book. This last Abram, having thanked him eagerly for all, stretched out his hand to examine.

"You see, Mr. Willie, I have not gotten over my old love," he said, as his fingers closed upon it. "Whittier? 'In

War-Time'? That is fine. I can read about it, if I can't do anything in it," and he lay for a while quietly turning over the pages. Mrs. Franklin had gone out to do an errand, and the two were alone.

"Do you know, Mr. Willie," said Abram, putting his finger upon the titles of two successive poems, "The Waiting," and "The Summons," "I had hard work to submit to this sickness a few months ago? I fought against it strong; do you know why?"

"Not your special reason. What was it?"

"I had waited so long, you see,—I, and my people,— for a chance. It made me quite wild to watch this big fight go on, and know that it was all about us, and not be allowed to participate; and at last when the chance came, and the summons, and the way was opened, I couldn't answer, nor go. It's not the dying I care for; I'd be willing to die the first battle I was in; but I want to do something for the cause before death comes."

The book was lying open where it had fallen from his hand, and Surrey, glancing down at the very poem of which he spoke, said gently, "Here is your answer, Franklin, better than any I can make; it ought to comfort you; listen, it is God's truth!

> 'O power to do! O baffled will!
>   O prayer and action! ye are one;
> Who may not strive may yet fulfil
> The harder task of standing still,
>   And good but wished with God is done!' "

"It is so," said Abram. "You act and I pray, and you act for me and mine. I'd like to be under you when you get the troops you were telling me about; but—God knows best."

Surrey sat gazing earnestly into space, crowded by emotions called up by these last words, whilst Abram lay watching him with admiring and loving eyes. "For me and mine," he repeated softly, his look fastening on the blue sleeve, which hung, limp and empty, near his hand. This he put out cautiously, but drew it back at some slight movement from his companion; then, seeing that he was still absorbed, advanced it, once more, and slowly, timidly, gently, lifted it to his mouth, pressing his lips upon it as upon a shrine. "For me and mine!" he whispered,—"for me and mine!" tears dimming the pathetic, dying eyes.

The peaceful quiet was broken by a tempest of awful sound,—groans and shrieks and yells mingled in horrible discord, blended with the trampling of many feet,—noises which seemed to their startled and excited fancies like those of hell itself. The next moment a door was flung open; and Mrs. Franklin, bruised, lame, her garments torn, blood flowing from a cut on her head, staggered into the room. "O Lord! O Lord Jesus!" she cried, "the day of wrath has come!" and fell, shuddering and crying, on the floor.

CHAPTER XVIII

"Will the future come? It seems that we may almost ask
this question, when we see such terrible shadow."
VICTOR HUGO

HERE it will be necessary to consider some facts which, while they are rather in the domain of the grave recorder of historical events, than in that of the narrator of personal experiences, are yet essential to the comprehension of the scenes in which Surrey and Francesca took such tragic parts.

Following the proclamation for a draft in the city of New York, there had been heard on all sides from the newspaper press which sympathized with and aided the rebellion, premonitions of the coming storm; denunciations of the war, the government, the soldiers, of the harmless and inoffensive negroes; angry incitings of the poor man to hatred against the rich, since the rich man

could save himself from the necessity of serving in the
ranks by the payment of three hundred dollars of commu-
tation money; incendiary appeals to the worst passions of
the most ignorant portion of the community; and open
calls to insurrection and arms to resist the peaceable
enforcement of a law enacted in furtherance of the
defence of the nation's life.

Doubtless this outbreak had been intended at the time
of the darkest and most disastrous days of the Republic;
when the often-defeated and sorely dispirited Army of the
Potomac was marching northward to cover Washington
and Baltimore, and the victorious legions of traitors under
Lee were swelling across the border, into a loyal State;
when Grant stood in seemingly hopeless waiting before
Vicksburg, and Banks before Port Hudson; and the whole
people of the North, depressed and disheartened by the
continued series of defeats to our arms, were beginning to
look each at his neighbor, and whisper with white lips,
"Perhaps, after all, this struggle is to be in vain."

Had it been attempted at this precise time, it would,
without question, have been, not a riot, but an insurrection,—would have been a portion of the army of rebellion, organized and effective for the prosecution of the
war, and not a mob, hideous and devilish in its work of
destruction, yet still a mob; and as such to be beaten down
and dispersed in a comparatively short space of time.

On the morning of Monday, the thirteenth of July,
began this outbreak, unparalleled in atrocities by anything

in American history, and equalled only by the horrors of the worst days of the French Revolution. Gangs of men and boys, composed of railroad *employées*, workers in machine-shops, and a vast crowd of those who lived by preying upon others, thieves, pimps, professional ruffians,—the scum of the city,—jail-birds, or those who were running with swift feet to enter the prison-doors, began to gather on the corners, and in streets and alleys where they lived; from thence issuing forth they visited the great establishments on the line of their advance, commanding their instant close and the companionship of the workmen,—many of them peaceful and orderly men,—on pain of the destruction of one and a murderous assault upon the other, did not their orders meet with instant compliance.

A body of these, five or six hundred strong, gathered about one of the enrolling-offices in the upper part of the city, where the draft was quietly proceeding, and opened the assault upon it by a shower of clubs, bricks, and paving-stones torn from the streets, following it up by a furious rush into the office. Lists, records, books, the drafting-wheel, every article of furniture or work in the room was rent in pieces, and strewn about the floor or flung into the street; while the law officers, the newspaper reporters,—who are expected to be everywhere,—and the few peaceable spectators, were compelled to make a hasty retreat through an opportune rear exit, accelerated by the curses and blows of the assailants.

A safe in the room, which contained some of the hated records, was fallen upon by the men, who strove to wrench open its impregnable lock with their naked hands, and, baffled, beat them on its iron doors and sides till they were stained with blood, in a mad frenzy of senseless hate and fury. And then, finding every portable article destroyed,— their thirst for ruin growing by the little drink it had had,—and believing, or rather hoping, that the officers had taken refuge in the upper rooms, set fire to the house, and stood watching the slow and steady lift of the flames, filling the air with demoniac shrieks and yells, while they waited for the prey to escape from some door or window, from the merciless fire to their merciless hands. One of these, who was on the other side of the street, coura- geously stepped forward, and, telling them that they had utterly demolished all they came to seek, informed them that helpless women and little children were in the house, and besought them to extinguish the flames and leave the ruined premises; to disperse, or at least to seek some other scene.

By his dress recognizing in him a government official, so far from bearing or heeding his humane appeal, they set upon him with sticks and clubs, and beat him till his eyes were blind with blood, and he—bruised and mangled— succeeded in escaping to the handful of police who stood helpless before this howling crew, now increased to thou- sands. With difficulty and pain the inoffensive tenants escaped from the rapidly spreading fire, which, having devoured the house originally lighted, swept across the neighboring buildings till the whole block stood a mass of burning flames. The firemen came up tardily and reluctantly, many of them of the same class as the miscreants who surrounded them, and who cheered at their approach, but either made no attempt to perform their duty, or so feeble and farcical a one, as to bring disgrace upon a service they so generally honor and ennoble.

At last, when there was here nothing more to accomplish, the mob, swollen to a frightful size, including myriads of wretched, drunken women, and the half-grown, vagabond boys of the pavements, rushed through the intervening streets, stopping cars and insulting peaceable citizens on their way, to an armory where were manufactured and stored carbines and guns for the government. In anticipation of the attack, this, earlier in the day, had been fortified by a police squad capable of coping with an ordinary crowd of ruffians, but as chaff before fire in the presence of these murderous thousands. Here, as before, the attack was begun by a rain of missiles gathered from the streets; less fatal, doubtless, than more civilized arms, but frightful in the ghastly wounds and injuries they inflicted. Of this no notice was taken by those who were stationed within; it was repeated. At last, finding they were treated with contemptuous silence, and that no sign of surrender was offered, the crowd swayed back,—then forward,—in a combined attempt to force the wide entrance-doors. Heavy hammers and sledges, which had been brought from forges and workshops, caught up hastily as they gathered the mechanics into their ranks, were used with frightful violence to beat them in,—at last successfully. The foremost assailants began to climb the stairs, but were checked, and for the moment driven back by the fire of the officers, who at last had been commanded to resort to their revolvers. A half-score fell wounded; and one, who had been acting in some sort as their leader,—a big, brutal, Irish ruffian,—dropped dead.

The pause was but for an instant. As the smoke cleared away there was a general and ferocious onslaught upon the armory; curses, oaths, revilings, hideous and obscene blasphemy, with terrible yells and cries, filled the air in every accent of the English tongue save that spoken by a native American. Such were there mingled with the sea of sound, but they were so few and weak as to be unnoticeable in the roar of voices. The paving-stones flew like hail, until the street was torn into gaps and ruts, and every window-pane, and sash, and doorway, was smashed or broken. Meanwhile, divers attempts were made to fire the building, but failed through haste or ineffectual materials, or the vigilant watchfulness of the besieged. In the midst of this gallant defence, word was brought to the defenders from headquarters that nothing could be done for their support; and that, if they would save their lives, they must make a quick and orderly retreat. Fortunately, there was a side passage with which the mob was unacquainted, and, one by one they succeeded in gaining this, and vanishing. A few, too faithful or too plucky to retreat before such a foe, persisted in remaining at their posts till the fire, which had at last been communicated to the building, crept unpleasantly near; then, by dropping from sill to sill of the broken windows, or sliding by their hands and feet down the rough pipes and stones, reached the pavement,—but not without injuries and blows, and broken bones, which disabled for a lifetime, if indeed they did not die in the hospitals to which a few of the more mercifully disposed carried them.

The work thus begun, continued,—gathering in force and fury as the day wore on. Police-stations, enrolling-offices, rooms or buildings used in any way by government authority, or obnoxious as representing the dignity of law, were gutted, destroyed, then left to the mercy of the flames. Newspaper offices, whose issues had been a fire in the rear of the nation's armies by extenuating and defending treason, and through violent and incendiary appeals stirring up "lewd fellows of the baser sort" to this very carnival of ruin and blood, were cheered as the crowd went by. Those that had been faithful to loyalty and law were hooted, stoned, and even stormed by the army of miscreants who were only driven off by the gallant and determined charge of the police, and in one place by the equally gallant, and certainly unique defence, which came from turning the boiling water from the engines upon the howling wretches, who, unprepared for any such warm reception as this, beat a precipitate and general retreat. Before night fell it was no longer one vast crowd collected in a single section, but great numbers of gatherings, scattered over the whole length and breadth of the city,—some of them engaged in actual work of demolition and ruin; others with clubs and weapons in their hands, prowling round apparently with no definite atrocity to perpetrate, but ready for any iniquity that might offer,—and, by way of pastime, chasing every stray police officer, or solitary soldier, or inoffensive negro, who crossed the line of their vision; these three objects—the badge of a defender of the law,—the uniform of the Union army,—the skin of a helpless and outraged race—acted upon these madmen as water acts upon a rabid dog.

Late in the afternoon a crowd which could have numbered not less than ten thousand, the majority of whom were ragged, frowzy, drunken women, gathered about the Orphan Asylum for Colored Children,—a large and beautiful building, and one of the most admirable and noble charities of the city. When it became evident, from the menacing cries and groans of the multitude, that danger, if not destruction, was meditated to the harmless and inoffensive inmates, a flag of truce appeared, and an appeal was made in their behalf, by the principal, to every sentiment of humanity which these beings might possess,—a vain appeal! Whatever human feeling had ever, if ever, filled these souls was utterly drowned and washed away in the tide of rapine and blood in which they had been steeping themselves. The few officers who stood guard over the doors, and manfully faced these demoniac legions, were beaten down and flung to one side, helpless and stunned, whilst the vast crowd rushed in. All the articles upon which they could seize—beds, bedding, carpets, furniture,—the very garments of the fleeing inmates, some of these torn from their persons as they sped by—were carried into the streets, and hurried off by the women and children who stood ready to receive the goods which their husbands, sons, and fathers flung to their care. The little ones, many of them, assailed and beaten; all,—orphans and care-takers,—exposed to every indignity and every danger, driven on to the street,—the building was fired. This had been attempted whilst the helpless children—some of them scarce more than babies—were still in their rooms; but this devilish consummation was prevented by the heroism of one man. He, the Chief of the Fire Department, strove by voice and arm to stay the endeavor; and when, overcome by superior numbers, the brands had been lit and piled, with naked hands, and in the face of threatened death, he tore asunder the glowing embers, and trod them under foot. Again the effort was made, and again failed through the determined and heroic opposition of this solitary soul. Then, on the front steps, in the midst of these drunken and infuriate thousands, he stood up and besought them, if they cared nothing for themselves nor for these hapless orphans, that they would not bring lasting disgrace upon the city by destroying one of its noblest charities, which had for its object nothing but good.

He was answered on all sides by yells and execrations,

and frenzied shrieks of "Down with the nagurs!" coupled with every oath and every curse that malignant hate of the blacks could devise, and drunken, Irish tongues could speak. It had been decreed that this building was to be razed to the ground. The house was fired in a thousand places, and in less than two hours the walls crashed in,—a mass of smoking, blackened ruins; whilst the children wandered through the streets, a prey to beings who were wild beasts in everything save the superior ingenuity of man to agonize and torture his victims.

Frightful as the day had been, the night was yet more hideous; since to the horrors which were seen was added the greater horror of deeds which might be committed in the darkness; or, if they were seen, it was by the lurid glare of burning buildings,—the red flames of which—flung upon the stained and brutal faces, the torn and tattered garments, of men and women who danced and howled around the scene of ruin they had caused—made the whole aspect of affairs seem more like a gathering of fiends rejoicing in Pandemonium than aught with which creatures of flesh and blood had to do.

Standing on some elevated point, looking over the great city, which presented, as usual, at night, a solemn and impressive show, the spectator was thrilled with a fearful admiration by the sights and sounds which gave to it a mysterious and awful interest. A thousand fires streamed up against the sky, making darkness visible; and from all sides came a combination of noises such as might be heard from an asylum in which were gathered the madmen of the world.

The next morning's sun rose on a city which was ruled by a reign of terror. Had the police possessed the heads of Hydra and the arms of Briareus, and had these heads all seen, these arms all fought, they would have been powerless against the multitude of opposers. Outbreaks were made, crowds gathered, houses burned, streets barricaded, fights enacted, in a score of places at once. Where the officers appeared they were irretrievably beaten and overcome; their stand, were it ever so short, but inflaming the passions of the mob to fresh deeds of violence. Stores were closed; the business portion of the city deserted; the large works and factories emptied of men, who had been sent home by their employers, or were swept into the ranks of the marauding bands. The city cars, omnibuses, hacks, were unable to run, and remained under shelter. Every telegraph wire was cut, the posts torn up, the operators driven from their offices. The mayor, seeing that civil power was helpless to stem this tide, desired to call the military to his aid, and place the city under martial law, but was opposed by the Governor,—a governor, who, but a few days before, had pronounced the war a failure; and not only predicted, but encouraged this mob rule, which was now crushing everything beneath its heavy and ensanguined feet. This man, through almost two days of these awful scenes, remained at a quiet seaside retreat but a few miles from the city. Coming to it on the afternoon of the

second day,—instead of ordering cannon planted in the
streets, giving these creatures opportunity to retire to their
homes, and, in the event of refusal, blowing them there by
powder and ball,—he first went to the point where was
collected the chiefest mob, and proceeded to address them.
Before him stood incendiaries, thieves, and murderers,
who even then were sacking dwelling-houses, and
butchering powerless and inoffensive beings. These
wretches he apostrophized as "My friends," repeating the
title again and again in the course of his harangue, assuring
them that he was there as a proof of his friendship,—
which he had demonstrated by "sending his adjutant-gen-
eral to Washington, to have the draft stopped"; begging
them to "wait for his return"; "to separate now as good citizens"; with the promise that they "might assemble again
whenever they wished to so do"; meanwhile, he would
"take care of their rights." This model speech was incessantly interrupted by tremendous cheering and frantic
demonstrations of delight,—one great fellow almost
crushing the Governor in his enthusiastic embrace. This
ended, he entered a carriage, and was driven through the
blackened, smoking scenes of Monday's devastations;
through fresh vistas of outrage, of the day's execution;
bland, gracious, smiling. Wherever he appeared, cheer
upon cheer rent the air from these crowds of drunken blas-
phemers; and in one place the carriage in which he sat was
actually lifted from the ground, and carried some rods, by
hands yet red with deeds of arson and murder; while from

all sides voices cried out, "Will ye stop the draft, Gov'nur?" "Bully boy!" "Ye're the man for us!" "Hooray for Gov'nur Saymoor!" Thus, through the midst of this admiring and applauding crowd, this high officer of the law, sworn to maintain public peace, moved to his hotel, where he was met by a despatch from Washington, informing him that five regiments were under arms and on their way to put an end to this bloody assistance to the Southern war.

His allies in newspaper offices attempted to throw the blame upon the loyal press and portion of the community. This was but a repetition of the cry, raised by traitors in arms, that the government, struggling for life in their deadly hold, was responsible for the war: "If thou wouldst but consent to be murdered peaceably, there could be no strife."

These editors outraged common sense, truth, and decency, by speaking of the riots as an "uprising of the people to defend their liberties,"—"an opposition on the part of the workingmen to an unjust and oppressive law, enacted in favor of the men of wealth and standing." As though the *people* of the great metropolis were incendiaries, robbers, and assassins; as though the poor were to demonstrate their indignation against the rich by hunting and stoning defenceless women and children; torturing and murdering men whose only offence was the color God gave them, or men wearing the self-same uniform as that which they declared was to be thrust upon them at the behest of the rich and the great.

It was absurd and futile to characterize this new Reign of Terror as anything but an effort on the part of Northern rebels to help Southern ones, at the most critical moment of the war,—with the State militia and available troops absent in a neighboring Commonwealth,—and the loyal people unprepared. These editors and their coadjutors, men of brains and ability, were of that most poisonous growth,—traitors to the Government and the flag of their country,—renegade Americans. Let it, however, be written plainly and graven deeply, that the tribes of savages—the hordes of ruffians—found ready to do their loathsome bidding, were not of native growth, nor American born.

While it is true that there were some glib-tongued fellows who spoke the language without foreign accent, all of them of the lowest order of Democratic ward-politicians, of creatures skulking from the outstretched arm of avenging law; while the most degraded of the German population were represented; while it is also true that there were Irish, and Catholic Irish too,—industrious, sober, intelligent people,—who indignantly refused participation in these outrages, and mourned over the barbarities which were disgracing their national name; it is pre-eminently true,—proven by thousands of witnesses, and testified to by numberless tongues,—that the masses, the rank and file, the almost entire body of rioters, were the worst classes of Irish emigrants, infuriated by artful appeals, and maddened by the atrocious whiskey of thousands of grog-shops.

By far the most infamous part of these cruelties was that which wreaked every species of torture and lingering death upon the colored people of the city,—men, women, and children, old and young, strong and feeble alike. Hundreds of these fell victims to the prejudice fostered by public opinion, incorporated in our statute-books, sanctioned by our laws, which here and thus found legitimate outgrowth and action. The horrors which blanched the face of Christendom were but the bloody harvest of fields sown by society, by cultured men and women, by speech, and book, and press, by professions and politics, nay, by the pulpit itself, and the men who there make God's truth a lie,—garbling or denying the inspired declaration that "He has made of one blood all people to dwell upon the face of the earth"; and that he, the All-Just and Merciful One, "is no respecter of persons."

This riot, begun ostensibly to oppose the enforcement of a single law, developed itself into a burning and pillaging assault upon the homes and property of peaceful citizens. To realize this, it was only necessary to walk the streets, if that were possible, through those days of riot and conflagration, observe the materials gathered into the vast, moving multitudes, and scrutinize the faces of those of whom they were composed,—deformed, idiotic, drunken, imbecile, poverty-stricken; seamed with every line which wretchedness could draw or vicious habits and associations delve. To walk these streets and look upon these faces was like a fearful witnessing in perspective of the last day, when the secrets of life, more loathsome than those of death, shall be laid bare in all their hideous deformity and ghastly shame.

The knowledge of these people and their deeds was sufficient to create a paralysis of fear, even where they were not seen. Indeed, there was terror everywhere. High and low, rich and poor, cultured and ignorant, all shivered in its awful grasp. Upon stately avenues and noisome alleys it fell with the like blackness of darkness. Women cried aloud to God with the same agonized entreaty from knees bent on velvet carpets or bare and dingy floors. Men wandered up and down, prisoners in their own homes, and cursed or prayed with equal fury or intensity whether the homes were simple or splendid. Here one surveyed all his costly store of rare and exquisite surroundings, and shook his head as he gazed, ominous and foreboding. There, another of darker hue peered out from garret casement, or cellar light, or broken window-pane, and, shuddering, watched some woman stoned and beaten till she died; some child shot down, while thousands of heavy, brutal feet trod over it till the hard stones were red with its blood, and the little prostrate form, yet warm, lost every likeness of humanity, and lay there, a sickening mass of mangled flesh and bones; some man assaulted, clubbed, overborne, left wounded or dying or dead, as he fell, or tied to some convenient tree or lamp-post to be hacked and hewn, or flayed and roasted, yet living, where he hung,—and watching this, and cowering as he watched, held his breath, and waited his own turn, not knowing when it might come.

CHAPTER XIX

"In breathless quiet, after all their ills."
ARNOLD

A body of these wretches, fresh from some act of rapine and pillage, had seen Mrs. Franklin, hastening home, and, opening the hue and cry, had started in full chase after her. Struck by sticks and stones that darkened the air, twice down, fleeing as those only do who flee for life, she gained her own house, thinking there to find security. Vain hope! the door was battered in, the windows demolished, the puny barriers between the room in which they were gathered and the creatures in pursuit, speedily destroyed,—and these three turned to face death.

By chance, Surrey had his sword at his side, and, tearing this from its scabbard, sprang to the defence,—a gallant intent, but what could one weapon and one arm do against such odds as these? He was speedily beaten down

275

and flung aside by the miscreants who swarmed into the room. It was marvellous they did not kill him outright. Doubtless they would have done so but for the face propped against the pillows, which caught their hungry eyes. Soldier and woman were alike forgotten at sight of this dying boy. Here was a foeman worthy their steel. They gathered about him, and with savage hands struck at him and the bed upon which he lay.

A pause for a moment to hold consultation, crowded with oaths and jeers and curses; obscenity and blasphemy too hideous to read or record,—then the cruel hands tore him from his bed, dragged him over the prostrate body of his mother, past the senseless form of his brave young defender, out to the street. Here they propped him against a tree, to mock and torment him; to prick him, wound him, torture him; to task endurance to its utmost limit, but not to extinguish life. These savages had no such mercy as this in their souls; and when, once or twice he fell away into insensibility, a cut or blow administered with devilish skill or strength, restored him to anguish and to life.

Surrey, bewildered and dizzy, had recovered consciousness, and sat gazing vacantly around him, till the cries and yells without, the agonized face within, thrilled every nerve into feeling. Starting up, he rushed to the window, but recoiled at the awful sight. Here, he saw, there was no human power within reach or call that could interfere. The whole block, from street to street, was crowded with men and boys, armed with the armory of the street, and rejoicing like veritable fiends of hell over the pangs of their victim.

Even in the moment he stood there he beheld that which would haunt his memory, did it endure for a century. At last, tired of their sport, some of those who were just about Abram had tied a rope about his body, and raised him to the nearest branch of an overhanging tree; then, heaping under him the sticks and clubs which were flung them from all sides, set fire to the dry, inflammable pile, and watched, for the moment silent, to see it burn.

Surrey fled to the other side of the room, and, cowering down, buried his head in his arm to shut out the awful sight and sounds. But his mother,—O marvellous, inscrutable mystery of mother-love!—his mother knelt by the open window, near which hung her boy, and prayed aloud, that he might hear, for the wrung body and passing soul. Great God! that such things were possible, and thy heavens fell not! Through the sound of falling blows, reviling oaths, and hideous blasphemy, through the crackling of burning fagots and lifting flames, there went out no cry for mercy, no shriek of pain, no wail of despair. But when the torture was almost ended, and nature had yielded to this work of fiends, the dying face was turned towards his mother,—the eyes, dim with the veil that falls between time and eternity, seeking her eyes with their latest glance,—the voice, not weak, but clear and thrilling even in death, cried for her ear, "Be of good cheer, mother! they may kill the body, but they cannot touch the

soul!" and even with the words the great soul walked with
God.

After a while the mob melted out of the street to seek new
scenes of ravage and death; not, however, till they had
marked the house, as those within learned, for the purpose
of returning, if it should so please them, at some future
time.

When they were all gone, and the way was clear, these
two—the mother that bore him, the elegant patrician who
instinctively shrank from all unpleasant and painful
things—took down the poor charred body, and carrying it
carefully and tenderly into the house of a trembling
neighbor, who yet opened her doors and bade them in,
composed it decently for its final rest.

It was drawing towards evening, and Surrey was eager
to get away from this terrible region,—both to take the
heart-stricken woman, thus thrown upon his care, to some
place of rest and safety, and to reassure Francesca, who, he
knew, would be filled with maddening anxiety and fear at
his long absence.

At length they ventured forth: no one was in the
square;—turned at Fortieth Street,—all clear;—went on
with hasty steps to the Avenue,—not a soul in sight.
"Safe,—thank God!" exclaimed Surrey, as he hurried his
companion onward. Half the space to their destination had

been crossed, when a band of rioters, rushing down the street from the sack and burning of the Orphan Asylum, came upon them. Defence seemed utterly vain. Every house was shut; its windows closed and barred; its inmates gathered in some rear room. Escape and hope appeared alike impossible; but Surrey, flinging his charge behind him, with drawn sword, face to the on-sweeping hordes, backed down the street. The combination—a negro woman, a soldier's uniform—intensified the mad fury of the mob, which was nevertheless held at bay by the heroic front and gleaming steel of their single adversary. Only for a moment! Then, not venturing near him, a shower of bricks and stones hurtled through the air, falling about and upon him.

At this instant a voice called, "This way! this way! For God's sake! quick! quick!" and he saw a friendly black face and hand thrust from an area window. Still covering with his body his defenceless charge, he moved rapidly towards this refuge. Rapid as was the motion, it was not speedy enough; he reached the railing, caught her with his one powerful arm, imbued now with a giant's strength, flung her over to the waiting hands that seized and dragged her in, pausing for an instant, ere he leaped himself, to beat back a half-dozen of the foremost miscreants, who would else have captured their prey, just vanishing from sight. Sublime, yet fatal delay! but an instant, yet in that instant a thousand forms surrounded him, disarmed him, overcame him, and beat him down.

Meanwhile what of Francesca? The morning passed, and with its passing came terrible rumors of assault and death. The afternoon began, wore on,—the rumors deepened to details of awful facts and realities; and he—he, with his courage, his fatal dress—was absent, was on those death-crowded streets. She wandered from room to room, forgetting her reserve, and accosting every soul she met for later news,—for information which, received, did but torture her with more intolerable pangs, and send her to her knees; though, kneeling, she could not pray, only cry out in some dumb, inarticulate fashion, "God be merciful!"

The afternoon was spent; the day gone; the summer twilight deepening into night; and still he did not come. She had caught up her hat and mantle with some insane intention of rushing into the wide, wild city, on a frenzied search, when two gentlemen passing by her door, talking of the all-absorbing theme, arrested her ear and attention.

"The house ought to be guarded! These devils will be here presently,—they are on the Avenue now."

"Good God! are you certain?"

"Certain."

"You may well be," said a third voice, as another step joined theirs. "They are just above Thirtieth Street. I was coming down the Avenue, and saw them myself. I don't know what my fate would have been in this dress,"— Francesca knew from this that he who talked was of the police or soldiery,—"but they were engaged in fighting a young officer, who made a splendid defence before they cut him down; his courage was magnificent. It makes my blood curdle to think of it. A fair-haired, gallant-looking fellow, with only one arm. I could do nothing for him, of course, and should have been killed had I stayed; so I ran for life. But I don't think I'll ever quite forgive myself for not rushing to the rescue, and taking my chance with him."

She did not stay to hear the closing words. Out of the room, past them, like a spirit,—through the broad halls,— down the wide stairways,—on to the street,—up the long street, deserted here, but O, with what a crowd beyond!

A company of soldiers, paltry in number, yet each with loaded rifle and bayonet set, charged past her at double-quick upon this crowd, which gave way slowly and sullenly at its approach, holding with desperate ferocity and determination to whatever ghastly work had been employing their hands,—dropped at last,—left on the stones,—the soldiers between it and the mob,—silent, motionless,—she saw it, and knew it where it lay. O woful sight and knowledge for loving eyes and bursting heart!

Ere she reached it some last stones were flung by the retreating crowd, a last shot fired in the air,—fired at random, but speeding with as unerring aim to her aching, anguished breast, death-freighted and life-destroying,—but not till she had reached her destined point and end; not till her feet failed close to that bruised and silent form; not till she had sunk beside it, gathered it in her fair young arms, and pillowed its beautiful head—from which streamed golden hair, dabbled and blood-bestained—upon her faithful heart.

There it stirred; the eyes unclosed to meet hers, a gleam of divine love shining through their fading fire; the battered, stiffened arm lifted, as to fold her in the old familiar caress. "Darling—die—to make—free"—came in gasps from the sweet, yet whitening lips. Then she lay still. Where his breath blew across her hair it waved, and her bosom moved above the slow and labored beating of his heart; but, save for this, she was as quiet as the peaceful dead within their graves,—and, like them, done with the noise and strife of time forever.

For him,—the shadows deepened where he lay,—the stars came out one by one, looking down with clear and solemn eyes upon this wreck of fair and beautiful things, wrought by earthly hate and the awful passions of men,— then veiled their light in heavy and sombre clouds. The rain fell upon the noble face and floating, sunny hair,— washing them free of soil, and dark and fearful stains; moistening the fevered, burning lips, and cooling the bruised and aching frame. How passed the long night with that half-insensible soul? God knoweth. The secrets of that are hidden in the eternity to which it now belongs. Questionless, ministering spirits drew near, freighted with balm and inspiration; for when the shadows fled, and the next morning's sun shone upon these silent forms, it revealed faces radiant as with some celestial fire, and beatified as reflecting the smile of God.

✳   ✳   ✳   ✳   ✳

The inmates of the house before which lay this solemn mystery, rising to face a new-made day, looking out from their windows to mark what traces were left of last night's devastations, beheld this awful yet sublime sight.

"A prejudice which, I trust, will never end," had Mr. Surrey said, in bidding adieu to his son but a few short hours before. This prejudice, living and active, had now thus brought death and desolation to his own doors. "How unsearchable are the judgments of God, and his ways past finding out!"

CHAPTER XX

"Drink,—for thy necessity is yet greater than mine."
SIR PHILIP SIDNEY

THE hospital boat, going out of Beaufort, was a sad, yet great sight. It was but necessary to look around it to see that the men here gathered had stood on the slippery battle-sod, and scorned to flinch. You heard no cries, scarcely a groan; whatever anguish wrung them as they were lifted into their berths, or were turned or raised for comfort, found little outward sign,—a long, gasping breath now and then; a suppressed exclamation; sometimes a laugh, to cover what would else be a cry of mortal agony; almost no swearing; these men had been too near the awful realities of death and eternity, some of them were still too near, to make a mock at either. Having demonstrated themselves heroes in action, they would, one and all, be equally heroes in the hour of suffering, or on the bed of lingering death.

Jim, so wounded as to make every movement a pang, had been carefully carried in on a stretcher, and as carefully lifted into a middle berth.

"Good," said one of the men, as he eased him down on his pillow.

"What's good?" queried Jim.

"The berth; middle berth. Put you in as easy as into the lowest one: bad lifting such a leg as yours into the top one, and it's the comfortablest of the three when you're in."

"O, that's it, is it? all right; glad I'm here then; getting in didn't hurt more than a flea-bite,"—saying which Jim turned his face away to put his teeth down hard on a lip already bleeding. The wrench to his shattered leg was excruciating, "But then," as he announced to himself, "no snivelling, James; you're not going to make a spooney of yourself." Presently he moved, and lay quietly watching the others they were bringing in.

"Why!" he called, "that's Bertie Curtis, ain't it?" as a slight, beautiful-faced boy was carried past him, and raised to his place.

"Yes, it is," answered one of the men, shortly, to cover some strong feeling.

Jim leaned out of his berth, regardless of his protesting leg, canteen in hand. "Here, Bertie!" he called, "my canteen's full of fresh water, just filled. I know it'll taste good to you."

The boy's fine face flushed. "O, thank you, Given, it would taste deliciously, but I can't take it,"—glancing down. Jim followed the look, to see that both arms were gone, close to the graceful, boyish form; seeing which his face twitched painfully,—not with his own suffering,—and for a moment words failed him. Just then came up one of the sanitary nurses with some cooling drink, and fresh, wet bandages for the fevered stumps.

Great drops were standing on Bertie's forehead, and ominous gray shadows had already settled about the mouth, and under the long, shut lashes. Looking at the face, so young, so refined, some mother's pride and darling, the nurse brushed back tenderly the fair hair, murmuring, "Poor fellow!"

The eyes unclosed quickly: "There are no poor fellows here, sir!" he said.

"Well, brave fellow, then!"

"I did but do my duty,"—a smile breaking through the gathering mists.

Here some poor fellow,—poor indeed,—delirious with fever, called out, "Mother! mother! I want to see my mother!"

Tears rushed to the clear, steady eyes, dimmed them, dropped down unchecked upon the face. The nurse, with a sob choking in his throat, softly raised his hand to brush them away. "Mother," Bertie whispered,—"mother!" and was gone where God wipes away the tears from all eyes.

For the space of five minutes, as Jim said afterwards, in telling about it, "that boat was like a meeting-house." Used as they were to death in all forms, more than one brave fellow's eye was dim as the silent shape was carried away to make place for the stricken living,—one of whom was directly brought in, and the stretcher put down near Jim.

"What's up?" he called, for the man's face was turned from him, and his wounded body so covered as to give no clew to its condition. "What's wrong?" seeing the bearers did not offer to lift him, and that they were anxiously scanning the long rows of berths.

"Berth's wrong," one of them answered.

"What's the matter with the berth?"

"Matter enough! not a middle one nor a lower one empty."

"Well," called a wounded boy from the third tier, "plenty of room up here; sky-parlor,—airy lodgings,—all fine,—I see a lot of empty houses that'll take him in."

"Like enough,—but he's about blown to pieces," said the bearer in a low voice, "and it'll be aw—ful putting him up there; however,"—commencing to take off the light cover.

"Helloa!" cried Jim, "that's a dilapidated-looking leg,"—his head out, looking at it. "Stop a bit!"—body half after the head,—"you just stop that, and come here and catch hold of a fellow; now put me up there. I reckon I'll bear hoisting better'n he will, anyway. Ugh! ah! um! owh! here we are! bully!"

If Jim had been of the fainting or praying order he would certainly have fainted or prayed; as it was, he said "Bully!" but lay for a while thereafter still as a mouse.

"Given, you're a brick!" one of the boys was apostro-
phizing him. Jim took no notice. "And your man's in, safe
and sound"; he turned at that, and leaned forward, as well
as he could, to look at the occupant of his late bed.

"Jemime!" he cried, when he saw the face. "I say, boys!
it's Ercildoune—Robert—flag—Wagner—hurray—let's
give three cheers for the color-sergeant,—long may he
wave!"

The men, propped up or lying down, gave the three
cheers with a will, and then three more; and then,
delighted with their performance, three more after that,
Jim winding up the whole with an "a-a-ah,-Tiger!" that
made them all laugh; then relapsing into silence and a hard
battle with pain.

A weary voyage,—a weary journey thereafter to the
Northern hospitals,—some dying by the way, and lowered
through the shifting, restless waves, or buried with hasty
yet kindly hands in alien soil,—accounted strangers and
foemen in the land of their birth. God grant that no tread
of rebellion in the years to come, nor thunder of contending armies, may disturb their peace!

Some stopped in the heat and dust of Washington to
be nursed and tended in the great barracks of hospitals,—
uncomfortable-looking without, clean and spacious and
admirable within; some to their homes, on long-desired
and eagerly welcomed furloughs, there to be cured
speedily, the body swayed by the mind; some to suffer and
die; some to struggle against winds and tides of mortality

and conquer,—yet scarred and maimed; some to go out, as
giants refreshed with new wine, to take their places once
more in the great conflict, and fight there faithfully to the
end.

Among these last was Jim; but not till after many a hard
battle, and buffet, and back-set did life triumph and
strength prevail. One thing which sadly retarded his
recovery was his incessant anxiety about Sallie, and his
longing to see her once more. He had himself, after his
first hurt, written her that he was slightly wounded; but
when he reached Washington, and the surgeon, looking at
his shattered leg, talked about amputation and death, Jim
decided that Sallie should not know a word of all this till
something definite was pronounced.

"She oughtn't to have an ugly, one-legged fellow," he
said, "to drag round with her; and, if she knows how bad
it is, she'll post straight down here, to nurse and look after
me,—I know her! and she'll have me in the end, out of
sheer pity; and I ain't going to take any such mean advantage of her: no, sir-ee, not if I know myself. If I get well,
safe and sound, I'll go to her; and, if I'm going to die, I'll
send for her; so I'll wait,"—which he did.

He found, however, that it was a great deal easier
making the decision, than keeping it when made. Sallie,
hearing nothing from him,—supposing him still in the
South,—fearful as she had all along been that she stood on
uncertain ground,—Mrs. Surrey away in New York,—and
Robert Ercildoune, as the papers asserted in their pub-

lished lists, mortally wounded,—having no indirect means of communication with him, and fearing to write again without some sign from him,—was sorrowing in silence at home.

The silence reacted on him; not realizing its cause he grew fretful and impatient, and the fretfulness and impatience told on his leg, intensified his fever, and put the day of recovery—if recovery it was to be—farther into the future.

"See here, my man,"—said the quick little surgeon one day, "you're worrying about something. This'll never do; if you don't stop it, you'll die, as sure as fate; and you might as well make up your mind to it at once,—so, now!"

"Well, sir," answered Jim, "it's as good a time to die now, I reckon, as often happens; but I ain't dead yet, not by a long shot; and I ain't going to die neither; so, now, yourself!"

The doctor laughed. "All right; if you'll get up that spirit, and keep it, I'll bet my pile on your recovery,—but you'll have to stop fretting. You've got something on your mind that's troubling you; and the sooner you get rid of it, if you can, the better. That's all I've got to say." And he marched off.

"Get rid of it," mused Jim, "how in thunder'll I get rid of it if I don't hear from Sallie? Let me see—ah! I have it!" and looking more cheerful on the instant he lay still, watching for the doctor to come down the ward once more. "Helloa!" he called, then. "Helloa!" responded the doctor, coming over to him, "what's the go now? you're improved already."

"Got any objection to telling a lie?"—this might be called coming to the point.

"That depends—" said the doctor.

"Well, all's fair in love and war, they say. This is for love. Help a fellow?"

"Of course,—if I can,—and the fellow's a good one, like Jim Given. What is it you want?"

"Well, I want a letter written, and I can't do it myself, you know,"—looking down at his still bandaged arm,— "likewise I want a lie told in it, and these ladies here are all angels, and of course you can't ask an angel to tell a lie,— no offence to you; so if you can take the time, and'll do it, I'll stand your everlasting debtor, and shoulder the responsibility if you're afraid of the weight."

"What sort of a lie?"

"A capital one; listen. I want a young lady to know that I'm wounded in the arm,—you see? not bad; nor nothing over which she need worry, and nothing that hurts me much; and I ain't damaged in any other way; legs not mentioned in this concern,—you understand?" The doctor nodded. "But it's tied up my hand, so that I have to get you to say all this for me. I'll be well pretty soon; and, if I can get a furlough, I'll be up in Philadelphia in a jiffy,—so she can just prepare for the infliction, &c. Comprendy? And'll you do it?"

"Of course I will, if you don't want the truth told, and

the fib'll do you any good; and, upon my word, the way you're looking I really think it will. So now for it."

Thus the letter was written, and read, and re-read, to make sure that there was nothing in it to alarm Sallie; and, being satisfactory on that head, was finally sent away, to rejoice the poor girl who had waited, and watched, and hoped for it through such a weary time. When she answered it, her letter was so full of happiness and solici-tude, and a love that, in spite of herself, spoke out in every line, that Jim furtively kissed it, and read it into tatters in the first few hours of its possession; then tucking it away in his hospital shirt, over his heart, proceeded to get well as fast as fast could be.

"Well," said the doctor, a few weeks afterwards, as Jim was going home on his coveted sick-leave, "Mr. Thomas Carlyle calls fibs wind-bags. If that singular remedy would work to such a charm with all my men, I'd tell lies with impunity. Good by, Jim, and the best of good luck to you."

"The same to you, Doctor, and I hope you may always find a friend in need, to lie for you. Good by, and God bless you!" wringing his hand hard,—"and now, hurrah for home!"

"Hurrah it is!" cried the little surgeon after him, as, happy and proud, he limped down the ward, and turned his face towards home.

CHAPTER XXI

"Youth on the prow, and Pleasure at the helm."

GRAY

J IM scarcely felt the jolting of the ambulance over the city stones, and his impatience and eagerness to get across the intervening space made dust, and heat, and weariness of travel seem but as feather weights, not to be cared for, nor indeed considered at all; though, in fact, his arm complained, and his leg ached distressingly, and he was faint and weak without confessing it long before the tiresome journey reached its end.

"No matter," he said to himself; "it'll be all well, or forgotten, at least, when I see Sallie once more; and so, what odds?"

The end was gained at last, and he would have gone to her fast as certain Rosinantes, yclept hackhorses, could carry him, but, stopping for a moment to consider, he

thought, "No, that will never do! Go to her looking like
such a guy? Nary time. I'll get scrubbed, and put on a
clean shirt, and make myself decent, before she sees me.
She always used to look nice as a new pin, and she liked
me to look so too; so I'd better put my best foot foremost
when she hasn't laid eyes on me for such an age. I'm fright
enough, anyway, goodness knows, with my thinness, and
my old lame leg; so—" sticking his head out of the
window, and using his lungs with astonishing vigor—
"Driver! streak like lightning, will you, to the 'Merchants'?
and you shall have extra fare."

"Hold your blab there," growled the driver; "I ain't
such a pig yet as to take double fare from a wounded soldier. You'll pay me well at half-price,—when we get
where you want to go,"—which they did soon.

"No!" said Jehu, thrusting back part of the money, "I
ain't agoin' to take it, so you needn't poke it out at me. I'm
all right; or, if I ain't, I'll make it up on the next broadcloth or officer I carry; never you fear! us fellows knows
how to take care of ourselves, you'd better believe!" which
statement Jim would have known to be truth, without the
necessity of repetition, had he been one of the aforesaid
"broadcloths," or "officers," and thus better acquainted
with the genus hack-driver in the ordinary exercise of its
profession.

As it was; he shook hands with the fellow, pocketed the
surplus change, made his way into the hotel, was in his
room, in his bath, under the barber's hands, cleaned,

shaved, brushed, polished, shining,—as he himself would have declared, "in a jiffy." Then, deciding himself to be presentable to the lady of his heart, took his crutch and sallied forth, as good-looking a young fellow, spite of the wooden appendage, as any the sun shone upon in all the big city, and as happy, as it was bright.

He knew where to go, and, by help of street-cars and other legs than his own, he was there speedily. He knew the very room towards which to turn; and, reaching it, paused to look in through the half-open door,—delighted thus to watch and listen for a little space unseen.

Sallie was sitting, her handsome head bent over her sewing,—Frankie gambolling about the floor.

"O sis, *don't* you wish Jim would come home?" queried the youngster. "I do,—I wish he'd come right straight away."

"Right straight away? What do *you* want to see Jim for?"

"O, 'cause he's nice; and 'cause he'll take me to the Theayter; and 'cause he'll treat,—apples, and peanuts, and candy, you know, and—and—ice-cream," wiping the beads from his little red face,—the last desideratum evidently suggested by the fiery summer heat. "I say, Sallie!"—a pause—"won't you get me some ice-cream this evening?"

"Yes, Bobbity, if you'll be a good boy."

Frankie looked dubious over that proposition. Jim never made any such stipulations: so, after another pause, in which he was probably considering the whole subject with due and becoming gravity,—evidently desiring to hear his own wish propped up by somebody else's seconding,—he broke out again, "Now, Sallie, don't you just wish Jim would come home?"

"O Frankie, don't I?" cried the girl, dropping her work, and stretching out her empty arms as though she would clasp some shape in the air.

Frankie, poor child! innocently imagining the proffered embrace was for him, ran forward, for he was an affectionate little soul, to give Sallie a good hug, but found himself literally left out in the cold; no arms to meet, and no Sallie, indeed, to touch him. Something big, burly, and blue loomed up on his sight,—something that was doing its best to crush Sallie bodily, and to devour what was not crushed; something that could say nothing by reason of its lips being so much more pleasantly engaged, and whose face was invisible through its extraordinary proximity to somebody else's face and hair.

Frankie, finding he could gain neither sight nor sound of notice, began to howl. But as neither of the hard-hearted creatures seemed to care for the poor little chap's howling, he fell upon the coat-tails of the big blue obstruction, and pulled at them lustily,—not to say viciously,—till their owner turned, and beheld him panting and fiery.

"Helloa, youngster! what's to pay now?"

"Wow! if 'tain't Jim. Hooray!" screeched the youngster, first embracing the blue legs, and then proceeding to execute a dance upon his head. "Te, te, di di, idde i-dum," he sang, coming feet down, finally.

Evidently the bad boy's language had been corrupted by his street *confrères*; it was a missionary ground upon which Sallie entered, more or less faithfully, every day to hoe and weed; but of this last specimen-plant she took no notice, save to laugh as Jim, catching him up, first kissed him, then gave him a shake and a small spank, and, thrusting a piece of currency into his hand, whisked him outside the door with a "Come, shaver, decamp, and treat yourself to-day," and had it shut and fastened in a twinkling.

"O Jim!" she cried then, her soul in her handsome eyes.

"O Sallie!"—and he had her fast and tight once more.

An ineffable blank, punctuated liberally with sounding exclamation points, and strongly marked periods,—though how or why a blank should be punctuated at all, only blissful lovers could possibly define.

"Jim, dear Jim!" whispering it, and snuggling her blushing face closer to the faded blue, "can you love me after all that has happened?"

"Come now! *can* I love you, my beauty? Slightly, I should think. O, te, te, di di, idde i-dum,"—singing Frank's little song with his big, gay voice,—"I'm happy as a king."

Happy as a king, that was plain enough. And what shall

be said of her, as he sat down, and, resting the wounded leg—stiff and sore yet,—held Sallie on his other knee,—then fell to admiring her while she stroked his mustache and his crisp, curling hair, looking at both and at him altogether with an expression of contented adoration in her eyes.

Frank, tired of prowling round the door, candy in hand, here thrust his head in at the window, and, unfortunately for his plans, sneezed. "Mutual-admiration society!" he cried at that, seeing that he was detected in any case, and running away,—his fun spoiled as soon as it began.

"We *are* a handsome couple," laughed Jim, holding back her face between both hands,—"ain't we, now?"

Yes, they were,—no mistake about that, handsome as pictures.

And merry as birds, through all of his short stay. They would see no danger in the future: Jim had been scathed in time past so often, yet come out safe and sound, that they would have no fear for what was to befall him in time to come. If they had, neither showed it to the other. Jim thought, "Sallie would break her heart, if she knew just what is down there,—so it would be a pity to talk about it"; and Sallie thought, "It's right for Jim to go, and I won't say a word to keep him back, no matter how I feel."

The furlough was soon—ah! how soon—out, the days of happiness over; and Jim, holding her in a last close embrace, said his farewell: "Come, Sallie, you're not to cry now, and make me a coward. It'll only be for a little while; the Rebs *can't* stand it much longer, and then—"

"Ah, Jim! but if you should—"

"Yes, but I sha'n't, you see; not a bit of it; don't you go to think it. 'I bear'—what is it? O—'a charmed life,' as Mr. Macbeth says, and you'll see me back right and tight, and up to time. One kiss more, dear. God bless you! good by!" and he was gone.

She leaned out of the window,—she smiled after him, kissed her hand, waved her handkerchief, so long as he could see them,—till he had turned a corner way down the street,—and smile, and hand, and handkerchief were lost to his sight; then flung herself on the floor, and cried as though her very heart would break. "God send him home,—send him safe and soon home!" she implored; entreaty made for how many loved ones, by how many aching hearts, that speedily lost the need of saying amen to any such petition,—the prayer for the living lost in mourning for the dead. Heaven grant that no soul that reads this ever may have the like cause to offer such prayer again!

CHAPTER XXII

"When we see the dishonor of a thing, then it is time to renounce it."
PLUTARCH

A LETTER which Sallie wrote to Jim a few weeks after his departure tells its own story, and hence shall be repeated here.

PHILADELPHIA, October 29, 1863.

DEAR JIM:—

I take my pen in hand this morning to write you a letter, and to tell you the news, though I don't know much of the last except about Frankie and myself. However, I suppose you will care more to hear that than any other, so I will begin.

Maybe you will be surprised to hear that Frankie and

I are at Mr. Ercildoune's. Well, we are,—and I will tell you
how it came about. Not long after you went away, Frank
began to pine, and look droopy. There wasn't any use in
giving him medicine, for it didn't do him a bit of good.
He couldn't eat, and he didn't sleep, and I was at my wits'
ends to know what to do for him.

One day Mrs. Lee,—that Mr. Ercildoune's house-
keeper,—an old English lady she is, and she's lived with
him ever since he was married, and before he came
here,—a real lady, too,—came in with some sewing, some
fine shirts for Mr. Robert Ercildoune. I asked after him,
and you'll be glad to know that he's recovering. He didn't
have to lose his leg, as they feared; and his arm is healing;
and the wound in his breast getting well. Mrs. Lee says
she's very sorry the stump isn't longer, so that he could
wear a Palmer arm,—but she's got no complaints to make;
they're only too glad and thankful to have him living at all,
after such a dreadful time.

While I was talking with her, Frankie called me from
the next room, and began to cry. You wouldn't have
known him,—he cried at everything, and was so fretful
and cross I could scarcely get along at all. When I got him
quiet, and came back, Mrs. Lee says, "What's the matter
with Frank?" so I told her I didn't know,—but would she
see him? Well, she saw him, and shook her head in a bad
sort of way that scared me awfully, and I suppose she saw
I was frightened, for she said, "All he wants is plenty of
fresh air, and good, wholesome country food and exer-

cise." I can tell you, spite of that, she went away, leaving me with heavy enough a heart.

The next day Mr. Ercildoune came in. How he is changed! I haven't seen him before since Mrs. Surrey died, and that of itself was enough to kill him, without this dreadful time about Mr. Robert.

"Good morning, Miss Sallie," says he, "how are you? and I'm glad to see you looking so well." So I told him I was well, and then he asked for Frankie. "Mrs. Lee tells me," he said, "that your little brother is quite ill, and that he needs country air and exercise. He can have them both at The Oaks; so if you'll get him ready, the carriage will come for you at whatever time you appoint. Mrs. Lee can find you plenty of work as long as you care to stay." He looked as if he wanted to say something more, but didn't; and I was just as sure as sure could be that it was something about Miss Francesca, probably about her having me out there so much; for his face looked so sad, and his lips trembled so, I knew that must be in his mind. And when I thought of it, and of such an awful fate as it was for her, so young, and handsome, and happy, like the great baby I am, I just threw my apron over my head, and burst out crying.

"Don't!" he said,—"don't!" in O, such a voice! It was like a knife going through me; and he went quick out of the room, and downstairs, without even saying good by.

Well, we came out the next day,—and I have plenty to do, and Frankie is getting real bright and strong. I can see

Mr. Ercildoune likes to have us here, because of the connection with Miss Francesca. She was so interested in us, and so kind to us, and he knows I loved her so very dearly,—and if it's any comfort to him I'm sure I'm glad to be here, without taking Frankie into the account,—for the poor gentleman looks so bowed and heart-broken that it makes one's heart ache just to see him. Mr. Robert isn't well enough to be about yet, but he sits up for a while every day, and is getting on—the doctor says—nicely. They both talk about you often; and Mr. Ercildoune, I can see, thinks everything of you for that good, kind deed of yours, when you and Mr. Robert were on the transport together. Dear Jim, he don't know you as well as I do, or he'd know that you couldn't help doing such things,—not if you tried.

I hope you'll like the box that comes with this. Mr. Robert had it packed for you in his own room, to see that everything went in that you'd like. Of course, as he's been a soldier himself, he knows better what they want than anybody else can.

Dear Jim, *do* take care of yourself; don't go and get wounded; and don't get sick; and, whatever you do, don't let the rebels take you prisoner, unless you want to drive me frantic. I think about you pretty much all the time, and pray for you, as well as I know how, every night when I go to bed, and am always

Your own loving

SALLIE.

"Wow!" said Jim, as he read, "she's in a good berth there." So she was,—and so she stayed. Frankie got quite well once more, and Sallie began to think of going, but Mr. Ercildoune evidently clung to her and to the sunshine which the bright little fellow cast through the house. Sallie was quite right in her supposition. Francesca had cared for this girl, had been kind to her and helped her,—and his heart went out to everything that reminded him of his dear, dead child. So it happened that autumn passed, and winter, and spring,—and still they stayed. In fact, she was domesticated in the house, and, for the first time in years, enjoyed the delightful sense of a home. Here, then, she set up her rest, and remained: here, when the "cruel war was over," the armies disbanded, the last regiments discharged, and Jimmy "came marching home," brown, handsome, and a captain, here he found her,—and from here he married and carried her away.

It was a happy little wedding, though nobody was there beside the essentials, save the family and a dear friend of Robert's, who was with him at the time, as he had been before and would be often again,—none other than William Surrey's favorite cousin and friend, Tom Russell.

The letter which Surrey had written never reached his hand till he lay almost dying from the effects of wounds and exposure, after he had been brought in safety to our lines by his faithful black friends, at Morris Island. Surrey had not mistaken his temper; gay, reckless fellow, as he was, he was a thorough gentleman, in whom could harbor no small spite, nor petty prejudice,—and without a mean fibre in his being. At a glance he took in the whole situation, and insisting upon being propped up in bed, with his own hand—though slowly, and as a work of magnitude—succeeded in writing a cordial letter of congratulation and affection, that would have been to Surrey like the grasp of a brother's hand in a strange and foreign country, had it ever reached his touch and eyes.

But even while Tom lay writing his letter, occasionally muttering, "They'll have a devilish hard time of it!" or "Poor young un!" or "She's one in a million!" or some such sentence which marked his feeling and care,—these two of whom he thought, to whose future he looked with such loving anxiety, were beyond the reach of human help or hindrance,—done alike with the sorrows and joys of time.

From a distance, with the help of a glass, and absorbing interest, he had followed the movements of the flag and its bearer, and had cheered, till he fainted from weakness and exhaustion, as he saw them safe at last. It was with delight that he found himself on the same transport with Ercildoune, and discovered in him the brother of the young girl for whom, in the past, he had had so pleasing and deep a regard, and whose present and future were so full of interest for him, in their new and nearer relations.

These two young men, unlike as they were in most particulars, were drawn together by an irresistible attraction. They had that common bond, always felt and recognized by those who possess it, of the gentle blood,—tastes and instincts in common, and a fine, chivalrous sentiment which each felt and thoroughly appreciated in the other. The friendship thus begun grew with the passing years, and was intensified a hundred fold by a portion of the past to which they rarely referred, but which lay always at the bottom of their hearts. They had each for those two who had lain dead together in the streets of New York the strongest and tenderest love,—and though it was not a tie about which they could talk, it bound them together as with chains of steel.

Russell was with Ercildoune at the time of the wedding, and entered into it heartily, as they all did. The result was, as has been written, the gayest and merriest of times. Sallie's dress, which Robert had given her, was a sight to behold; and the pretty jewels, which were a part of his gift, and the long veil, made her look, as Jim declared, "so handsome he didn't know her,"—though that must have been one of Jim's stories, or else he was in the habit of making love to strange ladies with extraordinary ease and effrontery.

The breakfast was another sight to behold. As Mary the cook said to Jane the housemaid, "If they'd been born kings and queens, Mrs. Lee couldn't have laid herself out more; it's grand, so it is,—just you go and see"; which Jane proceeded to do, and forthwith thereafter corroborated Mary's enthusiastic statement.

There were plenty of presents, too: and when it was all over, and they were in the carriage, to be sent to the sta-

tion, Mr. Ercildoune, holding Sallie's hand in farewell, left
there a bit of paper, "which is for you," he said. "God protect, and keep you happy, my child!" Then they were
gone, with many kind adieus and good wishes called and
sent after them. When they were seated in the cars, Sallie
looked at her bit of paper, and read on its outer covering,
"A wedding-gift to Sallie Howard from my dear daughter
Francesca," and found within the deed of a beautiful little
home. God bless her! say we, with Mr. Ercildoune. God
bless them both, and may they live long to enjoy it!

That afternoon, as Tom and Robert were driving,
Russell, noting the unwonted look of life and activity, and
the gay flags flung to the breeze, demanded what it all
meant. "Why," said he, "it is like a field day."

"It is so," answered Robert, "or what is the same; it is
election day."

"Bless my soul! so it is; and a soldier to be elected.
Have you voted?"

"No!"

"No? Here's a nice state of affairs! a fellow that'll get
his arm blown off for a flag, but won't take the trouble to
drop a scrap of paper for it. Come, I'll drive you over."

"You forget, Russell!"

"Forget? Nonsense! This isn't 1860, but 1865. I don't
forget; I remember. It is after the war now,—come."

"As you please," said Robert. He knew the disappointment that awaited his friend, but he would not thwart him
now.

There was a great crowd about the polling-office, and they all looked on with curious interest as the two young men came up. No demonstration was made, though a half-dozen brutal fellows uttered some coarse remarks.

"Hear the damned Rebs talk!" said a man in the army blue, who, with keen eyes, was observing the scene. "They're the same sort of stuff we licked in Carolina."

"Ay," said another, "but with a difference; blue led there; but gray'll come off winner here, or I'm mistaken."

Robert stood leaning upon his cane; a support which he would need for life, one empty sleeve pinned across his breast, over the scar from a deep and yet unhealed wound. The clear October sun shone down upon his form and face, upon the broad folds of the flag that waved in triumph above him, upon a country where wars and rumors of wars had ceased.

"Courage, man! what ails you?" whispered Russell, as he felt his comrade tremble; "it's a ballot in place of a bayonet, and all for the same cause; lay it down."

Robert put out his hand.

"Challenge the vote!" "Challenge the vote!" "No niggers here!" sounded from all sides.

The bit of paper which Ercildoune had placed on the window-ledge fluttered to the ground on the outer side, and, looking at Tom, Robert said quietly, "1860 or 1865?—is the war ended?"

"No!" answered Tom, taking his arm, and walking away. "No, my friend! so you and I will continue in the service."

"Not ended;—it is true! how and when will it be closed?"

"That is for the loyal people of America to decide," said Russell, as they turned their faces towards home.

How and when will it be closed? a question asked by the living and the dead,—to which America must respond.

Among the living is a vast army: black and white,— shattered and maimed, and blind: and these say, "Here we stand, shattered and maimed, that the body politic might be perfect! blind forever, that the glorious sun of liberty might shine abroad throughout the land, for all people, through all coming time."

And the dead speak too. From their crowded graves come voices of thrilling and persistent pathos, whispering, "Finish the work that has fallen from our nerveless hands. Let no weight of tyranny, nor taint of oppression, nor stain of wrong, cumber the soil nor darken the land we died to save."

NOTE

SINCE it is impossible for any one memory to carry the entire record of the war, it is well to state, that almost every scene in this book is copied from life, and that the incidents of battle and camp are part of the history of the great contest.

The story of Fort Wagner is one that needs no such emphasis, it is too thoroughly known; that of the Color-Sergeant, whose proper name is W. H. Carney, is taken from a letter written by General M. S. Littlefield to Colonel A. G. Browne, Secretary to Governor Andrew.

From the *New York Tribune* and the *Providence Journal* were taken the accounts of the finding of Hunt, the coming of the slaves into a South Carolina camp, and the voluntary carrying, by black men, ere they were enlisted, of a schooner into the fight at Newbern. Than these two papers, none were considered more reliable and trustworthy in their war record.

WHAT ANSWER?

Almost every paper in the North published the narrative of the black man pushing off the boat, for which an official report is responsible. The boat was a flat-boat, with a company of soldiers on board; and the battery under the fire of which it fell was at Rodman's Point, North Carolina. In drawing the outlines of this, as of the others, I have necessarily used a somewhat free pencil, but the main incident of each has been faithfully preserved.

The disabled black soldier my own eyes saw thrust from a car in Philadelphia.

The portraits of Ercildoune and his children may seem to some exaggerated; those who have, as I, the rare pleasure of knowing the originals, will say, "the half has not been told."

Every leading New York paper, Democratic and Republican, was gone over, ere the summary of the Riots was made; and I think the record will be found historically accurate. The *Anglo-African* gives the story of poor Abram Franklin; and the assault on Surrey has its likeness in the death of Colonel O'Brien.

In a conversation between Surrey and Francesca, allusion is made to an act the existence of which I have frequently heard doubted. I therefore copy here a part of the "Retaliatory Act," passed by the Rebel Government at Richmond, and approved by its head, May 1, 1863:—

"SEC. 4. Every white person, being a commissioned officer, or acting as such, who, during the present war, shall command negroes or mulattoes in arms against the

Confederate States, or who shall arm, train, organize, or prepare negroes or mulattoes for military service against the Confederate States, or who shall voluntarily aid negroes or mulattoes in any military enterprise, attack, or conflict in such service, shall be deemed as inciting servile insurrection; and shall, if captured, be put to death."

I have written this book, and send it to the consciences and the hearts of the American people. May God, for whose "little ones" I have here spoken, vivify its words.

CLASSICS *in* BLACK STUDIES SERIES

Anna E. Dickinson, *What Answer?*

Frederick Douglass, *My Bondage and My Freedom*

W. E. B. Du Bois, *Darkwater*

W. E. B. Du Bois, *The Negro*

Ida B. Wells-Barnett, *On Lynchings*